He walked the heaving horse into the trees, slid down, then lifted Edain down. He carried her to the tree and laid her on a bed of fallen leaves.

"We have a few moments," he said. His hands were in her hair, running his fingers through it. He bent his head and hot, eager kisses captured her mouth, her throat. He pushed her resisting hands aside to unfasten her cloak. When he did, the white cat jumped out of the front of her gown and raced off into the bushes.

Magnus rolled on top of her, pulling her bared legs up around him. It was madness, but she could not stop him; she was caught up in the fever herself.

"My beautiful golden witch," he gasped. "Holy Mary, I can never leave you."

At that moment they heard the distant blast of a horn. The stallion tossed its head. "Give me the accursed reins," Magnus shouted. But it was too late. The horse reared and bolted into the night-dark woods and disappeared.

When he turned back to her, Edain was standing in a pool of moonlight, her wool gown and loosened golden hair almost silvery. "I am not going with you," she said. She turned and walked into the woods the way the horse had gone. A small white shadow, the cat, got up from the ground and followed at her heels.

The trees and the darkness closed around her.

BOOKS BY MAGGIE DAVIS

writing as Maggie Davis

Eagles
Rommel's Gold
The Sheik
The Far Side Of Home
The Winter Serpent
Forbidden Objects
Satin Doll
Satin Dreams
Wild Midnight
Miami Midnight
Hustle, Sweet Love
Diamonds and Pearls
Tropic of Love
Dreamboat

writing as Katherine Deauxville

Eyes of Love
The Crystal Heart
The Amethyst Crown
Blood Red Roses
Daggers of Gold

writing as Maggie Daniels

A Christmas Romance
(*also a CBS movie with Olivia Newton-John*)
Moonlight and Mistletoe

Eyes of Love

Katherine Deauxville

KENSINGTON BOOKS
KENSINGTON PUBLISHING CORP.

KENSINGTON BOOKS are published by

Kensington Publishing Corp.
850 Third Avenue
New York, NY 10022

First Kensington Printing: May, 1996
10 9 8 7 6 5 4 3 2 1

Printed in the United States of America

One

"I don't need a *woman!*" It wasn't necessary for Magnus to look at the wooden tally board, he knew very well the taxes owed by the hamlet of Torsham Lea did not include young, live females. "What the devil is she doing here?" he wanted to know, peering down the beach where the girl sat with her trunks and boxes around her.

The Torsham bailiff, who did not have his vassal lord, Ivo de Brise, there to explain, licked his lips. "Well, ah, young sir—"

Magnus didn't have the time nor the patience for a long-winded story. "Come, man, why did you bring her?" he barked. "You should know women are never considered tribute!"

The moment the words were out of his mouth Magnus allowed that in the old days they probably *were.* Saxons had not been above dealing in slaves, and sometimes even the Northmen traded in boys, if that was a lord's pleasure.

However, he told himself, as he checked off the bags of millet the sailors were loading, England was an enlightened Norman kingdom now under the second King Henry, with a righteous church that dealt sternly in such matters. Even this far north, on the barbaric Scottish borderland.

"Where's de Brise?" The local knight was supposed to be present when the tax collector came. "Why hasn't he come down with the tax rolls himself?" Before the bailiff could answer Magnus growled, "God's wounds, don't tell me this girl is his castoff *concubine* he wishes to send away!"

The bailiff looked startled. "Oh, no, young sir. God and Saint Mary, the girl's not a whore!"

Behind them villeins were lining up the sacks of barley and oats just out of reach of the tide. The earl's heavily-laden freighter was drawn up on the beach and tilted slightly to one side, its keel deep in the strand.

The bailiff gestured with a big hand. "You see, it's a bit hard to tell the truth without going into the whole tale, but she's—ah, well." He flapped the hand in her direction. "Well, what you—ah, see here is a—uh, well you might say—pretty bride in her wedding dress."

Magnus lifted his head to stare at him. At that moment a gust of wind blew into the cove, tearing at their cloaks, pulling the hood back from the girl's face.

She sat in the midst of a pile of her possessions that included an iron-bound leather trunk and looked as though they'd brought her down in a great hurry and just dumped her there. But she was not a concubine. At least not according to the bailiff.

Yet to anyone's eyes she was astonishingly beautiful, Magnus couldn't help thinking. Her long, unbound hair was a deep gold color, not the nearly white usually found among these Norse-mixed people on the coasts. From a distance it seemed her strange eyes were emerald green rimmed with black around the irises. She wore a rather fine filet of gold and silver wire over a headdress of red transparent silk. The wind lifted the veil and her tawny hair and let both stream away on the air like a red and gold flag.

Magnus scowled. Curiously, he was remembering the last time he'd seen the statues of saints in Normandy cathedrals, in particular Saint Anne and Saint Bertrile, and the Virgin herself. Their holy images had been covered with gold leaf, their eyes set with precious jewels. Over their gilded skins they wore silken clothes. The gold leaf was a new custom, brought back from the East where the statues in the churches there were much adorned, and very elegant. The girl reminded him somehow of the same sort of image.

Well, Magnus told himself abruptly, she was not his worry. He supposed concubines were still common enough, but he'd never known them to be publicly traded. They were almost certainly never thrown in with the sheep, cattle, lumber, and grain of a village's annual tribute.

"No women," he repeated, and turned back to his tally board.

The sun was sinking in a cold November sky. The trip back to his base where the earl's other tax ship waited was best not done after dark; he did not trust the villainous riffraff the earl had hired as sailors.

"Thirty sheep, four dozen geese, four oxen," Magnus finished, correcting a number he'd written in chalk with a rub of his sleeve.

As far as he could tell all of Torsham Lea's tribute to the earl was there. Including a particularly fine set of long bows as tall as a man, for which this part of the borderland was famous.

The bailiff pulled his cloak tight against the wind, looking worried. "Sir Magnus, you must take the girl with you," he insisted. "I beg of you—we cannot return to the hamlet with her. My lord de Brise has commanded that no matter what you tell us, we are to leave her here!"

Magnus lowered the tally board to look at him.

De Brise's bailiff had no way of knowing how ill tempered he, Magnus fitzJulien, was, all because of this damnable duty. That is, grubbing for yearly tribute from half-savage tribes while commanding a boatful of riffraff that passed for sailors, and who were eager to seize all if they could but think of a way to do it. And at the same time, having to haggle, now, over whether to give passage to some petty noble's discarded trull!

Magnus opened his mouth to blister the bailiff for wasting his time with such nonsense. And then closed it.

God's bones, he had to admit that much as he was tempted to vent his temper, he had no one, really, to blame but himself.

He was there on that barbaric shore north of the Earl of Chester's domain because he'd played the fool, losing heavily at dice with a drunken crowd of Chester's Angevins only two nights before. At the time Magnus had not only lost most of his coin but had to take on the Angevins's tax duty to round out what he owed.

Now he was finding out just how much the dice game had cost him. For this confounded tribute collecting was something any honorable knight would avoid like the fires of hell. He was to take two ships and go north to collect from the earl's half-Norse, half-Scots—and certainly half-civilized—subjects. Many of whom would be eager to steal back what they'd just given up. No wonder the Angevins had been so eager to stick him with their rotten task! They were probably laughing themselves sick over it by now.

And that was not the worst of it. At the time, some drunken demon had made Magnus boast that he could gather cows, sheep, grain, arms, assorted geese, and chickens and return to the court at Chester faster than had ever been done before. Thus showing that an English knight, favored liegeman of their great king, Henry the Second, could best a stupid Anjou mercenary knight anytime.

Magnus winced. Talk about lackwitted! He'd had time since then to wonder why he'd ever opened his mouth. Just thinking about it brought back the painful echo of a three-day hangover.

"Milord—" the bailiff began again.

Magnus wasn't listening. Morosely, he considered there were times when he could admit that he was *not* always the elegant, lute-playing, poetry-reciting young firebrand all the court's ladies sighed over. Or the strong, brave, and currently undefeated champion of Chester's tourney lists. But merely a thoughtless dolt given to sudden lapses of intelligence. Just as his family sometimes accused him of being.

"—then milord de Brise," the bailiff was saying,

"thought to wed the girl to Jorem the drover, so that he could take the *droit de seigneur* at his pleasure."

Carefully, so as not to aggravate the hangover, Magnus opened his eyes. "The *what?*"

The bailiff nodded. "Oh, yes, young sir, de Brise comes from Coutence, they set much store by *le droit* in those parts of Normandy. Once milord saw the beautiful lass the nuns had raised at the convent of the Sacred Limb of St. Sulpice he talked of nothing but her looks, and that she is an orphan with nothing known of her mother or father from the day the sisters found her in a basket in the convent turnstile for unwanted babes. So nothing must do but milord de Brise must have her! That's the truth of it." He turned to look to his men gathered on the beach. "Since milord de Brise is already wed to the lady Horgitha, he schemed to marry the girl to a villein, Jorem the drover, in order to claim her first night for himself. Then afterward milord de Brise would have her close by when he wanted her, as Jorem could never say his own lord nay, now could he? That is, if milord de Brise wanted to visit, you know."

Magnus stared at him.

He knew his own father, a handsome man in his prime, would never dream of taking the *droit de seigneur,* the right of the lord to bring a villein's woman to his own bed on her first night of marriage; his mother, the countess, would never allow it. But Magnus knew of the custom. Even Earl Niall looked the other way when one of his vassals took an occasional serf girl, claiming *le droit.*

"They was coming up to the porch of the church to be married," the bailiff went on, "when Jorem the drover, a big man with never a sick day in his life, sudden has his face turn as red as a July apple and begins pouring gouts of blood from his ears and his mouth. A horrid sight to see. Jorem staggers and falls down to the ground and many of those that were around him ran away in fear. One moment you was looking at Jorem there in the bloom of health, and the next there he was, stretched out in the road gasping for his very life!"

Magnus whirled to stare at the girl. "God's wounds, man, they think she poisoned him?"

"Oh, the holy angels guard your tongue, sir!" The bailiff quickly crossed himself. "Watch what you say, or we can be brought as witnesses in a matter we've rightly no part of!" He lowered his voice. "Nay, it was not poison, how could it be? I know myself the girl had never set eyes on Jorem afore he was brought to her. She'd never so much as even brushed against him, there in the road before the church."

Magnus could imagine how the villagers had panicked at the bridegroom's sudden death. And Ivo de Brise didn't want her now.

He couldn't say that he blamed him.

The bailiff had not used the word *witchcraft;* after all, from what he'd said the girl was straight out of the convent. But whatever had struck her bridegroom dead at the very doors of the church had at least taken away de Brise's lust for her.

Magnus studied the cloaked figure sitting among her bundles, thinking he was glad she hadn't beseeched him to take her. When one came right down to it he had no excuse at all for doing so even if he wanted to. But he couldn't help feeling sorry for her.

One could guess her fate if the bailiff and his men abandoned her there on the beach. They were not far from Scotland; wild bands raided these parts when de Brise's men were not about.

She's not my burden, he told himself.

He gave the bailiff a few brisk parting messages for de Brise, who had unwisely not bothered to come down to meet his liege lord's tax collector. Which Magnus intended promptly to report to the earl. Then taking his leave, he strode to the water's edge.

The keel of the boat was deep in the shale. At Magnus's shout most of the crew, plus the four men-at-arms, jumped overboard into the shallow water to cast her off. Magnus waded out into the surf himself and put his back to the hull. The water was icy cold. The livestock bleated over the whine of the wind. As the cattle and sheep shifted, the ship turned sidewise, in spite of the efforts of the sailor at the steering oar, and caught a long roll of the sea.

For a moment it looked as though the boat would swamp. Then, with a jerk that nearly took Magnus off his feet, the ship's keel broke free of the shore.

The cursing sailors followed the ship into deeper water. Magnus found himself suddenly up to his neck in breakers, his mail and sword dragging at him. He grabbed at the boat's wooden side with both hands and got a knee up and hauled himself into the scuppers. He fell against a rowing bench and cracked his shins as the ship turned. Two of the boatmen climbed the mast to put up the sail. The bleating and mooing from the animals was deafening.

Magnus sat down on the grain sacks in the stern and rubbed his legs. The hunched figure of the girl in the blue cloak was still there on the beach. He remembered her eyes—jeweled green, filled with light. He shook his head again, and the annoying vision disappeared.

Ivo de Brise's bailiff mounted one of the pack mules that had brought the earl's tribute down to the shore and, followed by his reeves, took the path through dunes topped with grass now bending almost flat in the wind. At the crest, the bailiff reined in his mule and looked back.

The curving beach stretched away on both sides as far as the eye could see, a cold, purple sky over it. The girl appeared to be watching the Earl of Chester's freight boat wallowing into the channel. She sat straight-backed, her hood pulled forward to hide her face.

The bailiff could not help feeling a pang of regret. She was a lovely thing; he would take her for himself if he could. But what had happened there before the Torsham Lea church had settled that.

He sat watching as his tally reeves toiled up to the crest of the dunes and pulled their pack animals to a halt. They could see the redheaded young knight, the earl's tax collector, standing in the stern of the freighter looking back at the beach. They knew him as young fitzJulien, the Earl of Morlaix's heir, current cock of the walk at Chester's court. Now, even as the boat drew farther away, his eyes were on the girl on the beach. A voice among the bailiff's men said, "He's a goin' to come back for her."

Someone snorted. "A ha'penny says he ain't."

The bailiff said nothing. But he was thinking the young knight would not turn back. Not if he knew what was good for him.

From her place on the sandy beach Edain, too, could feel the young knight's eyes on her.

With the hood of her cape pulled forward to hide most of her face she had watched the sailors load the ship, and the boat pull away from the shore, expecting even to the last moment that the young knight captain would approach her and tell her to get aboard. But it had not happened.

Now, Edain saw with rising disbelief, they were going to leave her there!

It was her own inexperience, of course; since she had known only the quiet ways of the convent she was not used to the way things happened in the outer world. It had never occurred to her that she should have approached the energetic young knight herself and spoken with him to make sure he would take her when the boat left.

But then, she thought, it was hard even to think when one's whole body felt as though the skin had been peeled back, leaving only the tender nerve endings. The outer world was a difficult place, and it didn't seem to get much better.

Edain closed her eyes against the light and the buffeting wind. Above the sea's roar she could hear the sailors' shouts as they hoisted the leather sail.

She couldn't let this happen. Once the sail was up it would be hard to turn the boat in the whitecapped sea. She licked her lips, thinking of the young knight captain.

It was not wise to call to him, but she had no other choice; she had waited too long as it was. But she was afraid there would be questions—sometimes even the accusation that she had called.

Nevertheless, she had to do something.

She knew that it was like a whispering in one's ear. A whispering that one could not resist.

With a sigh, she reached for the power, to use it.

The sailors pulled steadily at the oars. The wind caught the half-raised sail. Then abruptly, the earl's young tax collector raised his hand. His shout was carried away by the gale, but the surprised sailors scrambled out of the way as the rudder oarman changed direction. The leather sail suddenly emptied of wind and flapped around them.

On the dunes above the beach one of the reeves cried, "He's doing it! He's turning back."

As though she'd been waiting for the moment they saw the girl below stand up, the wind billowing her cloak.

De Brise's bailiff quickly yanked at his mule's reins and the animal turned as he shouted to the others to follow him.

The wind was cold, but the back of the bailiff's neck and his scalp was prickling with a curious chill.

So the young knight would come back for her, after all. He wouldn't have believed it if he hadn't seen it himself. Holy Mother—it was almost as though she had reached out to him, across the sea to the boat, and *willed* him to return!

The bailiff kicked his mule in the ribs and the startled animal lunged into a trot. The bailiff could not wait to get away. Far away from the beach.

And the bewitched young fool who was returning.

Two

The tall knight staggered down the ship between the oarsmen, chasing two pigs that were loose. It was not easy work. While he was doing this the freight boat climbed the swells from the Irish Sea, taking the waves at an angle that made the boat stand on its stern end, then wildly drop nose down into the trough.

The sailors seemed to take this up-and-down motion as no great consequence; they rowed steadily, even when their oars failed to connect with the sea. But every once in a while the tall, redheaded knight captain was forced to grab the mast and wrap his arms around it to keep from being flung overboard.

Edain watched all this from her seat in the stern, the edge of her hood partly drawn over her face. This big, young knight was taking her away from her kidnapper, de Brise, who wanted to force her to wed a villein in order to take her into his own filthy bed. But she still did not understand why this long-legged, broad-shouldered young tourney knight had apparently been chosen for her rescue. He seemed far too young, hardly experienced for all that they were doing. But in spite of it all, the Feeling deep inside her assured her strongly that everything would turn out all right.

She watched as he scrambled under a rowing bench to grapple for a pig. Her rescuer was certainly not used to freight boats, nor the lowly task of chasing animals. She studied his handsome, arrogant features, the brows drawn together in an irritable scowl. The wind carried back his curses as the pig managed to make its escape under the feet of the oarsmen, who were enjoying the knight captain's difficulties. Some of them were openly grinning.

Edain did not smile.

She had expected the young lordling to say something to her there on the beach. But he only strode to her, scooped her up in his arms, and carried her out through the breakers without so much as a word. There he proceeded to dump her over the side of the boat onto the stern's grain sacks before hoisting himself topside. After that, he and the crew had been too busy getting the ship under way to even look at her.

So much for worrying, Edain told herself. Most people were usually puzzled when they were called; they sometimes explained it away as an idea to be someplace, doing something, whose meaning they'd curiously forgotten.

Perhaps this big knight hadn't even thought about it; certainly someone that muscular and strong was a creature of action, not much given to thinking. Perhaps he'd never questioned why he'd turned back the ship to fetch her from the beach.

Edain rubbed her nose with the back of her hand, wiping away some of the sea spray. The Irish Sea in winter was not a welcoming place; the gray water around them was full of what the sailors called white horses. God and the saints knew where they were going, she thought, biting her lip.

She folded her hands together under the cloak and shivered, knowing she had almost waited until it was too late to bring the redheaded knight back for her.

She did not call people very often. And then usually not to help herself, but others. As for instance when old Sister Jean-Auguste, the convent gardener, would be so busy with her vegetables that she would forget and be late for chapter meeting. When Edain called her, Sister Jean-Auguste would almost immediately leave the kitchen garden and arrive at St. Sulpice's chapter house where the nuns were settling themselves, throw up her fat arms and cry, huffing and out of breath, that she had no idea why she was there—she'd forgotten what she'd come for! As though the idea of chapter meeting had just popped into her head.

Then Sister Jean-Auguste would look around in her nearsighted way and realize that she *was* where she was supposed to be at that hour. That she'd somehow arrived in the nick of time in spite of her absentmindedness. Ah, Sister Jean-Auguste would say, it was almost like a voice whispering in her ear, telling her not to forget again or certainly she would feel the weight of Abbess Clothilde's displeasure and yet another string of penances!

Bless us, Sister Jean-Auguste would say, angels looked after fools or she'd never get where she was supposed to in this life. Except of course the places she loved, like the kitchen and convent garden.

Actually, Edain had decided that calling Sister Jean-Auguste in time for chapter meeting amounted to a blessing more than anything else. For when Sister Jean-Auguste missed chapter and was disciplined, all the nuns suffered for her. Abbess Clothilde gave penances Sister Jean-Auguste hated: four consecutive hours of prayer on her fat knees in the dark between matins and lauds when no one was about, everyone asleep except the gate watchman, and every creak and terrifying shadow full of demons and worse. Even in chapel.

So why not, Edain had always thought, a quiet little message sent to Sister Jean-Auguste working in her garden, blissfully unaware of the time? When you came right down to it, a quick, airborne whisper in her ear was really nothing.

She shivered again. This afternoon on the beach had been quite different, though; then she'd been really afraid. It was like nothing she'd ever felt before. The thought that she'd be abandoned there had made her shudder with quiet panic.

Edain was jolted out of her reverie when the freight boat met the sea head on and a wave poured in. One of the sailors climbed the mast to turn the sail. She shrank back against the grain sacks, spitting out a mouthful of salt water. After a quick, experimental swallow, she did not think she was going to be sick.

Nevertheless, she was hardly comfortable beyond the gates of St. Sulpice. There were times when the sound and feel of everything in the "outside" fell on her like blows: a sailor's hoarse shout, the waves battering the sides of the boat, the cold and the wet. As though her body was still tender and new, not yet hardened enough for the harsh world where she now found herself.

"Damn you, Rothgar," a voice shouted, "reach for him!"

The young knight captain had squeezed between the rowers' benches, using his sword to prod a pig toward one of his men-at-arms, who waited to catch it at the platform before the mast.

Edain studied his dark red hair, long and curling, that stuck out below his helmet, and the wide, youthful mouth clamped together in grim determination. That he was some privileged nobleman's son could be seen from his fine armor: the steel helm decorated with inlaid gold bands, and the mail coat that was alone probably worth the earl's entire tax boat and all the sailors in it. Not to mention the magnificent sword that hung from a gold-studded belt, and that kept getting in the way as he lunged after pigs.

The rowers stopped to watch as the handsome young knight dropped to one knee and reached under their legs to grab a shrieking piglet.

Edain was struck by the thought that in a way she had never considered before her life was changing, torn apart; being taken by the knight de Brise from the convent and then saved by the unexpected death of her bridegroom was only part of it. She now found herself on the seas, among strangers, not even knowing where she was going.

The nuns had taught her one must not give in to despair. She had to go ahead no matter what happened, with the sort of faith of the kind the priests so often spoke of.

Besides, she was not without her own special means of help. Not that she could explain it to others, but even when the knight de Brise had come to take her from the convent in spite of the sisters' protests, the Feeling had been there, reassuring her. It did not need to tell her there would be a terrible change in what formerly had been her quiet, protected life at St. Sulpice; whether she liked it or not, after so many years of tranquil, loving companionship from the sisters, everything was going to be very different, very quickly. Even the abbess had wept in despair.

Be calm, the Feeling had advised her. *Above all, do not grieve.*

Now Edain knew she would always miss the only life she could remember: the orderly march of days around a framework of devotions to God. The prayers at *prime,* while the cocks in the barnyard were still crowing in the blackness. *Terce* that one usually hurried to from the tasks of busy morning. *Sext* at midday following noon meal. *None*—a welcome rest in midafternoon in the dim chapel with the nuns' voices droning. Blessed *vespers* at dusk and the end of the convent's workday. *Compline* to send one to bed—

Even in the open boat with cold spray on her face, she suddenly found she could feel the stillness of St. Sulpice quite clearly, smell the candle smoke of the chapel, the open windows above the nave, the rich aroma of Sister Jean-Auguste's dinner cooking in the kitchen house. It brought a warm flame of comfort that she grasped at eagerly even while she knew that part of her life was finished.

Edain found she had been staring at the young knight, who was attempting to tie the feet of the squirming piglet while the other soldier held it. She was aware the light had strangely dimmed! The air about them was an odd, greenish color.

She viewed the two men with the pig with a sudden, uneasy sensation. When she blinked she saw an amazing view of the redheaded knight's body. As though he had somehow shed his ring mail and underclothes, or managed to make them invisible!

Edain blinked, and blinked again. God in heaven, in spite of her incredulity there was not the slightest change in what she was seeing!

She could not tear her eyes away. By the odd light from the lowering sky, the knight appeared to her astonished eyes as naked as a jaybird! The only thing her stunned brain could think was that with all the manifest visions and Feelings she'd ever had through the years, *this* had never happened before!

On top of everything else, she had never really seen a man naked. She was sure she was openly gaping. Because such sights were never encountered in a convent where there were no men at all. Except for the aged pensioners hired to guard the gate and help in the stables.

Now she could see that stripped of clothes he looked even more powerful, with big hands and feet, and the arms and shoulders of a born swordsman. The silky skin of his belly was unmarred by any scars, as was his dangling, rather huge private parts.

Edain suddenly knew somehow that he had not had many women; he was too highborn and proud, perhaps too particular, to take common whores. Yet he shied from virgins; there had been only one, a long time ago. The strange vision told her he was now twenty-six.

The pig kicked itself loose and, hobbled by its hind legs, managed to scramble away. With a roar, the redheaded knight started after it. At that moment a wave broke over the bow and a sheet of water rolled the length of the boat.

Edain sucked in her breath as a gray-green wall lifted the freight boat up until it seemed to stand on its stern end, then let it slide back down again. Everything in the boat that was not tied down came loose. As ropes and buckets filled the air she clung to the bulkhead with both hands.

The redheaded knight grabbed a rowers' bench to keep from being flung overboard. The pig darted through the sailors' legs and slid the length of the deck, coming to rest against the grain sacks.

Edain lifted her skirts. The pig burrowed under them and into the sacks as the boat took another wave over the bow.

For a moment she couldn't breathe. When the water receded there was a puddle in her lap. There was quite a lot of water, too, in the bottom of the boat, it came up to her ankles. The giant sailor at the steering oar bellowed out something. In the next second the boat turned.

Edain felt a hand grab her wrist. A sailor with tarred yellow braids thrust a leather bucket into her hands. He showed her how to push it down between the floorboards and into the water sloshing from side to side.

She nodded that she understood. She looked over

the boat's sides as she emptied the bucket. The sea between Ireland and Britain rushed into the narrow lochs of Scotland like water through a sluice. One could see the snakelike currents that tore along under the surface.

The boat had changed course. They were making for the shelter of the shore that was rimmed with cliffs. Edain rested for a moment, letting her hand trail in the icy water. She could feel the power as it rushed past but deep inside her the Feeling told her there was no need to be afraid, the boat's wooden sides were solid. The freight boat was not going to swamp even in the great swells. Besides, they were making for calmer water.

But there was something else.

In the stern the steersman leaned his big body to the steering oar. It took all a powerful man's strength to keep a ship on course; the steersman was a giant, and by the flaxen color of his beard and hair, a Norseman.

Now the light had turned a deep, eerie green.

Edain looked down and saw the deck of the steersman's platform suddenly clear as glass. The air was like water. And the water under the boat's hull was full of sandy shoals.

She licked her lips. It was like the vision of the redheaded knight's invisible clothes! Except now it was the earl's wooden tax boat that one could see through. Her skin was crawling with foreboding.

To her eyes there was no longer any rough wooden decking to support the Norseman's feet, only the view, through suddenly transparent wood, of a gray-green object that was clearly a rock. Then came a flashing school of herring, silver shapes stitching through the gray water. Then a glimpse of the sandy, grassy bottom itself near the shore.

The boat glided forward, carried on the current, the crew resting at the oars. A splayed beam of sunshine broke through the clouds and lit the sea. The high cliffs were full of wheeling seabirds, their cries piercing the air.

The young knight captain had sat down on the end of a rowing bench to stare glumly at the sacks where the pig had disappeared. Slowly, his tawny eyes lifted to Edain.

She felt his sudden regard like a shock. Was he considering now, for the first time, why he had turned back to the beach for her? And not finding any answers?

She saw his scowl deepen, puzzled. Yes, what *had* brought him back?

She saw him open his mouth to speak but in that moment the slate-colored clouds parted and a burst of sunshine lit the water between the mountains. With cold ghostly fingers on her back and neck Edain could see through the decking of the freight ship and into the depths as though into a looking glass.

Then she saw why.

She jumped to her feet. The knight had been watching, not expecting her sudden movement. He was too surprised to stop her and only turned his head as she started for the steersman's platform.

The fair-haired Norseman was leaning against his oar. He did not expect Edain when she mounted the platform and threw all the weight of her body against the oar, knocking it out of his grasp.

As the huge oar swung free it almost threw Edain overboard. She wrapped her hands around it as she felt her feet leave the deck. She could not hold back a small scream.

All around her sailors were shouting. The huge steersman leaned over the side and grabbed the oar before it came free of the oarlock. He dragged it and Edain back at the same time the redheaded knight captain reached the platform.

All three went to their knees as the earl's tax boat struck the shoal. Sailors were thrown from their rowing benches. The animals squealed as the keel ran aground. The earl's freighter came to a crunching stop. There was a brief second of silence broken only by the leather sail flapping in the wind. Then the boat, its bottom firmly locked on the sandbar, rocked in the swells.

The steersman reached out and, shouting Norse curses, seized Edain. He would have lifted her up and over the side but the redheaded knight pulled her away in the nick of time and set her on her feet.

"Thor's balls, you see what she did?" The steersman lunged for her again. "This trollop made us run aground. She's crazy, her wits are addled! She did it a purpose!"

The knight captain held onto Edain.

The Norseman reached for her again. "Throw her overboard," he ground out.

Three

The rock upon which the castle at Edinburgh stood was as carved with roads as knife marks in a wheel of Scottish cheese.

From the time before anyone could remember—that is, from the days of giants and other monsters—to the fairly recent time of the Saxons, there had been some sort of fort on castle rock as a refuge in times of war, and to defend the town below. As a result, the granite mountain had been cut with paths and roadways now lined, in the twentieth year of the reign of King Henry the Second, with wayside huts and encampments, peddlers' booths, merchants' stalls, inns and taverns and, for those who could not afford better, rude tents whose crowded insides barely gave shelter for the few coppers paid for it.

Because the king of the Scots, William the Lion and brother of the late, brave Malcolm, often made his home at the fort at the very top of the rock, there was a never-ending thread of court traffic that ascended and descended the roads from daybreak to nightfall. A tall man in the white tunic of a Templar knight, riding a bay stallion and leading a magnificent half-Arab black horse, chose the middle road.

After a while the jostling, close-packed crowds

forced the Templar to the shoulders of the road, which were just as congested. There were Norman men-at-arms marching up toward the fort under the command of a mounted knight captain, followed by a group of monks, and beyond them, a young girl in ragged dancing dress being pulled along by a length of rope around her neck held by her master. On both sides, the road was flanked by a line of Highlanders squatting on their haunches, their backs to the ditch.

Only in the land of the Scots, Asgard de la Guerche told himself as he viewed the scene. Edinburgh's castle seemed particularly squalid with mud and animals and the gallery of Highlanders watching. As Asgard's big bay put his feet down perilously close to the men they never moved, looking up at the Templar with incurious expressions.

That is, if one could find such a thing as an expression in all that hair, de la Guerche couldn't help thinking. Scots Highlanders apparently never shaved. Shapeless caps barely covered the uncombed bushes that joined even thicker mats of beard. Although there was snow on the ground, most were barefoot, the soles of their dirt-stained feet as hard as horn. To a man they wore the Irish-Scots saffron shirt that reached to their knees, and over it deer hide or fur cloaks. Beside them, Asgard thought, even the wildest heathen foe of the Holy Land would look fairly refined.

And yet, if one looked close enough one could discern exquisite jewelry. Ancient gold torques decorated unwashed necks, silver and gold armbands studded with amber and precious stones on hairy arms, even on ankles. Battle-scarred hands were adorned with gold and silver rings gleaming with bright enamel.

Asgard had been told in London that one could not tell the Highland chiefs from their men by their dress. But here and there he glimpsed a headdress of gold-tipped deer antlers, or a few upright eagle feathers held by a jewel, that showed the leaders.

The Scots returned his stares unblinkingly. They saw Asgard, a Crusader knight in his polished steel helm, his sword and shield tied at his saddle, wearing the white tunic of the Poor Knights of the Holy Temple of Jerusalem with its large red cross on his front and back. From the tone of their voices Asgard guessed they were discussing him.

It really didn't matter. The mission that brought Asgard to Scotland would, by his estimate, not keep him there past Christmas. Hardly enough time to make the effort to pick up more than a few words of their barbaric Gaelic. If that.

Beyond the Highlanders he came abreast of the scrawny young gypsy girl and her master. Somewhat absently, obeying the Templars' pledge to charity, Asgard reached into his leather purse and brought out a piece of bread and tossed it to her.

Although the girl walked with her head down, slim brown fingers suddenly reached into the air to deftly snatch the bread. Asgard caught the grateful flash of black eyes under a mop of dark hair.

Unfortunately, before the girl could cram the bread into her mouth the man holding the rope jerked her to him and snatched it out of her hand. "What yer get, yer gives to me," he shouted. He back-handed her across the face. "All this time, you ain't learned that?"

The girl stood stock-still, looking at the ground, while the gypsy broke off a piece of the bread with his teeth and made a great show of chewing it.

Asgard had watched all this impassively. Now he touched his spurs to the bay. The stallion hardly broke stride as the Templar leaned from the saddle and hit the gypsy in the middle of the back with his mailed fist.

It was all done so quickly, man and horse moving together, that the blow seemed only glancing. But the gypsy promptly flew up into the air with a squawk, then dropped into the laps of the Highlanders, who greeted him with roars of appreciative laughter.

Asgard reined in the bay. He sat for a moment adjusting his mailed gauntlet, settling it back over his knuckles. "Pick up the bread, girl," he told her.

The wild Highlanders, clacking and laughing in their odd language, threw the half-stunned gypsy from hand to hand, finally tossing him out onto the road. The girl did her best to get all of the bread into her mouth before the man got to his knees, spitting dirt between his teeth.

A tall figure stood up among the Scots and approached Asgard. "God's blessings on you, Templar," he said in reasonable Norman French, "you are a long way from Jerusalem. What brings one of Christ's true knights here to Scotland's castle rock?"

Asgard looked down. *Not Norman,* in spite of what his ears told him.

The Highlander was one of the biggest men Asgard had ever seen, a giant with reddish-gray hair who wore a cap decorated with eagle feathers, and about his body a long woolen drapery of red and black checks belted at the waist and drawn up between his knees to form a sort of skirt.

"Ruaig Mor," the Scot said. He gestured to the others. "And my men, the Lion's royal guard."

So they were the King of Scotland's men. And a "royal" guard at that.

The Templar worked hard to keep from smiling. "God's blessings on you also, Chieftain. I am Asgard de la Guerche of Mortrain of Normandy, lately of the Brotherhood of the Poor Knights of the Holy Temple that men call Templars. Were my eyes closed, I would bet my good mount under me that I heard a brother Norman speaking."

The other laughed. "The Norman speech comes easy after having served six years under good King Baldwin of Jerusalem." Sharp eyes swept over the horses and Asgard himself. "The Lion is not at home on the rock," he informed him, "if it is the king you seek."

Asgard nodded. "My business is not with King William but with one of his justiciars, Nigel fitzGamelin. I am told fitzGamelin holds office in the fort."

For a moment the other man's eyes showed a glimmer of something, perhaps only the recognition of yet another Norman to add to the numbers the king had brought to his kingdom. Then it faded.

Ruiag pointed the way, walking alongside Asgard's destrier, giving instructions to the royal enclave and the justiciar's office.

At the curve of the walled road the Templar bade the chieftain a good day, and urged his mount forward. The black Arabian followed, tugging at the lead and tossing his head. He passed the gypsy girl sitting on the step of a stone cross, wolfing down the last of the bread. The dark-faced man turned to glare at him.

That reminded him.

Asgard leaned out of the saddle to speak in a voice the rest could not hear. "Beat her," he said pleasantly, "and I will bring down God's terrible curse of rotting flesh on you so that you will spend the rest of your days in the company of the leprous accursed, carrying a begging bowl and ringing a bell."

Even before Asgard had finished speaking the look in his eyes had sent the gypsy cringing back, believing every word of it. Asgard straightened up and rode on.

Of course it was not within his power to curse anyone, only a fool or a gypsy would believe that. And he certainly could not curse anything or anyone in God's name.

Especially since, and even as God's truly chosen knight and Templar, Asgard de la Guerche no longer much believed in Him.

In the cobblestone courtyard at the top of the rock he found a sentry in a hauberk of Norman mail and showed his warrant signed by the Scots king's minister at King Henry's court. Two more knights ushered him past the guards to a small stone room set in the castle wall. Here, Asgard saw with satisfaction, everything was in excellent order; it might have been a fine Norman keep in London.

Outside the corridors had been filled with knights who had saluted him, could read his papers, and were properly clean-shaven and respectful. Most of all, the sound of Norman French was like music to his ears. So was the sight of the dour-faced captain, fitzGamelin, as Asgard was ushered into his presence.

"Welcome to the Lion's kingdom, Sir Templar." King William's justiciar seated Asgard at a table untidy with inkpots and vellum scrolls. "You are in the very heart of Scottish enlightenment here in Edwin's burgh," he said wryly, as he poured him a cup of wine, "why do you wish to go farther?"

"For more of it, of course."

The other barked his laughter as he offered the cup.

Asgard sipped at the wine, a good red brought from the east of France where red wine was a speciality. They discussed the vintage, agreeing that if one could not get French or Spanish or even Italian it was best to give up the idea and drink ale. England could not grow decent grapes, but even the Scots made an ale that was acceptable.

The justiciar expressed a wish for the good health and welfare of King Henry the Second, who was much plagued by the intrigues of his two oldest sons, the Princes Henry and Geoffrey.

Neither said anything for a long moment.

It was impossible even to talk of the English king's troublesome heirs, for to do so was to court the suspicion of treason. But all of England and a good part of Normandy now well knew it had been a mistake for the old king to crown young Prince Henry his co-ruler—a move thought to pacify the ambitious boy, but which had only served to aggravate Prince Henry's desires.

The prince had found that he would indeed be called co-ruler, but that he would not actually have any part in England's ruling. So he had departed for France in a fury to rally his father's enemies. He was joined by his younger brother, clever Prince Geoffrey. It had been war, sons against the father, ever since.

Thinking the same thoughts, Asgard and the justiciar avoided looking at each other. The future of England was worrisome, and all feared the consequences of King Henry's doting weakness for his unruly sons, not to mention Queen Eleanor's vicious meddling on the side of her offspring. Naturally they could not speak of it. Especially here in Scotland, where the very walls had hundreds of ears.

The justiciar poured more wine but Asgard refused a second cup. He had given the gypsy girl the last of his bread and it did not serve him to take too much to drink on an empty stomach. Also, he did not want to wait any longer to get to the matter that had brought him to Edwin's burgh as the king's emissary.

"Our blessed King Henry the Second," Asgard said, "who supports and honors his friend King William the Lion of the kingdom of the Scots, wishes to pursue a matter that has come to his august attention. Namely, a complaint he has received from the Abbess of the Convent of the Sacred Limb of Saint Sulpice, a community of Norman nuns under King Henry's own charter. There is a young novice whom the nuns regard as of such holy character that they are given to speaking of her as nearly in her sainthood. And she has been abducted by a vassal of the Earl of Chester's, one Ivo de Brise."

The justiciar put his elbows on the table and looked at Asgard. "The Convent of the Sacred Limb of Saint Sulpice is a long way from England. Above Wigan, is it not, on the banks of the River Ribble?"

Asgard said, "Yes, it is on land claimed by the Earl of Chester. But it is seldom clear in these border places to which king, English Henry or Scottish William, fealty is owed." Asgard expected the justiciar already knew of the matter. "The nuns at Saint Sulpice, however," he added, "pay a yearly tax to our blessed King Henry."

The justiciar lifted his eyebrows. "So do they, too, to King William."

Asgard sipped his wine. No doubt the confounded women, with their convent on disputed borderland, felt it prudent to pay two masters. "It is the English king the holy sisters have appealed to," he reminded him. "For it is a situation of much concern, when—ah, possible *sainthood* is involved. All Christendom echoes the pain of the wounding of one of the church's own innocents."

"Saint is not the term I had heard of this girl," the justiciar said. " 'Witch' is more like it." Before Asgard could interrupt he went on, "Whatever, I had not considered her so valuable. Especially to King Henry, so far away in—where has the English court moved itself now? To Winchester?"

Asgard fought down a surge of annoyance. He ought to be able to get a warrant to travel the land of the Scots as King Henry's special emissary; he had thought it all settled in London. "Yes, the king is always at Winchester this time of year."

They sat facing each other in the narrow stone room. Asgard was not at all sure, now, why the King of England desired to obtain some obscure novice from some equally obscure convent on a dreary stretch of the borderland coast. In London it had not been thought necessary to explain. Now Asgard was beginning to feel that he needed to know more. Much more.

"I am here," he said, "because my liege lord, blessed King Henry, believes his vassal de Brise is in Scotland. De Brise is something of a varlet, a fugitive from his lord, the Earl of Chester. I seek him in the land of the Scots because there is reason to believe he may have taken the—er, holy novice captive with him."

FitzGamelin looked skeptical. "De la Guerche, if someone abducted a novice from a convent of mother church it would be an ecclesiastical matter, would it not?"

Asgard reached into his tunic. "Yes, milord, and I carry a letter from England's highest prelate, the Archbishop of Canterbury, asking King William's full consent in this matter."

He handed over the sheepskin tied with a string and sealed with red wax. FitzGamelin took it and put it down on his desk. "You wish in return," the justiciar said, "a king's warrant to travel in search of Chester's vassal in Scotland?"

They regarded each other for a long moment. Asgard knew he must start somewhere. And yes, he needed King William's warrant. But he detected a note in what fitzGamelin was telling him as one Norman to the other, that wherever de Brise and his budding young saint had gone to King William the Lion of the Scots was not ready to turn her over to English King Henry.

Probably because William the Lion would like to take a look at her himself.

The Scot's king's justiciar lifted the wine pitcher. "Shall I fill your cup?"

Asgard de la Guerche regarded the other a long moment. He was going to get his warrant to travel Scotland and look for the girl; that he was fairly sure. But nothing, now, looked as simple as it had a few weeks ago in London.

Asgard nodded, and held out his cup.

A small boat and two rowers was sent out from the earl's freighter to pull it off the sandbar. But a choppy sea had set in. Even with the sailors' vigorous rowing the small boat was not enough to get the ship off the shoal.

Following the Norseman's shouts, the sailors returned to the larger boat, got its iron anchor, and took it out and dropped it into deeper water, then waited while the freighter's crew attempted to windlass their craft across the barrier.

The Norse steersman, who was in charge of the boats including the other freighter they were going to meet at the cove, still wanted to throw Edain overboard. Magnus sent the girl back to sit on the grain sacks, and put one of the men-at-arms to guard her.

The steersman had a right to be angry; Magnus still

was not clear on what had happened himself. Even when he went back to the beginning of it, when he had returned to the shore to take the girl away, he could not explain it. Why hadn't he just left her there, as he'd planned? All he remembered was that it had been like a voice whispering in his ear. A powerful voice that he could no more resist than he could stop breathing.

It had seemed in that instant like the most natural thing in the world to go back and get the girl. As if she had every right to be taken away with the rest of the tax goods. And yet now that Magnus thought of it, watching her shivering as she pulled her wet cloak around her, the thing made no sense at all.

Even more baffling was what he had seen happen when she had thrown herself at the steering oar, deliberately running the ship up onto a sandbar.

After he'd recovered his oar the Norseman, Olav, had seized her by the arms and had shaken her until her hood fell off and her gold-colored hair flailed around her like so much wind-tossed silk.

"Why did you do this?" the Norseman had bellowed. "Tell me why you have run us aground, or I will put you over the side and drown you!"

As if to make good his threat, he'd lifted the girl and held her stretched out at arm's length over his head. But her only reply had been a terrified scream.

It had seemed to Magnus that even as the girl teetered above the steersman's head, about to be thrown into the water, she obviously could not explain what she had done.

That made him step forward and drag the girl down out of the enraged Norseman's grip and set her on her feet. He called one of the men-at-arms to take her back to the stern.

"She's not addlewitted, she knows what she done!" the Norseman had howled. "Let me throw her overboard! Or you be sorry you keep her!"

Magnus couldn't bring himself to kill the girl outright. But now as the sailors windlassed in the anchor and as the hull of the ship shivered and began to move across the sandbar, he rested his arms on the ship's rail and stared out at the sea. The steersman was probably right. They would be sorry they hadn't got rid of the confounded girl, even as beautiful as she was. God's wounds, hadn't she been a great trouble to de Brise?

Running aground had delayed them. He didn't know now if they could make the cove above Wigan and the other tax ship before dark. The thought of another night camped on the open beach made Magnus groan.

There was no way he could make good his boasting, now, about returning in record time from the tax collecting. In fact, he winced when he thought of the jeers of the Angevins when he returned to Chester's court not only late, but with this strange girl in tow.

How in the devil, he wondered, bracing himself as the wind caught the sail, was he going to justify any of this? He supposed he could only do as good a job as had ever been done anytime, by anyone, and let it go at that. Once they were back at camp, he promised himself he would spend the rest of the evening in his tent putting the earl's tax accounts straight, and double-checking to make sure the vassals' tallies were true and that they had paid all they said they had.

As the cattle in the pen beyond bellowed he remembered another thing. There was the livestock to be fed, somehow; he'd already learned on this hellish voyage that if animals went without feed and water they raised the very demons in hell all night long and kept everyone from sleeping. As the boat beat along the waters close to the shore, Magnus looked up at the sky. The weather was growing even rougher; a gale was brewing. Those sailors not at the oars groped their way about the boat tying down the buckets and ropes that had come loose earlier.

Magnus braced his hands against the ship's rail. They were coming up on the point of land that hid the cove and the other freighter full of tax goods. Jesu, how he longed to have this over with and be back at court! His liege lord was young, blissfully unmarried, and when not with King Henry chasing the rebellious princes, the earl was at home holding a notoriously raucous, free-spirited court. Young knights from England and France flocked to Chester for tourneys, the nightly feasting, and the opportunity to maneuver through the matchmakers in the hopes of finding an heiress to wed.

Or the other way around, Magnus thought.

This autumn in Chester no end of toothsome young things had been proposed to him by an army of ravening beldames. As the eldest son and heir of the famed Earl of Morlaix he was favored husband material. But he'd avoided even the appearance of listening to go-betweens; when he had to marry his mother and father would do the arranging, his mother especially.

In fact, the Countess Emmeline had already mentioned she had her eye on the Earl of Winchester's youngest daughter, now thirteen, an heiress in her own right with much west of England property and according to the reports, very pretty. Although Magnus had heard his father seemed to be holding out for a continental marriage, perhaps to one of Queen Eleanor's young princess relations from Aquitaine or Castile.

Of course it would be difficult to reach the queen for such matchmaking, as that unlucky lady was still imprisoned for urging young Prince Henry's last attack on his father. But the whole world knew arranging marriages through Europe and back had always been one of the queen's great talents; that, and her sympathy with lovers. As in the case of her sister, and her sister's nearly outlawed marriage.

A sailor came stumbling up to where Magnus stood at the rail. "M'lord, look!" he shouted over the wind.

Magnus had already seen it.

They were rounding the point of land that hid their camp. A telltale plume of smoke, bigger than any campfire, blew out to sea. With a curse, Magnus shouted for his men-at-arms to take up positions in the bow.

They saw it as the ship passed the point.

Disaster had struck. The second tax freighter lay burning on its side in the shallows. They could see the beach and the bodies of the slain sailors. Boxes and bales of the earl's tribute had been broken open and plundered. The camp was scattered, and tents that had been set on fire were still burning.

As Magnus's ship rushed toward shore a straggling band of sailors and men-at-arms came running down to meet them, followed more slowly by the other boat's commander, Emeric, holding a bleeding and useless arm.

"Stand away, stand away!" Emeric shouted as he waded into the surf. "They're not finished with us yet—the bastards'll come back if they see you!"

Sailors crowded the rails to help drag the survivors into the ship. The knight was the last to follow. He sank to the deck, biting back a moan. "My arm's broken," he told Magnus. "They hit us hard. One of my best men, Longspres the bowman, is dead back there."

Magnus bent over him. "Is there anyone else? I am loath to leave the dead unburied."

The other cursed and shook his head. "They're just over the hill. A hundred Scotsmen on foot, perhaps twenty on horseback. If you had arrived a hair-breadth sooner they would have killed us all."

Magnus did not even lift his head. "Cast off," he shouted.

The sailors scrambled for their rowing benches. The girl came forward. She knelt by the wounded knight, her cloak spreading around her on the deck. After a searching look into Emeric's face, she lifted his arm and carefully pulled the shreds of cloth and mail away from the gash. In the midst of the blood white ends of bone stood up raggedly.

"You took a sword blow," she told him, "that could have severed your arm."

Emeric looked up at Magnus, his eyes wide with surprise to find a woman aboard. His eyes moved quickly back to her. "Yes, a sword blow, demoiselle," he agreed.

The Norseman was shouting the stroke, the sailors pulling hard to get away from the deadly beach. The wind snapped at the leather sail. The knight stared at the girl with the look of a man enchanted in spite of his pain.

She produced a strip of clean cloth from somewhere and talked softly to Emeric as she bound up his arm, explaining that it had yet to be cleaned of dirt and humors; the binding was merely to stop the flow of blood. Beyond the Norse steersman watched them with a baleful glare.

Perhaps, Magnus told himself, he and the steersman were thinking the same thing. That the girl's mad dash to the steering oar to make them run up on the shoal was not the folly it had seemed.

As Emeric had pointed out, if they had arrived at the camp any sooner they would have met the raiders that had come, apparently, to destroy them.

Sweet Jesus, was it possible that the girl had known what was waiting for them?

The thought made Magnus's hair stand up on the back of his neck. He realized that the steersman probably shared it.

That she'd run them aground deliberately.

Four

As soon as they were out of the cove the boat met the force of the gale. The big Norseman at his steering oar couldn't turn it. Wallowing heavily, the earl's tax freighter nosed north in the storm instead of south in the direction of Chester. Worse, night was falling. After a few minutes it was so dark they could no longer see the shoreline.

To be heading in the opposite direction from where they needed to go was madness. Yet they could not stay in the cove waiting to be attacked. Magnus stared at the huge waves rushing at them, well aware no one traveled the treacherous Irish seas at night except Danes, and mad Norsemen.

"Can nothing be done to turn us around?" He had to put his mouth to the steersman's ear to be heard over the wind and the terrified animals. "We are being blown north, into Scotland!"

As he looked into the Norseman's dripping face he could see the answer. The boat was well into the channel taking a following sea. The storm was driving it ahead while huge waves broke over the stern. It was perilous going: the bottom of the boat was already half filled with water.

"Unload," the Norseman shouted back at him. "We must lighten her!"

It was the only thing to do or they were in danger of going under. But in that moment Magnus couldn't help a wild, despairing thought for what was left of the earl's half-yearly tribute. And how he was *not* going to arrive at Chester in triumphant glory as he'd boasted to the Angevins, but virtually empty-handed.

Except—if they survived—for the damned girl. That was all he had to show for this. God and Saint Mary, it would be a wonder if Chester did not clap him in irons and send him to the bottom of the castle dungeons! He'd bring no taxes from this miserable foray, only a stray woman that the earl's subjects on the northeast coast clearly wanted to get rid of.

With fury in his heart Magnus turned and shouted to the men-at-arms to cut loose the livestock from their tethers and start getting them overboard. While they obeyed, the sailors from the other tax boat huddled together, looking frightened, as though they feared they might be next.

Magnus went down the middle of the boat to lend a hand. He helped his men-at-arms lift a sheep and throw it over the rail. Beyond in the towering waves some of the cattle were trying to swim. The struggles and terrified cries of the animals set his teeth on edge.

Magnus shouted to the four men-at-arms to begin on the grain sacks. As the soldiers began to toss the earl's grain overboard Magnus looked down. Night was on them, the only light an eerie nightglow from the storm clouds churning overhead, but he could see the water in the boat was up to the top of his boots. He sloshed forward to the huddled group of Emeric's sailors and shouted to them to find buckets and commence bailing. At the steering oar the Norseman was cursing the rowers, shouting at them to pick up their oars, that they needed to make headway if they were not to capsize.

In a frenzy of energy Magnus went from one end of the boat to the other, crawling over anyone in his way, forcing rowers back onto their benches, picking up ship's gear and tossing it overboard. The boat slowly emptied of everything except its human cargo. But even as it lightened it was clear the freighter was in dire trouble.

The night dragged on. The tired crew was half asleep, yet afraid to give in to any sort of rest. Magnus looked around thinking there was not a man aboard who could forget that with every hour they were being swept even farther north, and away from home. He found the girl helping Emeric with an injured oarsman. Even with his arm bound up the knight had managed to rig a half shelter with his cloak, and they had dragged two of the men under it.

Magnus crouched down to look in on them. "That one's dead," he yelled, "or will be shortly. It is best to put him over the side."

He heard the girl gasp. He supposed it was too bad, since she had been trying to save the poor bastard. He shouted to the knight, "Take off your mail and weapons, that will help. You can't swim much with that arm."

They might as well resign themselves to the fact that sooner or later they would be forced into the sea. Emeric apparently agreed, for he nodded, and started pulling at his hauberk lacings with his good hand.

The girl looked terrified. "No, it can't be!" she wailed. "Is the ship going to sink?"

Magnus started to tell her he didn't know, that his experience with ships was equal to her own. Instead, looking down at that beautiful face, the long gold hair plastered to her skull, he felt a sudden peevishness. What in the name of God and all the saints had pulled him back to the beach as though he had no *will* of his own? Had she cast some sort of spell on him?

He was damned if he knew how it had happened. He had the sudden, evil feeling that this blond witch had willed him to come back and get her by some sort of sorcery. That she had somehow known the camp was under attack. That she'd thrown herself against the steering oar deliberately and run the boat up on a shoal to delay them.

He stuck his face in hers. "The ship sink? I have a feeling that it is you I should be asking, demoiselle, since you seem to know more about what is happening than anyone of us!"

At that moment the steersman shouted, " 'Ware, 'ware, we are coming up on land!"

A huge sea broke in and swept forward to the mast, tangling men and oars and ship's lines in a wall of water.

Magnus grabbed for Emeric and the girl. There were shouts and screams from the hapless crew. As his feet left the deck, Magnus felt hands clutching at him.

The giant wave carried him over the side. The ship

struck a rock with a loud sound of breaking timbers. Half the Irish Sea seemed to pour over them. A bubbling, roaring filled his ears. When his head broke the surface of the water he could see the surf rushing him between shoreline rocks. In the dark he could barely make out the sea striking boulders and shooting white spume skyward.

His feet touched something and slipped off. The weight of his mail and his sword was dragging him under. He couldn't get his hands free. A body, slender but strong, clasped his and would not let go.

Another wave broke over Magnus and tumbled him along. The body he held in his arms—or that held him—was the girl; he could dimly see the top of her head, her floating pale hair. Icy water scraped them between rocks. Magnus got his feet under him again and touched a sandy bottom. Another wave promptly knocked him down.

Magnus fell with the girl's arms around his neck. His sword knocked against his knees. His helmet was gone and he was gulping mouthfuls of water. Drowning as the sea roared around him.

The best time of the day was at vespers, when the nuns sang.

From as early as Edain could remember, which must have been when she was about three years old, the evening worship after the last meal of the day was nearly always bathed in a glow of peace. At vespers the same peace filled the cloisters and halls of St. Sulpice with the wafting, sweet, threadlike sound of the nuns at evensong.

It was such a pleasure, the day's end when the sisters of St. Sulpice were permitted to sing, that the good nuns sometimes ran far beyond their allotted time. And of course were lectured by the prioress, herself a soprano of glorious range, and a prime offender.

The children who lived at the convent until they came of an age to accept the novice's veil or go to work as servants in the town, always bunched together at vespers to one side of the nave of the chapel.

The sweet, unearthly sound of cloistered women's voices in the twilight, the smell of candle smoke, and the shadows beyond the flickering lights, stayed forever in a child's mind. It was a time when the sun set and the cool night began, so still that it seemed the angels came down to listen. After the joyous singing at vespers the day was finally over. Three hours later, at compline, when the venerable sister abbess herself went about checking the doors and the gate, the children were all in bed, asleep.

There were, naturally, times when the day was not so sweet, the nuns not so harmonious, and the cold winds blew, making the choir's voices as sour and complaining as a winter gale in the chapel rafters. Then the endless chants could try one's patience, and even the sister prioress sounded bad.

Edain opened her eyes.

It was not the nuns' voices she heard, but the wind, a cold sound wending its way among the boulders of some seashore. Lying there she could look straight up and see purple scudding clouds racing in a sunlit sky.

It was day, Edain told herself. Not twilight vespers at the convent of St. Sulpice. She'd been dreaming of nuns and peaceful evensong, but what was real was this, and the sound of the wind in the cliffs.

She remembered the storm. She was alive, she thought, tremulously.

She hadn't been sure she'd survive, no matter how the Feeling tried to calm her and tried to assure her that she would live. Now in the bright glare of the sun she remembered the ship breaking up, the waves pounding and breaking about them, the night so dark they could not see where to go except drag themselves away from the raging water.

Slowly she moved her legs. Her whole body was sore from the sea's pounding. She remembered trying to help the young knight and finding she could not do much because of his size and weight, his mail and sword.

Yet it seemed they had managed somehow to crawl into a shelter between the rocks. Sometime later, in the stormy light of dawn, the tide had come up and lapped at their feet. It woke Edain, and she urged the knight to move to higher ground under an overhang of rock. There they found sand and boulders mixed with dead broom sedge as springy as hay. They'd fallen down in it, mindless with weariness, and gone to sleep.

She sighed and rolled against the big body next to her. They seemed to be alone. She did not even want to get up and look.

Overhead, gulls wheeled and screamed. The sun made the sheltered spot almost comfortable. Wherever the rest were—the Norseman and his crew,

Emeric the knight, all the sailors and men-at-arms—they were not on that stretch of beach. The place was locked in silence.

Edain could not help a small shudder. Perhaps none of them had survived. At her movement the man next to her stirred but did not wake.

Edain squirmed closer. The sun was drying their clothes, sticky with seawater. Where sunlight touched their skin it made a lovely heat.

The young knight captain lay with his sword and belt twisted under him. At some time or other during the night Edain had pulled his mail hauberk up above his hips and hauled close enough to snuggle against his warm belly. Even now her hands grasped bare skin at his back and under his padded jacket. Where she had dragged his hose down in front, his muscular belly pressed against her groin and legs, the skirt of her gown hiked up to meet it.

Her bare legs, Edain realized with a start. Her shoes were gone, lost in the storm, and so were her stockings. She sighed. The young knight's body was too comfortable to pull away; she did not intend to move for a while.

He slept a deep, exhausted sleep. And barely moved except to twitch where her fingers explored him. She remembered his running up and down the length of the boat, shouting commands.

But he'd not been able to keep the ship from foundering, she thought as she looked down at his face. She supposed he'd be made to account for that, as well as the loss of the second ship back in the cove. Plainly this had been a most disastrous venture for him, no matter how fortunate he was to survive.

She rubbed her fingers along the smooth flesh of his back, and he shifted a little. If and when they ever managed to get back to Chester, this brave young lordling might find that his liege would have been more pleased if he had done the honorable thing, and gone down with his ship and his men.

Edain lifted herself on one elbow to look into his face.

He had a gold earring stud in one ear, she saw, peering at it. It was mostly hidden by his thick dark red hair so one would not notice it at first. The hair itself was beautiful, wavy, slightly curling even if sticky with seawater. The long russet eyelashes that turned up in starry spikes at the tips were just as enviable.

But he was very much a man, she thought, resting her chin on her hand. She touched the gold earring with the tip of her finger. The waving red hair, the earbob, his finely crafted mail coat, his sword marked him very much the young nobleman.

Edain lowered her hand and slid it into the opening at his belly, the warm spot between his mail and his hose. Her legs were warm where his groin pressed against her.

On board the boat she had had a strange vision of him naked, the most startling she'd ever had; she was not sure even now the reason for it. Yet his clothes had turned as transparent as the blue water around him, and she had seen his fine soldier's body.

He was so *warm,* she thought. Her hand could not seem to stop exploring smooth skin in the gap between his hauberk and belt. Her fingers were telling her it was true, that he was not hairy like some of the old gatemen at the convent who bathed stripped to the waist at the stable yard well.

He was firm and smooth and very well-muscled. He had trained hard; from where she could reach he was layered with lean muscles. Below that her hands found slowly breathing ribs, and the softer flesh of the indent of his waist.

She ran a hand down and touched his hose, sandy and damp, and under the cloth the flat strength of his buttocks. His leg twitched slightly in response.

Edain suddenly wished the handsome knight would go on sleeping for a long time. She was surprised that his body so fascinated her. But then she'd never in her life had had one to explore. She felt very wicked; she was fairly sure the nuns would not approve. Even though, of course, she had never discussed with them exploring a man's body while he slept.

Above them gulls circled with their catlike cries. The brisk wind added its moan. They were not far from the sea; she could hear the surf booming on the rocks. It would be prudent for her to be up and about looking for the others. Although she was fairly certain there were no survivors about, or they would have heard them.

At least she could survey the cove to see what could be found. Perhaps find a road to take them to some town or hamlet. Even driftwood for a fire. They would be needing dry driftwood badly if they hoped to dry out their clothes.

Edain lay still. She had just discovered something.

When she shifted away slightly she could see down the knight's front. His smooth bare belly with the hauberk pulled up from it showed a fine line of russet hair that disappeared into the drawstring of his hose.

A vivid picture of him naked on board the boat came back to her. The drawstring was wet and would not give, even when she picked at it with her fingernails. But the hose sagged open enough to look down.

It was only a matter of looking again, she told herself. If she just leaned forward and pulled the top of his hose out a little . . .

A voice from the body she was pressed to made her jump. She lifted her head and looked up into the tawny eyes of the knight. His hand grabbed her wrist and held it away from him.

"I—I—" Edain cried. "I was just *curious!*"

It was the God-given truth. But she could see by the way his eyes widened that it was not the best answer she could have thought of at that moment.

He slammed the offending hand against her breast with a thump.

"Christ in heaven," the knight captain said through stiff lips, "you're even more wanton than I thought you were. No wonder de Brise was eager to get rid of you!"

Five

When they got to the top of the hill Magnus stopped and looked around. Below lay the cove where they'd spent the night of the storm, its boulder-strewn shore extending as far as one could see.

Later someone was to tell them this part of the Scots' coast was called the famous Teeth of Kirkinner, home of many a ship's grave. But from the knoll Magnus could see no trace of a floating spar or even a torn piece of sail to mark where the earl's tax boat had broken up. Only the rock-strewn shoreline and the Irish Sea whipped to whitecaps by the wind.

He kept dismay from his face. There was no need to alarm the girl, but he had hoped they would find someone alive. Perhaps one of the sailors who could tell them where they were and help them get back to the borders of the Earl of Chester's lands.

He looked out to sea, shading his eyes. Since the storm had blown them northward, his guess was that they were somewhere on the south coast of Scotland. But it was only that—a guess. He didn't think they had gone as far as the wild highlands, or the western islands beyond.

Still, Scotland was bad enough.

He looked down at the girl. Her clothes were still

wet for she stood shivering, her teeth clamped together to keep them from chattering. She had bound up her hair in a torn veil, but the gold tendrils escaped around her face, stirred by the wind. She was slender, tall for a woman, her curves nicely revealed even under the sodden cloak. Seeing her like that, beautiful in spite of having nearly drowned, Magnus couldn't help thinking that the bailiff's story of de Brise's attempts to marry her off so that he could claim his *le droit de seigneur* was meant to put a good face on another, more likely tale: that this extraordinarily beautiful little piece had been de Brise's mistress or concubine. And de Brise's wife had wisely made him get rid of her. She reminded Magnus more than ever of a jeweled image with those slightly tilted emerald eyes. She looked foreign, not like the women of France or England; he couldn't put his finger on it. Of course the bailiff had sworn she was an orphan, raised by the nuns at St. Sulpice convent and brought there at such an early age that no one had any idea of her origins.

Magnus said, "It can do no harm if we travel north along the shore for a while, to see if any of the others have survived the wreck."

He did not think they had, but there was no other course of action he could think of except to throw themselves on the mercy of the nearest Scots' villagers if there was a town nearby. And that would undoubtedly prove foolhardy: these shores were notorious for wreckers who kidnapped survivors for ransom, killed those who were penniless. The Scottish king had settled many Norman families on fiefs here in an attempt to civilize the place. There were now Norman Bruces in Annandale, de Morvilles in Ayrshire. And the fitzAlans in Lauderdale, of whom it was said that William the Lion had raised their barons to the position of hereditary "stewards" or "stewarts." And that the ignorant Scots were already calling the fitzAlans by that name.

He decided it was probably best to go along the coast in the hope of finding some of the crew. At the same time they would look for the manor houses of any Normans settled in the district. Magnus remembered that if they were anywhere near Ayrshire he had a claim of distant kinship with the de Morvilles, who'd come from the same town in Normandy as his grandfather's people.

He rubbed his jaw, covered with the morning's fine stubble. Making their way through this part of Scotland was not going to be easy. For one thing, there was the way they looked. Although he had lost his fine, heavy tourney helmet in the shipwreck, he was still wearing mail of a quality seldom seen this far north. It would not be hard to find a barefoot Scot who admired his Spanish-made hauberk enough to kill him for it.

Jesu, Magnus thought, the same thing was true of his sword! His father had given it to him when he was knighted, along with his steel spurs. The weapon was intended to be a treasure for all time, the very thing an earl would bestow on his firstborn and heir. Even King Henry had admired the blade, hinting that he would like one like it if the Earl of Morlaix was ever so generously inclined. Unless he could do something about his possessions, Magnus realized, he was a walking invitation to robbery and murder.

And that was not the only thing. There was the girl.

He studied her profile as she stood beside him looking anxiously out at the sea. She was wearing a silver circlet on her brow and silver bangles at her wrists. Her gown was salt-stained and torn, but it was silk, elegantly embroidered. She was barefoot, her slippers ripped away at some time during the night, but the cloak she wore was of the finest wool.

Dressed as a bride, he was reminded. Part of the *droit de seigneur* story. Although from the way she looked and acted—especially when he'd caught her boldly peering into his hose at his privates—his first opinion, that she was de Brise's concubine, was more nearly the right one.

Magnus rubbed at his unshaven jaw again, wondering what in the devil he was going to do with her. He was going to have enough trouble taking care of himself, and the girl was like a red flag, inviting attack from brigands and lechers of every variety. Unless he wanted to spend all his time defending her, it would be wiser to leave her right here.

God knew, he thought, studying her, that it was a temptation to leave her. As he should have done there on the beach the first time he saw her. But in some strange way he was coming to believe that God was seeing to it that this girl was his burden. His penance.

The remains of his hangover echoed through Magnus's skull as he faced the terrible truth that God was undoubtedly punishing him for his dissolute ways. For the drinking and gambling and boasting that had led him to this fix. He'd had plenty to regret since he'd begun his roistering life at the Earl of Chester's court.

He could see why the Almighty would be angry with him over the loss of the tax ship, the earl's cargo thrown overboard and abandoned, the crew probably all gone to their deaths.

Inwardly he groaned. In the harsh light of day what could be a clearer task than to return to Chester with the only thing that had been saved from this disaster? His only witness, the girl. Who could testify that he had tried to do his best in spite of blows of massive ill-fortune.

Magnus knew if he did this, he was accepting trouble without limit. But he also knew that if he ever hoped to be in the Earl of Chester's good graces again he must bring her back. And tell the whole story from beginning to end.

He took a deep breath. "What do they call you?" he said.

She started, then gave him a wary look, no doubt remembering that he had shouted at her for pawing him while he was asleep back on the beach.

"Edain," she whispered.

"Edain?" It sounded vaguely Irish. "Is there more?" When she did not answer, "Come, no other name but 'Edain'?"

She shook her head, no.

Magnus made an impatient sound between his teeth. "Well, girl, in my opinion we are somewhere in the land of the border Scots. You must realize we have no food, no water, except what we can find or steal until we can make our way to the nearest manor house. And we will have to discard some of our possessions or we will be set upon and robbed just for what we have on our backs."

She lifted her head. Magnus gazed into wide green eyes, not wanting to tell her something else he'd just remembered. That if the Scots along the coast discovered that he, the son and heir of the Earl of Morlaix, had fallen into their hands, their piratical lust for ransom would go sky high. He only said, "Follow me down among the rocks here, to where the dead tree stands."

He started down the path. She padded after him. He knew her bare feet were cold on the rocky ground but he could think of nothing to do about it at the moment. He needed to buy or steal her a pair of shoes somehow. Or fashion something from a cloth and straw, like the villeins, when they had time.

But first, he told himself, they needed to get rid of anything that might tempt thieves.

Standing by the dead tree, Magnus shrugged out of his hauberk. He pulled off the mail cowl from around his neck and stuck it in his padded jacket, thinking he might need to fight again somewhere, sometime. It was bad enough to have to sacrifice the precious mail coat.

When he had scraped a hole with his dagger in the base of the dead tree, Magnus folded the hauberk and laid it in it. Then he sat down and took off his spurs, and put them on top of the mail.

Quickly, so that he would not have to look at the symbols of his knighthood, Magnus scraped dirt into the hole, then stood up and tamped it down with his boots. When this was done he rolled a nearby rock into place at the foot of the dead tree and covered it.

The girl had watched every move. "No one will find it."

He had almost forgotten about her. While he'd been digging with the sun warm on his back he'd been filled with thoughts of home. Of Castle Morlaix, of his mother and brother and sisters, the fine horses his father raised, the rolling fields of golden corn, what the land looked like there. And not the life he'd led at Chester's court since leaving them all.

Magnus hoped with all his heart that God was truly not punishing him for being empty-headed, a roisterer, a waster of his youth and strength. But here he was, shipwrecked and abandoned with nothing except the clothes on his back, his sword and a small purse of silver he'd kept back from the damnable dice game. The coin was hardly enough to buy a loaf of bread and a cup of beer.

Then he remembered, squinting at the sun, they'd yet to break their fast. It was approaching high noon. There was nothing to eat or drink and he was starving.

"Stand still," he told the girl. He stripped off her silver bangles, the silver headband with the small ruby stones, and finally the small silver chain about her neck.

Her ornaments were only as much as he could hold in one of his big hands; he found he hated to take them away from her. But he knelt and dug another hole with his poignard and put them in and covered them with dirt.

She looked so woebegone Magnus felt compelled to say something. "We will come back for them," he said. "See, I have marked the spot, under this dead tree, on this knoll that overlooks the cove."

As they left the hill he noted that she kept looking back. He told himself they were undoubtedly the only gewgaws she'd ever had.

His wrathful God was being merciless.

We will not be coming back here, Edain knew as she turned away from the dead tree. It made her feel strangely empty but there was nothing they could do because their path led far away, perhaps to the east.

The Feeling had been strong when she'd watched him bury his spurs. She had a vivid picture at that moment that a tall man with dark red hair like his, who seemed both strong and impetuous and good, had given the spurs to him, probably when he was knighted. His father?

His father, the Feeling agreed.

While the knight was burying his possessions she'd had a glimpse of many people—young girls who were probably his sisters, another young man, perhaps a brother; the mother and father, a jumbled sense of a mist-filled land and horses and townspeople and a castle. Overall there was a spirit of love and youth and growth and happy discord. Looking into his thoughts like that, he did not seem so spoiled and aware of how handsome he was, as he had before.

And he still had his sword, Edain told herself as she picked her way down the rocky path from the cliff.

It was his sword that was important, after all.

* * *

A long time later they came through a mountain pass and found a small valley with a herd of sheep. The shepherd was not in sight. They could hear him away calling to his flock, and the barking of a dog. Magnus gave Edain his sword to hold and slithered down the grassy incline to gather up a furry pouch that, from its reek, was the shepherd's lunch.

As he came zigzagging back up the mountainside he broke into a run. The woods there were sparse and offered little cover; they could hear the shepherd's dog now, yapping frantically at unseen intruders.

Running as hard as they could, they followed the mountain path, going north, leaving the coast behind. They ran for a long time, far away from the shepherd's valley, until they could run no more, and finally let themselves slide into a steep ravine filled with rowans and holly trees, and a shallow, swift-running brook.

"Did you leave him silver?" Edain panted, thinking of the hungry shepherd without his food.

He flung her a look. "Yea, and knighted him while I was at it. Jesu, did you think I'd announce our thieving presence with a coin for payment?"

She was silent. She supposed he was right, that they needed to keep themselves hidden from the common folk as well as the inevitable robbers. And look for what any Norman would regard as safe territory, the abode of other Normans. He seemed to be sure there were several fiefs the Scottish king had bestowed on some Norman knights there in the borders.

Edain got down on her hands and knees and

drank from the stream until she was breathless. The water was wonderful, even more so than food. Since she'd wakened with her mouth full of salt from the sea she'd been so thirsty she'd thought she'd die of it.

She sat back on her heels and wiped her lips with her hand. The young knight peeled back the goatskin wrappings of the shepherd's food, then stopped, staring at the sinewy white globe he'd uncovered.

If it hadn't been for her own aching hunger Edain would have laughed at his expression.

"What is it?" He looked as though he couldn't believe his eyes. Or his nose. "Saint George save us, surely it's not meant to be eaten?"

At that moment Edain knew this handsome knight had never been hungry in his life. At least not so much as to have to eat rough peasant fare. She sat back on her heels. "You've had meat scrap pudding before," she told him. "This is the same, with barley and ground oats mixed in, cooked in a sheep's stomach."

"Cooked in a sheep's stomach," he muttered. "I've had pork and beef tripe, it's a favorite dish of mine. But this doesn't look anything like it."

He lifted the shepherd's food and smelled it. She saw him recoil slightly. "Holy Mother, how do you know? That this is what you say it is?"

Edain shrugged. "Anyone who lives on this coast knows haggis. The shepherds make it after they slaughter a sheep. They say it even keeps well. The herders sometimes have a whole season of haggis buried for the—"

"Never mind," he said quickly. "Enlighten me no

more." He sliced open the outer skin and cautiously cut himself a sliver. He had it in his mouth for a while before he finally swallowed it. Then, with eyebrows raised, he offered her a slice.

Edain took the piece and ate it. She was hungry and also used to shepherds' food. The mountain people sometimes shared haggis with the orphans at St. Sulpice's convent when they drove in the flocks for slaughter in the autumn.

Anyway, haggis was not as potent as the hard sausage the Scots made of sheep gut stuffed with offal meats and wild garlic and acorn meal that kept for months in any weather. One could usually tell a herder with his store of mutton sausage somewhere in his shirt when the wind blew downwind from him.

After they had eaten and drunk from the stream, the knight pulled off his cloak and hung it on a tree branch. "We must try to wash the salt from our clothes and our skin," he told her. "If we do not, it will make sores. The sailors warned me."

He went down to the little brook, sat on the bank, and took off his boots. Then he waded through the stream, peeling off his padded jacket but keeping on his sword until he was out of sight.

Edain followed him down to the water, glad of a chance to wash the haggis from her hands. She, too, took off her cloak, and with a sigh hung it in a tree.

It really was too cold to wash. Or to even think about baring one's body in the brisk wind. The water in the stream was like ice. But her salty damp gown and her woolen shift stuck to her skin. Slowly, she undid the laces of her gown and let the garment drop into the stream.

As she stared at the gown at her feet she wondered how she would get warm while her other garments dried. Even standing full in the sun was not enough; she was already shaking with chill.

She peeled off her shift and threw it after the gown. If her clothing ever dried, at least she would be clean and comfortable.

She scooped water with both hands onto her legs, trying not to gasp at its touch. Then her arms. At the last she splashed her breasts and stomach, unable to keep from making small screams of pain.

Dear God in heaven, the salt clung to her flesh in spite of her frantic efforts! Even after she rubbed with handfuls of sand from the streambed she still felt sticky.

She picked up her shift and wrung it out and used it to wipe her stinging skin, noting that everywhere she scoured she turned red as a crabapple. Finally the gummy sea salt washed away.

In a fever of shivering Edain stamped on the gown, forcing water through it, then picked it up and wrung it out and threw it up on the bank. All that was left were her linen drawers that tied at the knees. She undid the ribbons and the waist drawstring with red, stiffened fingers, and peeled off the undergarment.

It was not just a matter of stamping on the drawers to get them clean; she was now so cold she had to do a veritable jig to keep going at all! Her feet in the brook were so chilled she could hardly feel them.

The noon sun was moving in the sky. That part of the little stream and its bank was now in shadow. The wind whined under the trees, making gooseflesh stand up on her arms and legs.

Edain kicked her knees higher as the shepherds did when dancing, her feet pounding the under-drawers. She clapped her hands and shook her arms over her head and in a few moments her heart was pumping madly. She tingled all over and feeling had returned to her toes.

The drawers were thoroughly washed, but Edain did not stop. Saints in heaven, she was finding if she kept on she might actually get warm! She whirled around, sending sheets of water into the air. Then her feet slipped a little on the stones.

She came to a stop, gasping but definitely warmer. And hoping that she had not trampled her drawers beyond repair.

When she stopped she sensed something. And realized she was not alone.

She saw he was standing there in the stream not too far from her, barefoot, wearing only his hose, his unsheathed sword in his hand.

His hair was still wet and hung to his shoulders in dark red strings. He was staring at Edain, transfixed. As if he had come on a woods wraith, or ghost.

"I heard you screaming," he said hoarsely.

Six

It was true, Magnus had thought the girl was being attacked.

He'd heard her cries from where he was bathing only a few feet around the bend of the stream, and had yanked on his hose and come splashing through the shallow brook like a madman, envisioning wild Scots tearing off her clothes, throwing her down, perhaps already on top of her subjecting her to their lusts.

Instead, he plunged through the stream and found a scene that brought him up short. What he encountered there in the midst of the Highland brook was something one never expected to find in this world if one was a good Christian. And certainly not in broad daylight.

It was, he saw, a hair-raising vision, a kelpie or water troll that the old tales said inhabited such streams.

There it was, a hell-spawned spirit from dark pagan days, spinning and stamping crazily in some demon-dance. But at the same time golden and slender, stark naked, incredibly beautiful, flinging herself about in the flickering light under the trees. And all the while making sharp, shrieking noises.

It took a moment, but Magnus recognized the sounds as the screams of peril he'd thought he'd heard.

At exactly the same moment the kelpie or water demon caught sight of him and stopped in midspin. She gazed at him, wide-eyed and panting. Too startled, apparently, to cover herself.

Naked, was all Magnus's numbed brain could think.

There, standing ankle-deep in the mountain stream, lit by dappled light through the autumn trees, was the most beautiful body his eyes had ever beheld.

No wonder he had thought her a water sprite! The same haunted feeling he'd had a moment ago made the hair prickle again on his neck.

While she stood wide-eyed, still as a statue, his avid gaze took in her golden skin, the slender form that was perfection itself with thrusting, rosy-tipped breasts, a tiny waist, and gently curving hips. The long legs were enough to entice any saintly monk from the depths of his cloister.

The vision shuddered, breaking the spell. She turned quickly toward the bank, but Magnus was there ahead of her.

De Brise's concubine, he reminded himself, stepping to block her.

He only wanted to put his hands on her, to make sure she was real. The spirit of the glen had him enchanted. He had never seen a woman so dazzlingly beautiful in his life.

Magnus reached out to catch her by the arm. As he did his hand brushed the cool perfection of her breast. A drop of water hung from the rosy nipple. Without thinking, he touched it with his fingertip.

She went perfectly still, turning her head to look up at him with her light-filled, emerald eyes. "No," she whispered, "you can't."

Magnus did not dare answer; the blood was pounding madly in his ears.

Can't?

He *could*, and he *would!* Just the touch of her, and he was burningly, instantly aroused!

He could not get de Brise out of his mind. He told himself that by all the saints she was much too good for Chester's petty knight. Much too exquisitely, glowingly lovely. Even if de Brise had a jealous wife he could not see how the man could bear to send her away.

And then somehow the vision was in his arms. He pulled her quickly against him, and the sensation of her silky wet body, chilled from the stream, against his own half-bare one, was almost more than he could bear.

With a groan Magnus found her soft, yielding lips. His own were suddenly shaking, wanting to devour her sweetness. Their mouths ignited a fire that shot through him, and drew a muffled, breathless sound from her. When he pulled back and looked down he saw the surprise in her eyes.

There was no time to think about it.

"Come," he croaked, "we can't do this here, standing in a stream. Let me take you to a better place."

He bent and picked her up, and carried her to the bank and laid her down in a spot of sunshine.

He couldn't wait; he was out of his own soggy hose and sword belt in a trice.

It was still cold even in the sun, and the wind raked their bare flesh. But lying there before him, in full sunlight, the beautiful naked girl heated Magnus's blood to the boiling point. When he knelt down before her, she took one startled look at his uncovered groin and his massive readiness, and quickly clapped her hands over her eyes.

"Ah, sweetheart, don't do that," he begged her.

What in the devil did de Brise look like under his chausses anyway? This was no way for her to act!

And what was it she was trying to see when she peeped into his hose earlier? If she was looking for a deformity, he could certainly allay her fears. Outside of some few complaints that he erred on the large side, what he had there was perfectly formed, and normal.

Besides, Magnus told himself, none of the wives and serving girls he'd bedded at court in Chester had ever complained. On the contrary, there were some who professed to be so deliriously fond of his privates that he'd had the devil's own time getting rid of them. But Jesu, he'd certainly never faced one who couldn't bear to look at them. For a kept woman, de Brise's concubine was strangely timid.

Smiling reassuringly, Magnus lowered himself onto her and kept her busy for several delightful moments kissing her and stroking and caressing her lovely body. His own passion was strong and painfully urgent. He cupped her beautiful breasts in his hands and kissed them, then lightly nipped the rosy buds with his teeth until she gasped.

"Does this excite you?" he whispered. "Sweeting, I desire only to give you pleasure. Tell me if what I do does not please you and I will stop."

She seemed not to hear him. A little distracted moan broke from her lips when his hand slid between her thighs, and his fingertip lightly caressed the little nub of her desire. By this time Magnus was in flames. He had a hectic thought that never, in all his experience with women, had there been one that so wildly and quickly enchanted him. She lay in his arms in tantalizing surrender, her jewel-like eyes heavy-lidded. She opened her body like a flower to him, tremulous, a little reluctant—and yet he could not mistake the response in the hand that crept to the back of his neck to caress him softly, nor the clasp of her thighs against his.

She wanted him, he was sure of it. Yet she was hardly showing a courtesan's practiced arts.

For a moment in the midst of his fevered burning, Magnus considered that he should be flattered. That he had taken this beautiful, experienced passion's toy by storm, and so roused her that she had no time for artifice.

"Magnus," she whispered, her eyes closed.

He didn't remember telling her his name. It didn't matter. "Dearling, sweetheart," he murmured as he settled himself between her legs, "I want to adore your beautiful body. I want to pleasure you with mine."

It was what Magnus always said, with a few variations. He slid his hands under her rounded bottom to lift her. His head was spinning. She was exquisite, soft but fiery. In a second he would breech that tight, luscious portal of her flesh and bury himself in her. He couldn't wait.

He gave her an all-possessing kiss at the same time he skillfully thrust into her. She gasped. He felt her hands holding tightly to him, her body straining against his as though they were about to begin a voyage, experience another shipwreck, and must seize each other and hold on to survive.

That alone should have warned him. A passing thought told him to pull back, be cautious, but it was too late.

He felt the barrier break but not as one usually experienced these things. There was a tingling shock. Before he could know his mistake and withdraw, the vibrant power seized his flesh in a hot-cold sensation that burst into numberless shards, deliciously, brilliantly piercing every sinew of his being. Like colors. Like music. Exquisite pleasure exploded behind his eyes. In his groin.

Shuddering, Magnus thrust in and filled her warm, luscious tightness. He did not feel her flinch, or hear any cry of discomfort. And yet he knew what had happened.

Before he could marshal his wits—if he could do such a thing considering the convulsions of ecstasy tearing through him—the tingling shock radiated out again from where he was buried in her golden flesh. It was as sharp and mind-shaking as a lightning bolt.

Magnus couldn't stop. He felt himself swelling, growing even more urgent, while his naked body was besieged by an invisible shower of sparks. He felt himself being lifted as, wrapped in each other's arms, he and the golden girl fell through the heavens among the shooting stars, the blazing rays of the sun. He was in her, possessed by her, the center of his body locked into her, and they were on fire. She was an eternal, searing flame twined around him, whimpering her desire, her tongue in his mouth, her legs tight about his waist.

Battered by waves of such passion, he knew it could not last long. Magnus heard his lustful bellow, her soft cry as their bodies reached their peak. It took but a giant, wrenching moment. And then he felt the earth reel, the stars and the sun and the moon slide back into their places in the unearthly golden afterglow.

It was over. He could not believe it. He shook his head to clear it, breathing hard. It was like nothing he had ever experienced, and he could not wait to have her again. He lowered his sweating body gently to kiss her mouth.

He looked down at her. She, too, was wet and thoroughly tousled, her eyes closed, her delicate lips swollen from his eager kisses.

Where had they been? This passionate lovemaking had not just taken place on the bank of a stream in some place in wild Scotland, Magnus was sure of it.

Jesu, he thought as he lifted his head rather foggily, there was even a perfume, like summer wildflowers, on the November wind! And unless his eyes deceived him, gold motes danced in the air around them, a pleasure veil whose remnants floated away like jewel-dust under the limbs of the trees and over the surface of the running brook. As Magnus watched, disbelieving, the gold dust drifted away and disappeared.

A second later the wind touched his bare shoulder blades with the shock of ice water. He shuddered, and the girl stirred under him. Wincing, he slipped out of her.

She opened her eyes.

That emerald blaze always enchanted him, the long lashes thick as glossy miniver, against her cheek. But now Magnus found with what was left of his muddled brain that she could cast an even greater spell. Because she smiled.

He had never seen her smile. It left him speechless. It was as golden, as glorious, as the mysterious lovemaking. He could do nothing, either, when she lifted herself slightly and touched her lips to his.

"I didn't know." She lifted her hand to touch his sweaty hair and brush it back from his brow. "Magnus." She sighed. "Wonderful, Magnus, it is so strange that I am here in your arms."

He felt the same tinge of unease when he heard her speak his name. "Lie still," he told her.

Magnus got to his feet and fetched his cloak where he had hung it in the trees. It was almost dry, warm from the sun.

She sat up, but he quickly knelt beside her and folded the cloak around them, and they lay back together in the dry leaves. She put her hands on his chest to warm them and snuggled against him. Since they wore no clothes and their bare bodies were twined together, they were soon warm and comfortable.

Magnus looked up through the branches of the tree above them, thinking hard. He had lain with a reasonable number of women since he had attained his manhood, but none had ever been like this. Already he was dreading turning her over to whoever would care for her at the Earl of Chester's court.

Sweet Mary, he thought, his life became more complicated at every turn! How could he leave this angel beauty, who was enough to dazzle any man under the age of ninety, when he had survived shipwreck and imminent death with her? Jesus God, when he had taken her *virginity?*

He knew nothing about her, except the most damnably intimate knowledge, of course. The rapturous little moans of her desire. The feel of her hands on his most tender organs. The clasp of her tight, hot luscious little channel of feminine flesh as he possessed her. And she possessed *him.* And always, the memory of the sight of her, beautiful as a woods goddess, dancing naked in the stream.

She was no concubine. He had been a fool even to consider it. Now, he thought, almost groaning aloud, when he brought her to Chester's court there were those who would use her like one.

The thought gave him a cold chill in the very core of his being. Sweet Jesus, he was responsible for *that,* too! If it had not been for his stupidity she would still be untouched.

Still, he must bring her back with him, there was no way to explain the disaster of this voyage without her. Now that he had lain with her, now that he had experienced a sweet ecstasy that one seldom found on this earth, this beautiful girl had become both his blessing, and his curse.

Perhaps he should marry her.

The thought added a cramp of sheer dread to the other pain in the pit of Magnus's belly.

He knew full well she was not such a girl, an orphan from a convent in the wild borders, that either his mother or his father would consent to his marrying. God and Saint Mary, he would wound the angel in his arms even further to subject her to his family's rejection! Magnus cursed himself. He had practically made a whore of her.

He looked down at her, lying so trustingly by his side. *Wonderful Magnus,* she had said. The words were like knives cutting into his flesh.

He saw she had gone to sleep.

She was sleeping in his arms. He felt an anguish so deep he could have wept. He wanted to wake her to ask, "Where do you come from? What is this strange magic that seems to follow you, to tell you of events that have yet to occur? And have you no knowledge of your lineage, other than that you were an orphan, left with the nuns to be raised?"

It was warm where they lay. Even warmer to be holding her now. Magnus rested his chin on the top of her golden hair, smelled the flowery scent of it, and yawned.

No matter what the troubles that assailed them, they were still greatly wearied from the ordeal of the shipwreck. He could feel tiredness dragging at him. He closed his eyes.

He woke sometime later with a start. The sun was going down and the wind was still, but it was colder.

He knew at once the girl was not there with him under the cloak.

He sprang up, feeling the absurdity of being there, naked, in the empty woods with sunlight fading. First he had to get his clothes. She could not have gone far.

He started toward the stream, thinking that she, too, had gone to collect her garments. On the way he gathered up his hose where he had dropped them, and stepped into them. He found the jacket, the padded gambeson he had hung in a rowan tree.

"Edain," he called. He called again, softly, because there was no telling who might be about.

She was not at the brook. He turned back, thinking she had gone into the woods to relieve herself. Or to look for berries. Anything.

Magnus was beginning to feel cold fear like a knot in his chest. She would have left to find her clothes and dress herself because night was coming on. She would have come back. After what they had done in that golden afternoon it was madness to think that now she would run off into some unknown land and leave him.

He was sure of it. Even before he saw the trampled ground by the clump of alder bushes, the hoofprints of unshod horses where they had seized her and carried her off.

Seven

As soon as Asgard left the justiciar's quarters in Edinburgh Castle and started down the crowded road into the town he was joined by a serjeant of his order.

"Sir Asgard?" The youth saluted him smartly. His white tunic had only a red border at the throat to mark that he was a Templar; of the knights, serjeants, chaplains, and servants of the order of the Poor Knights of Christ and the Temple of Solomon, only the knights were allowed to wear the red cross blazoned on the front and back of their surcoats.

The serjeant, who couldn't have been over twenty, tried to look properly austere. "Brother Tristan de Montville at your service, sir. I am to escort you to our local commandery."

Asgard nodded. It solved the problem of finding an inn for the night. He had just not expected to be greeted so promptly.

He had supposed it would be logical to find a Templar compound in Edinburgh; since King William the Lion had introduced so much that was Norman French into his country, why not Templars, too?

Besides, Asgard thought as the serjeant guided them through Edinburgh's narrow streets, no doubt

King William was making good use of Templar funds. Every Templar commandery these days was also a bank. His order's original business, protecting travelers in the Holy Land, had led to caring for pilgrims' money, transporting it back to Europe when necessary, changing currency, and finally, investments and lending money to Europe's monarchs and kingdoms. After all, the feeling went, it was better for Christians to borrow from the famed fighting monks of the Holy Land than from moneylenders like the Jews. Or worse, the clever Italians.

"Has the commandery been here long?" Asgard called out.

The serjeant turned in the saddle. "Long enough to do God's work and be blessed by it, brother."

Asgard almost snorted. He couldn't help remembering himself at that age: the same piety had oozed from him like sweat. Although he was damned if he could remember looking so smug about it.

There was a little fog in the lower streets of the town. Asgard drew his cloak about him, thinking of all the time that had passed. Twelve years. It seemed he had known everything at the serjeant's age—and nothing. Old Brother Robert had been the one who had interviewed him when he applied to become a Templar. Green and arrogant, Asgard hadn't known what the old man meant when he'd said, "You seek what is a great thing, to become a Templar, but you do not yet know the strong precepts of the Order. For you see us from the outside, well dressed, well mounted, and well equipped, but you cannot know the austerities. For when you wish to be on this side of the sea, you will be beyond it, and vice versa. And when you wish to sleep you must be awake, and when you wish to eat you must go hungry. Can you bear these things for the honor of God and the safety of your soul?"

Ahead of him the serjeant trotted his horse into a market square. Beyond the town walls there was a glimpse of the autumn countryside.

"We do not live in Edinburgh, Sir Asgard," the boy called. "We have built a commandery in the country, where there is room for the growing of crops and the practice of arms."

Asgard studied the helmeted back of the serjeant's head.

To apply to be a Knight Templar was simple: one had to believe in the Holy Catholic Faith, to be born legitimate and of knightly family, not be married nor in holy orders, not be in debt, be strong in mind and in body, and must not have bribed anyone to gain admission to the Order.

Yes, simple enough. Many youths could qualify to become Templars in the north of France, especially younger sons like himself. And oh, holy Jesus in heaven how he had wanted it! He'd dreamed of nothing else since he was twelve. Templars had seemed like gods to him then.

When the day came, he'd knelt before the brother of the commandery swearing to obey the Master of the Temple in the faraway Holy Land and all superiors, to preserve his chastity, the good usages and the good customs of the Order, to own no property, to protect, defend, and enlarge the kingdom of Jerusalem, and never to permit Christians to be murdered or unjustly disinherited, and not to leave the Order without permission.

When Brother Guigo had raised the new knights to their feet and placed their white Templar mantles with the red crosses over their shoulders, kissed them, and welcomed them into their new life, Asgard had felt exalted, transported with holy ecstasy. This was for him indeed a new life!

Now he could not think about it without a deep bitterness.

Sinless, innocent—totally unblemished at that tender age—God and St. Mary, what did he need with a new life? He pitied the poor young fool he had been; it had been stupid for him to be so carried away. A "new life" for a twenty-year-old who had not even had a woman, was still growing his first scraggly beard, who played the harp and shawm surpassingly well but had not spilled his first blood in combat?

A taste of what it was going to be like came when they were marched into a room and stripped embarrassingly naked before the brothers, who gave them two shirts, a long-sleeved tunic, two pairs of shoes and drawers, a long surcoat open at the front from the waist down, a cape, two mantles, one for summer and one lined with lambswool for winter, a leather belt, a cap and a hat. And in addition two towels, bedding, a suit of mail, helmet, leggings, and white surcoat with red cross, plus a sword, lance and shield and three knives, one for eating. Each young knight was provided with three horses, the serjeants and men-at-arms having only one.

Standing there in that cold, bare barracks room of the Falaise commandery with the eyes of his brother Templars upon him, it was plain to Asgard that in spite of his fear and trembling he would become by divine grace a warrior and a monk, a member of the order so nobly dedicated to Christ and the defense of the Holy Temple that his faith would never swerve from that goal.

The trouble was, of course, that he had not really listened to what Brother Guigo had told him. That when a Templar wished to be asleep he would be awake, that when he wished to eat he must go hungry, and that when he wished to be on that side of the sea, in France most especially, he would be sent instead to the bloody nightmare of Outremer, immersed in the corruption not only of the Holy Land's savage and warring countries, but the unspeakable, secret outrages of the Knights of the Holy Temple itself.

Asgard could not now remember when it had begun, this soul sickness. Perhaps at Acre. Perhaps even when he had first set foot on the Palestine shore.

Ahead, the serjeant reined in his horse. He turned to look at him. Asgard supposed the boy had spoken, but he hadn't been paying attention. They were outside a gate in a high stone wall and a bell was ringing for vespers. He was suddenly hungry, knowing he could look forward to a decent Templar meal.

Although his order followed the Rule of St. Benedict, Knights of the Temple were allowed red meat and any other foods that would add to their strength. A good dinner was really the only thing Asgard looked forward to: the commander here had sought him out—indeed, knew somehow that he was in Edinburgh, when Asgard had purposely not sent a message that he would be visiting Scotland. He was not looking forward to an evening of questions.

The Templars' evening meal, following vespers, was taken in silence in a great stone refectory with a vaulted ceiling that magnified the smallest sounds of chewing and swallowing and the occasional scrape of boots against the stone floor. From the stares sent his way Asgard guessed that his reputation had been told to the assembled tables of knights and their servants and men-at-arms by the commander.

He took a cup of goat's milk instead of the wine, and sat sipping it, watching the men of the commandery. His brother Templars could stare their eyes out for all he cared; it changed nothing, least of all what they had heard of him. Asgard de la Guerche, the great Crusader. Named by Salah al Din himself as the firebrand of the Franks, and as such marked for death.

And how they loved that story.

So great had been the Saracen leader's belief that if the Templar Asgard de la Guerche could be caught that the back of the assaults to capture Jerusalem could be broken, that for a time the siege had focused on just one Templar. On him. The troubadours had sung the fame and glory of it all over Europe: Asgard de la Guerche, greater Knight Templar than any other before. Or since.

As they were filing in silence into the round church that was the symbol of the Templars' order, the commander took Asgard by the arm.

"Come into my office," he told him. He steered

him away from the rest going for compline, nightly prayers, and down a cloister corridor. "We have," the commander said in a loud, conspiratorial whisper, "what you seek."

Asgard pulled back to stare at him. For a moment he entertained the wild thought that the Templars had the mysterious girl there, in the commandery, in Edinburgh. In the next moment he told himself he was a fool.

It took a few minutes to light the small pottery lamp on the table in the commander's office. The stone room was full of mementoes of the East. The other man went to a brass brazier and lifted the pierced lid and stirred up the coals, then added more charcoal from a basket nearby. Both lamp and brazier were Saracen work, as were the fine tapestries with Christ and the apostles garbed in mail as knights and riding war horses, that hung on the whitewashed walls. The room was what was becoming the unique Templar mix of the eastern exotic and the monkish austere.

As one could say, Asgard thought, the Templars were themselves.

He sat down on a bench and the commander poured wine from a Saracen brass ewer and handed a cup to him. "The girl," he said abruptly, "is being sought by more than the English king."

Asgard made his face noncommittal.

The commander paced to the table and back. He was a Norman in his fifties, with pale eyes that fixed themselves on Asgard. "Tell me, brother, did you think the English king could send any Templar into Scotland—or any other land—and the brotherhood not know of it?"

Asgard looked down at his cup. "It had occurred to me." As far as he was concerned he was on king's business; it was not necessary to explain to Edinburgh's master.

"Hnnnh." The other turned away, rebuffed. "Henry Plantagenet will not find it clever to be devious. A messenger from the Grand Master rode across France to bring me the news of your coming."

So, Asgard was thinking, not just King Henry of England and William the Lion of Scotland, but also the Grand Master of the Knights Templar. God's wounds, who was she— *What* was she to any of them?

"The Grand Master," the other man went on, "has an interest in this girl who is said by the nuns of Saint Sulpice to be a saint. And whom English King Henry has heard of and wants enough, now, to send a famed brother of the Temple into the kingdom of William the Lion to fetch her."

Asgard lowered his eyes. "The Brotherhood serves many monarchs, my commander. In many ways." Inside the collar of his gambeson he felt an unpleasant sprinkling of sweat.

The commander lowered himself to a bench and put his elbows on the table. He was wearing his white surcoat with red cross, but kept on his woolen cape. The stone room, in spite of the glowing Saracen brazier, was not very warm.

"It is clear they have not told you much," he said heavily. "There is not much to tell—only stories from servants and the like who talk even when the nuns have them sworn to secrecy. Stories one finds intriguing but hard to credit. One such story says that when the babe was found in the turnstile of the convent and could not have been more than two or three days old, it was making sounds more intelligible than any newborn the nuns had yet to know of. And was, of course, of surpassing beauty even then.

"As the child grew she was so docile and sweet of nature that by the time she had learned to walk the nuns were besotted with her, and would not allow her to be sent into the town to be adopted by a family there, as was the custom. The child was the apple of their eye, they wished to keep her to themselves. They even held a special chapter meeting to consider names for her. Many were considered before they chose Edain."

Asgard murmured, "A queen of Ireland."

"Is that so?" The Templar shot him a look. "Is that what the name is? But there is no indication the girl is Irish, the sisters must have made it up. They say that when she was old enough to reason the nuns foolishly asked if she knew at all where she came from and the child responded, 'Through the clouds.' "

Asgard looked up. "Through the clouds?"

"So the sisters swear." The commander looked exasperated. "I confess I feel they have lost their heads, these women. The story of clouds is but a little girl's fancy such as many orphans make up who have no claim to known origins. Besides, it would be impossible for a newborn babe to have knowledge of where it came from. Pah, the cloud story only adds to the ridiculous gossip about her!"

The commander poured himself some more wine. "These women have called her a saint," he said, wiping his mouth with the back of his hand, "because they have been sore afraid to have her called else.

After all, it is better to think a saint than to think a witch, now isn't it?"

"There are more stories?" Asgard said.

"She controls animals. Yes, I know what you are thinking, but there are those who have been witnesses. For some years now this Edain has been more or less mistress of the orphans, guiding them and teaching them, seeing to their meals and general welfare. A story goes that one day an ox that a carter had been yoking got loose in the road and, being an ill-tempered beast, would have charged the children. But the girl stepped in between and calmed it by speaking to it, and led it away holding it by the horn."

Asgard smiled. "I've seen a few horses and cattle tamed in my time. It is not all that difficult to do if one is accustomed to animals, and masterful."

"Masterful?" The other turned his head to stare at him. "They say the girl merely looked at the charging, bellowing beast and it fell to its knees as though it had been struck with an ax! A glance—no more than that, and the ox came down obediently, bowing its head to her."

Asgard waited a moment before he said, "It sounds as though the good sisters of Saint Sulpice are making ordinary acts into miracles."

The commander shook his head. "Even the herdsmen who come to the convent rattle on and on about her. That she has the gift of calling. Nay, no one will testify to it—the nuns are closemouthed as clams for fear of having a flock of Roman bishops come to investigate. But the villagers who serve at the convent whisper that when the girl calls you it's as though a little voice sounds in your ear, and you must obey."

Asgard had heard miraculous stories of girls taming wild animals before; all of Christendom celebrated the symbol of the virgin and the unicorn. But a secret voice calling to one to make one obey? At least it was different.

He couldn't resist asking, "Does she cast spells? The stories say that they cast spells after they are seen flying through the air on the branches of oaks or willow trees. Or after they have made hens stop laying eggs, or cows stop giving milk. Umm, tell me, can the girl foresee the future?"

The commander lowered his cup and looked at him. "Superstition is ignorant, Brother Asgard. Our order has never condoned the oppression of women with gifts that may not be easily explainable. We do not use the word witch, that is for vulgarians. Yet there is much we do not know of the natural laws of God's earth. If you have lived in the East with us you know the brotherhood has not failed to inquire into God's mysteries—of which there are many."

Asgard felt a faint ringing in his ears. The words brought the unease again, along with the beads of sweat on the back of his neck. He could have told the commander that yes, he had lived in the East. Had not Salah al Din made his reputation for him there for all time? And yes, the man was right, the Brotherhood of Templars in the Holy Land were not timid about inquiring into God's mysteries. He could not, even now, shake some of the terror.

The commander had seen him quiver, and raised his brows.

"An old wound," Asgard said quickly, "from the last siege at Acre. It continues to afflict me." He added, "Milord, you said before that you have what I seek?"

The Templar paced back to the table. "It is true, then, de la Guerche, that you come here from London on English King Henry's mission? Which is to know more of the postulant who was taken from the convent of Saint Sulpice?"

Asgard nodded.

"Then know she was taken from a shipwreck by a band of Scots who call themselves the Sanach Dhu, who serve their leader, one Constantine of Loch Etive. They have sent a messenger to me to say their Lord Constantine wishes the Templar sent by King Henry to come to ransom the girl. Since it is the English king who wants her, they know he will pay a large ransom. Much more than William the Lion, who has only Scotland for a kingdom and is therefore poor. The girl is held in a fort across the firth, some fifty leagues from here."

Asgard put down his cup slowly, trying to get his thoughts sorted out. "Why do they not bring her here? Ransom is paid this side of the water as well."

"The ransom is fifty gold crowns."

He pursed his mouth in a whistle. "Fifty crowns? They're mad. I do not have it, and King Henry will not pay that much just to satisfy his curiosity. Even for the saint or witch the girl may be."

The other man turned away. "I'll send a squire with you. Constantine's Scots are from the outer islands and wild as foxes, they will not come here to Edinburgh and risk ambush and seizure."

Asgard stood up. He had not agreed to any of this in London. Now he found himself caught between the schemes of two kings and his own order's interest in this strange affair. What did the Knights Templar want with a woman who any man in the street would condemn out of hand as a witch? God's wounds, why did *anyone* want her, when the best place for her was back in the convent of St. Sulpice, where the nuns could revere her as their resident miracle worker?

"And to whom do I deliver her when I return?" he wanted to know. "To the Templar Grand Master, or William the Lion of Scotland? Or the one to whom I gave my oaths in this quest, King Henry Plantagenet of England?"

The commander of the Templars of Edinburgh stood up and put his arm around Asgard's shoulder and walked with him to the door.

"Find the girl and bring her here," he told him soothingly. "All will be settled then."

Magnus came skidding down the grassy knoll on his heels so fast he nearly fell. The fog was thick, but not so much so that he could not make out the blob of bright color that he had seen from the top of the hill and that he was sure was the red silk scarf he had seen Edain wearing.

He kept it in his sights as he nearly fell over a huge rooting sow that just managed to get out of his way. Dogs barked, and figures in the fog called out to one another, warning that someone was charging into their camp.

Magnus looked around at the foggy outlines. Something like this passed for a hamlet in Scotland. Although it was a sorry place, even cloaked in mist.

He could make out three or four houses of wattle and mud, something that might have been a barn, and a stockade of tree trunks and dead branches. He had come in by the only entrance, lunging on the heels of the giant hog.

He immediately found himself surrounded by squat people with black hair and black eyes, wearing pieces of cowhide for clothing. Their faces, even those of the females, were liberally decorated with blue tattoos.

And there she was, he saw as his heart leaped with excitement. A fairly young girl, although it was hard to tell with these gnomish people, with Edain's precious red silk scrap of a veil wrapped around her head!

Under his cloak, Magnus put his hand on his sword. There were four or five bare-legged males in the band, all carrying spears pointed at him.

"Where is the other girl?" Magnus said in Norman French. He pointed to the female wearing the scarf. He wanted the beautiful blond girl who had worn *that.*

As if they hadn't noticed her before, the crowd turned and surveyed the female wearing the scarf. Several of the spear carriers spoke to one another in a language Magnus had never heard before.

Looking around, he had a sinking feeling. Two other women were on the edge of the crowd; he thought he recognized the blue bride's dress with the embroidery at the neck and sleeves. And one woman was clad in the top part, while the other wore the severed skirt.

She's dead, Magnus thought. These Scottish trolls had stripped her of her things and killed her!

The thought was like a blow to his stomach. Then he felt a thunderous surge of rage. Well, he'd kill a few of them himself before he was through!

Magnus threw back his cloak, baring his sword-arm. At the same time an old man in goatskins threw himself at him, shaking his head and waving his hands wildly. Someone caught Magnus to stay him.

Girl. The old man shouted the Saxon word. He grabbed Magnus's arm and hung onto it, pointing with his free hand. The others gathered around. *Girl. Go.* They gabbled it fiercely.

Magnus stopped. He could hardly make himself understood as he had almost no Saxon, an uncouth tongue. And from the sound of it, neither did the others. They stared at one another, not knowing where to begin.

One thing was clear. They wanted to tell him the girl Edain, was gone. Not dead then, but gone.

He did not wait for the feeling of relief to strike but strode to the young female wearing the silk scarf and pulled it roughly from her head. The crowd made a menacing sound. He carried the scrap to the old man and stuck it in his tattooed face.

The old man's look was shuttered. After a moment he held up two handfuls of blue-marked fingers and counted off ten. Then he made a gesture with the fingers for horses galloping.

Magnus raked his hand through his hair. What did it mean? Ten horsemen had brought Edain to the village and taken her away? God help him, he wanted so much to believe she was still alive!

The old man reached out and fingered the silk in Magnus's fist. Then he motioned for one of the skin-clad women to come forward, one of the younger ones with a blue-decorated, pug-nosed face, who stood stealing coy glances at Magnus from under her lashes.

The old man raised his hands above his head and stamped his feet as he turned around twice to show that he had become a fighter, a warrior, a horseman, one of those who had come through the village. He stopped and looked at Magnus.

The entire village looked at Magnus, who hesitated, then nodded. Yes, he supposed he understood that much.

The old man took the red silk and laid it on the girl's head, and then snatched it off. With the scarf in his hand he careened a few steps, laughing mirthlessly. Then in a movement so swift Magnus almost did not see, he pounced on the girl and tore at the front of her hide vest. A pin or a lacing gave way and her full breasts spilled out. The old man barely touched her as he waved his hands, still cackling.

He held up ten fingers again. Ten horsemen. For Magnus's benefit he carefully pointed out the women wearing parts of Edain's bridal dress. The spearmen, excited, were shouting at one another.

Magnus let himself slump against the corner of the ramshackle barn.

Holy Mother Mary, he hoped he had understood the headman's dumb show correctly. Ten horsemen had brought the girl he sought to this hamlet to barter for food and water, apparently not too long after they had kidnapped her from his side.

Once they had stopped at the village, according to the old man, they'd stripped the clothes from her. To *look* at her.

The thought of it made a roaring pulse beat in Magnus's skull. He hadn't realized until that moment how precious and private her body was now that she'd given it to him. He remembered her delicate legs, her golden belly and breasts, that luminous flesh. It drove him mad to think of her manhandled in front of gawking villagers—in front of anybody—just because brigands had wanted to see if she was *beautiful!*

He lifted a trembling hand and rubbed at his burning eyes. This offal, whoever they were, thought they'd defiled Edain, but they hadn't yet learned the lesson he was going to teach them! He would catch up with them and spend the better part of the night digging their eyeballs out with his dagger.

The old man was making a gesture, lifting the edge of Magnus's heavy war cloak.

"Cloak," Magnus said.

The headman nodded.

They'd left her only her cloak to wear. They'd given the rest of Edain's clothing to the villagers in return for food and water. She'd be freezing.

Magnus bit his lip, wanting to howl his fury. They had no right to take her clothes away from her to satisfy their filthy curiosity. And, dear Jesus, a terrible thought had just occurred to him; he couldn't bear to think of it. What they might do to her, a naked girl they were dragging across the countryside.

He turned, scraped against a spear blade pressing against his back and recoiled, an oath on his lips.

The old man in the beard, joined by another ancient, was trying to tell him something. Not much Saxon, just a lot of shouting and gesturing.

"Confound it, stop bellowing!" He couldn't understand them. But the moment he put his hand on the pommel of his sword the swarthy, skin-clad youths jammed their spear tips in a circle around his body so that he couldn't move.

The old man stuck his face in Magnus's. *You*— He mouthed the Saxon word. *Go.*

Magnus would be glad to go. He had no greater desire right at that moment than to leave these hobgoblin folk to their miserable lives and follow the horse tracks left by Edain's abductors.

And he would. As soon as they took the spears out of his back.

As he looked around he could see it wasn't going to be that simple. Bulbous little women crowded around him, touching his legs, pressing the muscles in his forearms—they even lifted up the back of his war cloak to pinch the curve of his buttocks.

"Stop that," Magnus said to the one wearing the scrap of silk scarf. The sight of it caused a wrenching sensation in his heart, remembering the beautiful girl who'd worn it, and who'd lain so lovingly in his arms.

The slightly older female wearing the bodice of the bridal dress was exploring his chest and arms.

"Desist, I said!" Magnus tried to push the women away. He drew a length of his sword from his scabbard to show he was serious; if he had to fight his way out of the village he would do it. But when he moved, the spear carriers, their blue-inked faces fierce, lifted their weapons.

Magnus tried to calculate the odds of his big sword against the dozen or so undersized spearmen when a handful of old women pushed the warriors out of the way. Led by an old crone with bare breasts, their hands were suddenly all over him. It was impossible to draw his sword now to defend himself. He felt scrabbling hands in the waistband of his hose. Several of the crones hung on his arms, squeezing his biceps and exclaiming. The spear carriers, circling around them, made a barrier.

Magnus struggled but the women pushed him step by step toward one of the huts. An old beldame had wormed her hand into his hose and had it around his shaft and was hanging on for dear life. The effort to pry her hand loose and at the same time keep his free one on his sword was almost impossible. Magnus staggered, and nearly went down. At once hands dragged him back to his feet.

Desperate, he yelled at the top of his lungs for help—from anyone—but no one was listening. Out of the corner of his eye he saw a man sit down by the barn to milk a goat. In some dim part of his mind he was remembering stories of these tribes in the unknown far north, of how they once practiced blood sacrifice. Tortured their captives, dismembered them, and burned them.

That they ate each other.

Inside the hut he tripped and went down on both knees. He tried to get his sword free of its scabbard, but the screeching old women hung onto his arms. He couldn't believe how strong they were.

The old man with the tattooed face came in and shouted at all of them. Magnus lay flat on his back on the floor while four old women sat on his shoulders and arms and three others worked to pull off his boots. He tried to throw them off, but the headman had two spear carriers put the points of their spears at his throat, forcing him to lie still.

The old man bent over him and said something Magnus couldn't follow. Then he seized the girl wearing the blue wedding bodice and put her arm around the shoulder of the spearman standing next to her. Lined up, the three stood staring at him expectantly.

"God rot all of you!" Magnus tried to get up again and was pushed back. "Just let me up and out of this accursed place!"

The old man shook his head. Panting, Magnus let his weight fall back on his elbows. The faces of the spearman and the wedding bodice girl were exactly alike. Their black eyes regarded him with snakelike intensity.

The old man abruptly turned and found the girl in the red silk scarf and drew her to the first couple. He put another spearman beside her. As the five stood together the old women squatting on the floor made hissing sounds, and nudged one another.

Magnus sat all the way up, keeping a hand on his sword. All those the headman had pulled out of the group looked exactly like the others. It was, unfortunately, a tribe or clan where there was not much contrast between squat, muscular male and squat, muscular female, even when they were young.

Holy Jesus in heaven, Magnus thought, *that was it!*

The whole village was a family. Brothers and sisters. The rest perhaps first cousins at best. No wonder the old women turned to him, as eager as butchers at a lamb slaughter!

The crones weren't about to let him go. They pounced on him, slammed him flat on his back once more, and his sword disappeared. With a roar, he tried to capture it, but one of the women held his precious Toledo blade above her head while the others stripped off his cloak, his shirt, and his hose, and tossed them away.

The rest was mayhem.

The first girl to throw herself on his naked body was the one wearing Edain's silk scarf. In spite of her mouth and hands on his flesh, Magnus was only able to do what she wanted because he thought of golden Edain somewhere, and knew that once again she would be his. And his body responded.

It couldn't have been anything else, he knew, gasping; this was some sort of war—not even lust. The female in the red scarf lifted her cowhide skirt and straddled him as one would a bucking stallion. She bounced up and down on him so thoroughly that Magnus went from outrage, fury, then speechlessness as his very breath was pounded out of him.

After the girl had what she wanted from him, the old women called for a rest. Magnus lay still, head spinning. He needed to lunge out from under their hands and grab his sword and get out of there somehow. At that moment the sister in the bottom part of the wedding dress hauled him to her. Her black braids flapped as she settled herself on his stomach and held his ears in both hands so that he could not get away while she kissed him.

Magnus let out a roar of desperation. He felt as though he was drowning. Hands were all over him, holding him down. He wanted to kill every one of them. He had no accursed sympathy for these women wanting to mix the six feet four, redheaded fitzJulien family seed with their own hobgoblin strain, even though he could see the need for it.

As the last girl, the one in the wedding bodice, pounded up and down on his crotch with her great buttocks, Magnus moaned. He was exhausted, with murder in his heart. And as for these women who'd had their way with him—after much rooting about and slamming their bodies down on him, he hoped each one of them had a babe. Not boys. He would not give this troll village what they wanted if he could help it.

Magnus hoped they all had girls. All of them as big as his father and with the earl's famous disposition. Babes who would grow into big-footed, red-haired giantesses all resembling Earl Niall fitzJulian.

It would serve them all right.

Eight

It was raining hard, as it had for days. Across the loch there was another matching stone broch, one of the round towers that dotted the western highlands, and the downpour all but obscured it behind a steady, silvery curtain.

Edain had never seen a place where it rained so much. It even made the children restless although you would think, born and bred in such a land, that they would become used to it.

After a morning of tormenting the chieftain's wife and her maidservant, the bairns had tried pestering the clan's warriors, who had soundly pummeled all but the smallest ones and chased the lot out off the barracks level. Now all eight or nine of them from a toddler to a girl and a boy nearly twelve, towheaded and redheaded and some with hair the color of tar, had come scrambling up the wooden ladder to Edain, looking for something or someone to entertain them.

Yesterday Edain had told them stories, and after that the biggest boys had found a store of fresh straw at the bottom level where the horses were penned, and brought it up so that they could use it to make little dolls and mannikins.

It had been a pleasant occupation; even the boys liked making soldiers of straw. And even though the stone fort, jammed with tribesmen and the chief's family, was a rough, bare place sadly lacking in a household's cloth and beads and the little scraps that made dollmaking such a fine rainy-day occupation.

Today, Edain saw, looking them over, the children were more than just restless. They had been quarreling since daybreak, with one fight after another. The girls, too, not just the boys. Edain lifted the baby, Duncan, into her lap to get him out of the way of his two brothers, Rory and Callum, as they traded blows.

It was hard to keep the children quiet since the chieftain of the Sanach had waked. Constantine was drinking early, nursing the foul mood that had settled on him after days of waiting for the messenger from Edinburgh to arrive. They could hear his voice raised below and occasionally the sound of things being thrown—probably at his long-suffering wife. After a particularly loud outburst followed by a crash and a woman's shriek, one of the little girls began to cry.

"Now, now," Edain tried to soothe her.

She stared somewhat helplessly at the children clustered around her. She'd been told Constantine of the Clan Sanach had a much better house at the head of the loch, the manor where he did his farming. But he preferred to stay in the tower fort, which could be better defended in case the king was not going to pay her ransom.

God knows, Edain thought, putting the baby down so that she could wipe a little girl's nose, what would become of any of them if *that* happened. The clan looked as though they could use a fat ransom. The ragged children standing before her needed warm clothes for the winter and something to cover their feet. Even Constantine's own offspring were scarcely better dressed.

It was strange the way the Highlanders lived. Constantine himself wore a handsome red woolen tunic and furs, sealskin boots and gold jewelry. Even his wife was finely dressed by their standards: her gold armbands and brooches were worth a fortune. From somewhere they had even managed to find Edain a long, white woolen gown of surpassing softness, doeskin rivlins for her feet, a pair of gold and silver wire bracelets. And she still had her blue cloak, the wedding gift from the de Brise.

But the children of the broch were dressed like beggars. No one seemed to care. They were always underfoot like the hunting dogs, or the tower's cats.

Up there at the top the room was fairly warm but so smoky one could hardly see. Edain sent one of the boys to pull back the cowhide at the arrow slit so that some of the murk from the brazier could pass out. When the slit opened, they heard the roar of the deluge outside.

With a sigh, Edain picked up the baby and put him back into her lap. "Tell the story of Naoise and Deirdre," one of the little girls said, leaning both sharp little elbows on her knee.

The children had heard the story of Naoise, the most beautiful and bravest of men, and his love, Deirdre of the golden hair, twice that morning. The second time the boys did not sit still but fell on one another and wrestled on the floor, liking the tales of the warrior Finn McCool and his band much better.

They played finger games and cat's cradle with pieces of string leftover from the dollmaking. And because they were finally quiet, Edain took their hands one by one and stroked a blue glow into each finger.

There was enough of the substance anyway in the sea and the waters of the lochs, so it was easy enough to call it out of the air. She made them stand quietly around her, promising on pain of terrible punishment not to utter a word or a squeal or any sort of noise that could be heard down below, as she gently stroked the small fingers until each child's glowed at the tip like a blue fire candle. Even the baby sat in her lap with his starfish hands opened, silently staring at his glowing fingers, until he finally popped his thumb into his mouth.

Edain pulled it out, extinguished it, and lit it again with quick strokes of her forefinger. Some of the boys tried to rub their fingers on their faces and make their cheeks and lips glow, which of course didn't work. "Candle fingers only," she told them. "And a secret all around now not to tell anyone, or the fun will be gone."

They liked that.

They came back to Edain and stood with wide, awestruck eyes as she relit the tips of their fingers and made them glow brightly. After a while the baby went to sleep. The children's fingers began to dim, and she did not keep the glow going. The broch's children seemed to understand the play could last only a while. Edain murmured to them to see if they could curl up against one another for warmth, and take a nap.

As for herself, she leaned her head back against the wall of the broch and closed her eyes. It had been sweet fun to watch the children with their blue, glowing candle fingers. Not for the first time that day she tried to bring the Feeling, but it would not come.

It had been this way since she had been taken from the young knight who had made love to her at the stream. Dear Holy Mother, she thought suddenly, she hoped he was not gone forever!

From that instant when the tax boat had pulled away from the shore, leaving her on the beach, there had been the strange certainty that the tall, russet-haired young knight would be with her from then on. Yes, even that he would make love to her.

With the boat pulling out to sea, Edain had been calm in her certainty that this, too, was foreordained. Although she did not have the slightest understanding of the *why* of it.

Then it had not become necessary to understand. His warm, solid strength as she clung to him in the terrible storm gave her an unshakable faith that grew even stronger. All through that night and the next day the Earl of Chester's brash young captain was a rock of courage, dauntless, handsome—the Feeling had showed her his impressive body on board the ship even before they'd reached the stream where they'd made love. And she found him, close up, in her arms, making love to her, even more splendid.

A picture presented itself in her mind's eye. How his wide mouth curved enchantingly at the corners when he talked. She loved to watch it. His eyes were tawny brown flecked with dancing lights of amber. And one could only marvel at the length of his lashes that would be the envy of any maid. He was tall and strong and his body was perfect in those private places she had examined with great curiosity. Even there he was big, and potent and magnificent.

And oh, she mused wistfully, he had been passionate and tender and almost worshipful in the act of lovemaking. She moaned softly, remembering, and the sleeping baby in her lap stirred.

She had never envisioned anything like it, even in her most fantastical dreams.

So this was what men and women did together when they wished to create "love"! It was as though when her body met with his they left the earth and drifted in a golden, searing haze. She could not wait to be with him again.

Beyond her three of the boys were playing at dice they had stolen from the spearmen below. When they met her eyes they put the dice down and got quickly to their feet.

They'd all heard someone coming up the ladder from below.

The little girls scrambled out of the way as the head and shoulders of the chief of the Sanach appeared. Constantine stood in the hole at the top of the ladder and looked around, scowling.

"What are you doing up here?" he shouted to the children.

He pulled himself up out of the stairwell and leaped into the middle of the room. At once the children scrambled to dodge his blows and get to the ladder. Below, the voice of the chief's wife anxiously called out. The oldest girl ran back to get the baby.

Constantine stood before Edain, his hands braced in his leather belt. He was very drunk, and it was not yet noontide. It was plain he was tired of waiting for the messenger from Edinburgh, and like the children looking for something to entertain him.

Edain pressed back against the stone wall. No stories of Naoise and Deirdre nor any dollmaking were going to satisfy the chief of the Sanach. She saw it in his bloated red face.

For the first time she considered, not without some shock, that the glorious lovemaking she had known with the young knight could turn into something evil, and hurtful.

When she lifted her head she saw it there in the chief's eyes. "What do you want?" she whispered.

It was a stupid thing to ask. On the floor below them things had gone very quiet. She licked her lips, thinking of the chief's wife. Thinking of the children, who would hear everything. She began to tremble for what seemed sure to happen.

"It's time you made yourself useful, girl." The chief of the Sanach squatted down in front of her, pulling the edge of his long shirt back to show his bare legs. "Lying about, playing with the bairns, eating my food. You can do more than that, can't you?"

She stared at his feet, thinking the chief's body was made the same as Magnus fitzJulien's, it had the same parts, but one would not think of it in the same way. Where the handsome young knight was all powerful grace, Constantine was round as a barrel, so clogged with muscle his arms stuck out from his sides. Black hairs sprouted on the backs of his hands, and his legs were covered with it like fur.

She knew, without actually seeing, that what was between his legs was not handsome, not for pleasure. It was twisted and brutal and he had always used it that way.

"Come," he rasped, reaching for her cloak. "Get rid of this, I want to look on you."

Edain tried to slide out of his grasp but he put his hands under her arms and dragged her to her knees. As she crouched in the straw he seized the hem of the woolen gown and pulled it over her head.

She had on nothing underneath. As he well knew. In the dim light from the arrow slits she was a slim, beautiful wood nymph, a fairy being. Her bright, unkempt hair fell about her shoulders and arms and hid her thrusting breasts.

Constantine's face flushed a deeper red as he pushed her hands away.

"Gold," he whispered hoarsely. "They said you were gold all over, Saint Sulpice witch, with gold skin and green-jewel eyes, and by the cross, they did not lie. Christ protect me, with you naked like that it's like looking at one of the Enchanted Ones!"

He heaved himself closer to her and thrust his big fingers between her legs to fondle the gold-colored hair there, while his other hand pushed her knees apart so that Edain was completely exposed to him.

She tried to cringe away from that punishing, invading touch, but the Sanach chieftain was visibly aroused, breath snorting through his nose. The odor of the rank whiskey he'd been drinking was like a cloud around them.

"Let me go," Edain cried. She was telling herself that it was best to let him know she was not afraid. The trouble was, she was desperately afraid.

This was not like the other times; it had not even been like this with Ivo de Brise when he had threatened her with the *droit de seigneur.* When he had almost forced her to marry one of his vassals so that he could take her to bed.

Then Edain had had a Feeling that fate was moving her along in the stream of life's happenings; that nothing, even as dire as it looked, would seriously harm her.

Now, all was different.

She was in peril from this gross-bodied chieftain of the Sanach who wanted to stick his flesh in hers, root cruelly in her body, right above the room where his wife and children were listening!

She had to do something, she thought as his hands closed over her breasts and squeezed them. But there was no power inside her anywhere that she could sense; that she could call on. Nothing like the Feeling, that she could draw on to save her.

"Come on, come on," he was saying. "You've magic in you all right, sweeting, in that wee little cleft. And I've got the tool that's going to open it wide as Loch Linnnhe. Ah, you'll feel it, I promise that you will!"

He yanked up the front of his long shirt and she saw a mat of hair that stretched from his belly through his crotch to his upper thighs, so thick it was like a beast's body, not a man's. In the middle of it a huge rod of bluish-red flesh dangled, not quite erect.

The chieftain dragged her hands to him and wrapped them around his shaft. Edain's fingers were cold and limp; she could hardly bring herself to touch him. In answer he hit her on the side of the head—a stinging blow with his open hand that robbed her of breath for a long moment, and made her ears ring.

"Squeeze it," he hissed. His face was right in hers. "Squeeze it and stroke it like a lovely pet you want to take between your legs. Or I'll fetch you another smack what'll do more than make your head sing!"

Shaking with fright, Edain put both hands around him and squeezed as hard as she could. She saw his eyes narrow with pleasure. She kept on squeezing frantically until her fingers grew tired. Finally he took her hands away.

"Softly, softly," Constantine muttered. He looked down at his organ with a faintly puzzled air. It seemed less aroused than when she had begun.

Abruptly he took his flaccid shaft in his hand and gave it several brisk up-and-down jerks, then stopped to look again.

He swore under his breath. "I'm burning mad for you," he muttered, "aye, fit to burst, me balls are aching like a bad tooth. But Jesu—what's the matter with it? It should be hard as a rock!"

He lifted his head to look at her. Bewilderment turned to rage. He grabbed her by the arm and dragged her to him. "God rot you—what have you done to it?"

"N-n-nothing! Only what you told me to," Edain cried. It was only the truth.

"A curse on your tricks." He slapped her again, hard. "Now get me hot, or I'll beat you until you can't move, do you understand?"

He grabbed her by the hair and shoved her face down into his groin.

He was rank, Edain found, trying not to breathe too much of him, and needed washing badly. He pushed his limp flesh into her mouth, his fingers opening her jaw and prying open her lips to get it all inside. She started to gag.

It lasted only a second.

And it took only the bare touch of her tongue and lips on his most intimate flesh. Just as he had wanted. Instantly Constantine, chieftain of the Sanach, drew back with a shrill scream.

Edain had a brief glimpse of his agonized face above her, mouth open and teeth showing in his beard, before he scrambled to his feet still holding his shaft. He held up one side of the long Irish shirt and looked down at his drooping tool.

"Christ and the angels, it's burned!" he bellowed. He did a little dance of pain. "Blistered, my cock's blistered! It's been dipped in hell's fire, I tell you!" He turned to her, looking wild. "You whore's demon—you *burned* me!"

Edain stared back at him, her mind churning. All she could remember were his words: "Get me hot, or I will beat you."

Hot, that was it.

A calm feeling suddenly flowed over her, banishing the terrible fear. She sat back on her heels, picking up her cloak from the floor to pull it around her.

He should never have said it. She almost smiled.

It was plain some powers were still following her, protecting her, although she had lost faith there for a while. Besides, one never could tell how they would help. The chief of the Sanach had wanted to be hot. And hot he had gotten.

She was not quite sure what he would do. From the look on Constantine's livid face he wanted to do her great bodily harm. But not kill her; that would spoil his chances of King William's ransom.

Below them the voices of the spearmen were shouting something, followed by the pleading voice of the chief's wife. Then sounds of someone coming up the ladder. One of the tribesmen stuck his head and shoulders into the room.

"Sanach, he is going to do it!" The man was grinning from ear to ear. "William the Lion has sent his messenger. Look ye out, and see them coming up to the tower on the loch road!"

Constantine hesitated for only a second. Then he hobbled to one of the arrow slits and stuck his face into it.

What he saw evidently pleased him for in the next second he flung himself to the ladder hole in the floor, barely giving the spearman time to get out of the way. The chief disappeared into the room below, shouting at the top of his voice to his clan.

Edain picked up her woolen gown from the floor where Constantine had flung it and went to the arrow slit in the stone wall and pressed her face to it.

It was still raining, not the torrents of the night and early morning, but enough to have made the small party coming up the road huddle in their soaked cloaks. The leader, though, had thrown his aside.

One could see why. The big Templar knight rode a black destrier, bridle and trappings embellished with pure silver. Without his cloak the world could see his white surcoat with the large red cross emblazoned on front and back.

Edain drew in her breath.

Somehow she had not expected this. It was not that the Templar was not pleasing to the eye—on the contrary that fair, marble beauty was perfection. She had never seen anyone handsomer.

The beautiful knight rode with his great helm tucked under his arm and the falling rain had plastered his corn-colored hair against his skull. He looked like St. Michael the Archangel with his pure, noble brow, that faintly severe, unforgiving look in his blue eyes.

Behind the Templar was a servant leading a packhorse, and beyond the servant the knight's rather motley escort, five men-at-arms, and a tall figure in a mud-smeared cloak who made his way haltingly in worn horseman's boots.

Edain could not take her eyes from him. She had seen him take the spurs from those very boots and bury them, along with his hauberk. With a sob, she mashed her face against the stone.

He had no helmet, it was lost in the shipwreck. The hood of his fine cloak was partly thrown back and the rainy light made his curly, dark red hair a spot of color. And his face—

Edain bit her lip to keep from crying out.

Ah, that wonderful face, that wide, wide mouth

with its youthful, sardonic smile. The swing of his shoulders in the rain-soaked cloak! He looked absurd picking his way among the stones in his useless boots. She wondered why he was there; anyone would know Magnus fitzJulien was not a common soldier.

Then she remembered he no longer had his mail, and probably no coin at all after the wreck. Nothing to buy bread or something to eat. He was alone in a strange land. She wondered if he had managed to keep his sword.

Whatever, she knew he was looking for her. She looked down at the road where Constantine and his men were stumbling out of the tower entrance to greet them. Magnus could not hear her even if she called to him.

She pressed her cheek against the stone, thinking that whatever happened now, they could not be parted again.

Never, Edain told herself. She would not let it happen.

Nine

William the Lion, King of Scotland, stepped out of the copper cauldron where he had taken his bath, and into the arms of two young maidservants who were waiting for him.

Before the girls could wrap their linen towels around the king, the people who were in the bath chamber with him—the Norman justiciar, fitzGamelin, the steward of the castle, fitzAlan, the mailed knights of the king's guard, and a dozen Highland tribesmen squatting on their haunches—were treated to a view of the monarch's well-made, naked body. Which William doubtless intended. It was wise at any time to remind one's subjects that it did not hurt for a king to look quite impressively kingly.

The Lion was well over six feet, his flesh abundantly marked with battle scars, making him visibly a brave warrior and worthy successor to his late brother, Malcolm. Pushing the girls away, the king took time to scratch in his most intimate places, aware that eyes followed every move. He then reached his arms above his head to stretch, long and powerfully.

William overtopped most of the men in the room; the squatting Highlanders had to tilt their heads back to see him. Like the late king his brother he desired to be a powerful monarch, and especially to regain parts of the Scottish borderland from the English king, Henry Plantagenet, who had seized them.

That was why he took such interest in the present scheme that he had heard, interestingly enough, about the English King Henry. That he had sent to Scotland for a girl, a novice in one of the new Norman convents.

He allowed the girls to towel him until his big body was red and tingling, then stood while his body servant, a swarthy gillie half his size, dressed him in a fine white linen shirt, a leather kilt, and sheepskin cape embroidered with red and blue yarn.

When the king was finished with his bath the Highlanders gathered around the cauldron, rolling it over on its side to empty the bath water into the drain set in the stone floor. Then they carried the vessel out and down the stairs, the bath girls following them.

The king led the others into a larger room.

"Consider the marvels one could achieve," he said, as he sat on the edge of his bed and let the gillie lace him into heelless deerskin shoes, "if this fey saint has half the powers they say she has. God is my judge, she would be like the strength of a standing army to any king! She has but to—what? Look in her golden mirror, or toss her divining sticks and instantly reveal the peril to be faced? Such as how many men and how many knights and how many horses are arrayed against one in wood or field? And how to waylay and successfully slaughter them?" He slapped his knee enthusiastically. "God's wounds, she could even tell the time when a besieged castle will fall! With her, a king could conquer any land."

FitzGamelin and the Norman steward exchanged looks.

"A wondrous gift, if true, sire," the justiciar said carefully, "and most valuable to any monarch. But even I have heard only that the girl seems possessed of 'powers.' And those that I have met are loath to describe in any exactness what these may be."

William looked at him sharply. "Ah, but with a little persuasion the abbess of the convent of Saint Sulpice has managed to be quite—exact."

He raised his hand at the others' expressions. "Nay, nay, I have only sent the Bishop of Aberdeen to examine the good sisters of Saint Sulpice to be sure they have not fallen into any serious error. Cloistered life," the king observed, "is most concerned with error of any sort. Bishops and abbesses are constantly alert to maintain purity of belief. At any monastery or convent you will find multitudes of penances for lapses. The task is to find out which—ah, error—has been committed."

FitzGamelin looked down at his feet. He had no doubt the Bishop of Aberdeen, who had once been an ironfisted Crusader had thrown the fear of never-ending hellfire into the nuns of St. Sulpice to make them talk. He said, "And what did the abbess admit to?"

William the Lion accepted a cup of wine from the servant. "Anything the bishop desired of her, short of calling the girl a witch." He barked his laughter. "Is it ever thus?"

FitGamelin said he supposed not. He could imagine the nuns of St. Sulpice, when faced with their king's wishes as conveyed by the bishop, would agree to anything.

FitzAlan said, "So the bishop has listened to the abbess's account, and found evidence that their former charge is a saint full of miracles, and not an evil-doing daughter of Satan?"

The king frowned. "You may joke, fitzAlan, but the Saint Sulpice nuns would not be shaken from their testimony. According to the sisters their little novice has accomplished many miraculous things. They say the girl has the true gift of 'calling.' " He paused, looking far away. "My own grandmother, God rest her soul, an Orkneywoman of the islands where such things are well known, used to talk of it. That some of the folk there had that very gift, the women especially."

FitzAlan looked nervously at the justiciar, who did not meet his eyes. The steward lifted his hand and crossed himself.

The king accepted a cup of wine from the gillie and sipped it before he said, "I myself believe it is solely a faculty confined to women. According to my beloved grandmere, the Orkneywomen were known to call to their men out in their fishing boats when there was a storm coming so far away that it could not yet be seen. And the men would be warned by this mysterious message that passed through the air until it reached them, and would put their boats safely to shore."

The justiciar was having a hard time believing his ears. Henry Plantagenet of England, that wise and learned man, was anything but gullible. And yet William the Lion had learned that Henry had sent de la Guerche to Scotland to find this girl. From what the Templar, de la Guerche, had told him, it would seem that both monarchs wanted the girl to use as a weapon of statecraft.

Or war.

FitzGamelin waited a moment before he said, "The bishop of Abderdeen, then, has questioned the good sisters and found out where she has gone?"

William the Lion gestured for the servant to pass around a plate of roast meat. After his bath he was hungry. "The good bishop could find nothing of her, alas. But Abbess Clothilde made a long complaint to him that a vassal of Chester's by name Ivo de Brise"—he turned to his justiciar—"who's established a foothold most illegally at Wigan, I want you to note, fitzGamelin. That this de Brise kidnapped the girl from Saint Sulpice's convent for lecherous purposes and lost her. From de Brise, the girl fell into the hands of Constantine of Sanach, a chieftain of Loch Etive. Who sent a message to me that he has her, and that he is willing to give her over to his liege lord and true monarch for a suitable sum."

Both men leaned forward. "Milord," the steward began, "Sanach is your sworn—"

William waved him away. "Oh, I will pay it, fitzAlan, among Scots such ransoming is not dishonorable. On the contrary, it is considered clever, and just. Besides, Sanach is related to my youngest sister by marriage. The sum is not too great. Expensive, but not insulting."

FitzGamelin said, "Sire, at some point might not the church—"

The king shook his head firmly. "Cease, fitzGamelin, and give us peace. I am assured by the bishops of Aberdeen and Edinburgh that there is no reason for an ecclesiastical interest in our golden sibyl at this time."

Not as long as the king wishes it, fitzGamelin thought.

He had to admit the scheme was enough to make any hardheaded Norman shudder. A chase after a girl who was thought to have magical powers? The King of Scotland had apparently forgotten that he, as his justiciar of the western districts, had issued a pass to the Templar, de la Guerche, as emissary of the King of England, for permission to search for the girl. Although fitzGamelin did not think it was the proper time to remind him of it.

He could not avoid, though, the steward's troubled look. William of Scotland had recently been thinking of commencing another war for the borderlands, especially now that King Henry of England was no longer a vigorous young man and sorely troubled by his warlike sons.

It suddenly seemed to the fitzGamelin that a mad, fanciful Celtic spell had seized all of them. What else would explain their serious contemplation of a seeress who could foretell the outcome of battles? And when a fortress would fall? Even which monarch would retain his throne, and which would not? Yet Holy Mother in heaven, that was virtually what the monarch of all Scotland had said!

Inwardly, fitzGamelin stifled a groan. With William the Lion in this frame of mind they were in for perilous times!

* * *

The rain had stopped as the column, headed by Asgard de la Guerche on his great black charger, left Loch Etive and ascended the halls above it. Constantine's round stone broch and its twin across the water began to fade into the mists.

Edain longed to turn in the saddle and look back to the end of the column where the foot soldiers marched, and where she knew Magnus was, with his eyes always on her. But the Templar moved his horse up beside hers and wanted to engage her again in talk.

Edain used as an excuse the trouble she was having with the mountain pony she'd been given to ride to keep from answering him. It was true, she was not a good horsewoman to begin with, having spent most of her life in a convent, and all traveling was strange to her. Besides, she really did not wish to talk.

Handsome as the Templar was with his long blond hair and chiseled features, she had seen how ruthlessly he'd parlayed with the chieftain of the Sanach over her ransom. And she had known there was something dark and very alone inside him that the fighting monk did not wish to reveal to the world.

She hid in the briefest of answers, keeping her eyes downcast. Although she feared he knew this for what it was—and it was not womanly shyness.

She did not want the Templar's company. She wanted to think of Magnus there behind them, so full of thwarted fury that she could almost feel it chasing after her like a thundercloud. And how he had come to be limping along across the hills of Scot land with the mercenaries of the Templar's escort. When she allowed the memories of their hours together after the shipwreck to come flooding back, she was filled with sensuous warmth.

Oh, what a torment it was to have her lover back there with the men-at-arms, pretending he was something he was not—when he should have been riding beside her! She was sure he felt the same way. She could almost feel the impact of his tawny gaze on the back of her neck.

Holy Mother, could it be that he was thinking the same things?

Locked in each other's arms, their lovemaking there by the icy brook had been like falling through the heavens among the shooting stars. He was in her, possessed by her, the center of their bodies locked to one another as if spinning through eternity.

What a blasphemous thought, to make love *forever!* And yet the golden light of their passion that had bathed them for those short, sweet moments was exquisite. He had never experienced such a thing, she knew that without his telling her. And neither had she.

"Ah, the sun," the Templar said beside her.

They had reached the top of a ridge. All about them the folds and valleys of the western highlands, cut by deep inlets of the sea, were lighted with sunshine. A few clouds rolled away to the east and the sky above them suddenly became a canopy of dazzling blue. Ahead, the road entered a thick forest.

"That is the way we are going," the Templar said, pointing. "The way to Edinburgh takes us through the Cromach wood. But first we will stop, and feed and water the horses."

He called to the others, who came up to help the servant with the packhorse and destrier. In a few minutes even the pony had been hobbled and set out to graze, and they sat down on a ring of small stones that overlooked the water to a meal of smoked fish and bread that the people in Constantine's fort had supplied.

Edain sat as close to the men of the escort as she dared. She watched them as they ate and then lay back on the dry winter grass to rest in the sun. Magnus, with his big, strong hands, was given the cask of beer to open. He and one other man looked what they were: destitute knights without their horses, working for hire as foot soldiers.

The Templar was saying, "The Sanach chieftain was certain he had made his fortune when he found you, demoiselle. That was why the haggling took so long." He gave her a handful of smoked herring wrapped in leaves that one of the men had warmed over the fire. "Is Chief Constantine's story to be believed? That is, that an outlaw knight of the Earl of Chester's service kidnapped you from a convent, and that you were shipwrecked, and Constantine found you in the forest?"

"Found?"

Mother of God, she had not been "found"! The chief of the Sanach Dhu had been following them after they'd left the coast and had seen everything. He had boasted to her of it. That he had waited in the woods with his tribesmen to observe what happened there by the stream, all of it, up until the time she fell asleep in Magnus's arms!

Then when Edain woke and went down to the brook to get her clothes, the Scots had fallen upon her and dragged her through the woods to their horses, where they had thrown her over the back of one, to lie bouncing on her stomach like a haunch of venison all the way to the broch!

She said, "I was not found, no matter what the treacherous chief of the Sanach might say."

There was no reason to tell all her story. The Templar might be her rescuer but he had not been open with her, either. He had not told her where they were going, except to point out the way to Edinburgh. The rumor at the broch had been that the Scottish king himself, William the Lion, had paid the ransom. So Edain was not going to say anything until more of the others' plans were revealed to her.

She hesitated, her eyes seeking out the group of mercenaries. Magnus was passing around the beer. If only she could talk to him; surely he would not let things go on the way they were. She wanted to go with this handsome, brooding young knight who had made love to her, not the stern-faced Templar who, she gathered, might be taking her as some sort of prisoner to the Scottish king. But Magnus's warning signals were plain: They were not to give the smallest clue that they knew each other.

After they had eaten, Magnus helped Eudo, the broken knight who acted as serjeant for the Templar's escort, to put out the fire and round up the grazing animals.

"Nice piece of horseflesh," the other man observed as they led the destrier over to the groom. He ran his hand over the big charger's rump. "Been bred out of a Saracen mare?"

Magnus nodded as the groom took the stallion away to saddle him. The Templar's huge mount was a fine specimen of warhorse, heavy and strong for combat, but fast, with probably enough endurance with his Arab blood to outrun an entire field, if necessary.

The thought gave Magnus ideas.

The column formed a straggling line and followed the mounted party into the dimness of Cromach wood. Small talk died. Magnus kept his eyes on the girl. He never tired of watching her; his thoughts now were only of how to get her away from the Templar. How they were going to escape.

The November wind soughed in the trees. The gloom of the forest reminded them of the tales of wood spirits, trolls, and giants, and the terrible things that could befall them there. As well as the dangers from wolves and bears and robbers.

Magnus twisted his head to look up. Brown leaves drifted down on them from high branches. Here in the Scots Highlands the trees grew very old. Many of them were still held to be sacred—oak and rowan and tall beech, and on the higher slopes the whispering giants of pine trees. Eudo gave the order to those who carried bows to string them and keep them at the ready, and for the others to take out their spears or swords.

Magnus unsheathed his sword as he watched the girl and the Templar, de la Guerche, riding together. He'd already noticed how the blond knight looked at her. De la Guerche did not appear the type to fawn over women, the Templar's manner was too lofty, but it was plain he was drawn to Edain.

Watching them, Magnus did not pay attention to where he was going and stumbled on a tree root. His boots were coming apart; he would soon have to discard them and he was damned if he knew what he would do for foot covering after that.

As the sun slanted down through the trees he was finding it made great shafts of sunlight and shadow, fooling the eyes, making ordinary things appear what they were not. Once Magnus thought he saw a file of strange white deer bounding through the wood, but when he blinked, they were no longer there.

The Templar called back to them, "I want to be out of here by nightfall. It will be too easy to wander from the track here, and be lost."

No one lifted his voice to disagree. The escort did not relish spending the night in the forest with unknown things that could sit just outside the light of their campfires. When they stopped to water the horses at a small meandering stream the men worked quickly. Even de la Guerche, going to relieve himself, did not walk very far into the woods.

Magnus sauntered in the direction of the girl. There was not much time to talk to her, the Templar would be back at any moment. She was sitting on the ground, rubbing legs that were unused to so much time in the saddle.

Magnus took his sword and made a show of cutting down a small willow tree to make a walking staff. But the sight of the girl he had lain with by the stream that first day clad in the familiar blue cloak, her yellow hair spilling over her shoulders, her emerald eyes wide with fear and joy and alarm at the sight of him, his heart was set to pounding so much he could hardly speak.

When he did, all the wrong words came rushing out.

"Are you enjoying talking to this wonderful Templar who has bought you your freedom?" he said in a harsh whisper. "Do you even know or care where he is taking you?"

She did not look as though she heard; her look traveled over him anxiously. "Oh, Holy Mother, what has happened to you?" she whispered back. "Are you hurt? Look at your fine clothes!"

She would have jumped up then to fling herself at him, but he made a warning gesture.

"Listen," Magnus began. He wanted to tell her about his plans for their escape, but out of the corner of his eye he could see de la Guerche coming back.

She saw him, too. "Help me," she whispered.

"Yes," he promised just as softly.

Gazing into those beautiful eyes, he wanted to take her in his arms and kiss her senseless. He wanted to lie with her in a woodland bower and caress her and love her through long, golden days. Some place where no one could find them, or hinder their endless pleasure.

"Yes," he vowed huskily, "I promise."

He turned quickly away, swinging the new-made staff. The Templar stopped and looked after him, frowning, but said nothing. De la Guerche motioned

Edain to her pony, and gave her a hand up into the saddle. The men got up from the ground and gathered up their weapons. The party started through the trees toward the last of the dying light.

They had not gone half a league before something came bounding out of the forest and ran under the feet of Edain's pony, making it rear.

She screamed, and would have lost her seat but the Templar quickly leaned over and grabbed her reins, hauling the pony's head around until it stopped its panicked rearing.

Magnus came running up. He never took his eyes from her, anyway; he was at her pony's head almost at the same time that de la Guerche reached for the reins.

The Templar sat back in his saddle and regarded him, eyebrows lifted.

"I heard her scream, milord." Magnus did not give a tinker's dam what de la Guerche thought. "I wished to prevent an accident."

"Ah yes." Again that look. "The out-of-pocket knight. I've seen you back there, where Eudo has set you to guarding the rear."

The pony still danced and bobbed. Edain, looking shaken, hung onto the pommel with both hands.

Eudo came running up with the rest of the men-at-arms and bent and picked up something from the ground.

"Here is the culprit." The serjeant held a ball of white fur at arm's length. "This is what has caused the trouble, milord. One of Satan's own."

"A cat?" De la Guerche looked down his long nose at it.

They all craned to see. The girl bent from the saddle, hanging onto the pommel with her other hand, and extended her arm and the cat clawed up the side of her cloak quite daintily, jumped onto her thighs, and settled itself.

No one said anything for a long moment. De la Guerche brought his destrier up alongside and stared down at the white cat nestled in her lap. "It is someone's lost pet," he observed. "It is in too good repair to have been long astray. Look, someone has taken the trouble to fix a lady's bauble in its ear."

The men crowded closer. From the white cat's ear hung a small finger ring set with a red stone.

"Let us ransom it," Eudo said, "before the accursed Sanach Dhu come and do it for us."

The men all laughed. Magnus stood at the edge of the group watching as Edain stroked the top of the cat's head with the tip of her finger. It closed its eyes, and began a loud, rough purring.

"Fomor," she said to it.

The men turned to her, mouths slightly open.

"The last of the Fomorians," she explained, scratching behind the cat's ears. "The Fir Bolg, they call themselves. After them, my own people came."

Ten

A cold hand was put over her mouth and a voice whispered in her ear: "Don't move, don't make a sound."

Edain had been sleeping lightly. The ground was hard in spite of the piled dead leaves under her, and did little to ease her aching body. She came quickly awake.

"Can you see my face?" The whisper was hoarse.

Yes, the moonlight was bright and she could see him. But she'd know that voice anywhere. She nodded.

"Good," Magnus told her. "Get up quickly, and follow after me."

All around them the men-at-arms were wrapped in their cloaks and sheepskins. The night watch, sitting against a tree, had nodded off and was faintly snoring. The big body of Asgard de la Guerche lay on the other side of the fire, facing away from the red glow of the coals.

Magnus put his finger to his lips and like shadows they passed silently into the trees, away from the camp.

Edain wanted to ask about the horses. They couldn't get far without them. But Magnus stepped into a pine needle-covered gully and they skidded down a slope until they came to the end in a stand of bracken. There she saw de la Guerche's unsaddled destrier with a knight's padded jacket over his head, standing quietly tied to a pine branch.

Edain gasped. "You can't steal his warhorse!"

"I already have."

He gave her a boost up on the stallion's back. Then, keeping its head covered so that it would allow itself to be led, he pulled it on down the hillside.

Edain held onto the destrier's mane with both hands, her heart pounding. The pine needles muffled the sound of the destrier's hooves. Hopefully no sound would wake the men at the camp and raise the alarm.

But the daring of it all, she couldn't help thinking. The Templar's horse was a fine animal—if she had to guess, worth a fortune. They were not only escaping from the king's emissary, who'd paid a ransom for her, but they were stealing a Templar knight's warhorse!

They traveled through the woods that way, passing in between the dark of the trees and the light of the full moon, with Magnus leading the destrier. Then at last the woods ended and a great meadow spread out before them, the tall dry grass like a silver sea in the moonlight.

"Move back," Magnus whispered to her.

Edain shifted on the destrier's broad back to make room, and he bounded up in front of her.

"Hold my belt," he told her. He reached forward and pulled his jacket from the stallion's head.

Instantly the big horse shuddered at the sudden

sight of the strange meadow and the feel of the bit hard in his mouth, the riders on his back. With a neigh that sounded like a clap of thunder he reared, then charged forward in a great bound.

Edain hung onto Magnus's sword belt with both hands and bit back a scream. It was like a nightmare, the shock of the powerful horse suddenly bolting across the grassy, moonlit shieling, the feel of the muscles of its big legs and massive back drawing and bunching under her. The destrier's body flattened like an arrow shot from a bow.

Seconds later, as she clung to him, her mouth dry with terror, she realized Magnus was laughing!

Edain could not believe it.

Their very lives were in danger as the stallion bolted into the night. A runaway horse could step into an unseen hole, or stumble on a rock, and they could die. And yet to him it did not seem to matter!

She let go of Magnus's belt and flung her arms around his body. The same feeling was there in the man—of a powerful, straining animal, muscles bunching in a frenzy of headlong turbulence. He was meeting challenge with mastery, and loving it!

It could not last forever. Gradually, the destrier's pace slowed. Sweat, and foam from the horse's jaws splattered back on them. Its big ribs heaved. Finally its gallop faltered, and then, snorting and shaking its head, the stallion began a ragged canter. As it did so Magnus pulled in on the reins, talking to it softly, calling it boy, and lad, telling it there was nothing to be afraid of.

Edain took a deep breath. Her arms had clutched

his body so tightly during their wild ride that they could not stop quivering. Her legs, too, were shaking.

When he turned to look at her the moonlight struck his face. She saw he was still laughing.

Edain could have hit him. And yet he had ridden down the Templar's fine horse and conquered it; she could not fault him for that. If Magnus had not been a superb horseman they would have been bucked off and walking through the night woods by now. And probably lost.

Nevertheless, she almost hated him.

He walked the heaving horse into the trees and slid down and took the reins and tied him to an overhanging branch. The destrier tamely bent its head and began to crop a patch of dry grass.

Magnus lifted Edain down, and carried her to the tree and laid her on a bed of fallen leaves. She was still shaking. She watched as he pulled off his cloak, then stripped off his shirt and tossed it after it.

Edain sat up. "You almost killed us!"

"Never." He grinned at her. "I am too good a horseman for that." He sat down beside her and pulled at her cloak. "You are such a ninny. I can tell you've spent all your life in a convent."

She knew what he wanted, and started to protest, in spite of the quick stir of her blood at the sight of him, bare-chested and still full of a vibrating energy from mastering the big horse.

She tried to push him away. "What if the Templar is awake, and they are even now following us?"

He pulled her to him. "We have a few moments." His hands were in her hair, running his fingers through it. Then he bent his head and hot, eager kisses captured her mouth, her throat, dropped to the cloth gown stretched taut over her breasts.

When she moaned, he whispered, "Ah, God, how I have dreamed of this moment, to hold you again! I have burned with it. I have spent the day walking in the back and choking in the dust of our lord Templar's horses including your fat-arsed pony and thinking of how you would look in my arms, naked and gleaming and beautiful. How I wanted every minute to fit myself into your body as I did before, and taste the exquisite sweetness of it!" Mouth against hers, he groaned, "To think such thoughts—to think of *you*—is enough to drive one mad! Jesu, how I need you!"

He pushed her resisting hands aside to unfasten her cloak. When he did, the white cat jumped out of the front of her gown where she had put him when she lay down to sleep.

He recoiled. "Accursed cat! You can't bring that thing with us!"

He picked up the animal and flung it into the bushes. Then he dropped to his knees and peeled her cloak away in a passionate, trembling hurry, and lifted the hem of her gown to her waist. He rolled on top of her, pulling her bared legs up around him.

"Magnus," Edain choked.

It was madness, but she could not stop him; she was caught up in the fever herself. His mouth was over hers, swallowing her gasps as the tip of his big shaft probed her tight entrance, then pushed with urgent force inside her.

It was a rough possession, the same way he had conquered the warhorse. He filled her to stretching almost painfully; for a moment she could not match the violence of his unleashed desire.

But even as Edain squirmed under him, her hands pressing at his shoulders, he showered tender, heated kisses across her face. His body began to move as his mouth seized hers and dragged at her underlip with his teeth.

"My beautiful golden witch," he gasped. "I want to fill you, make you my prisoner, devour you—I want all of you!"

His words came true as he drove into her.

It was a greedy, sensuous coupling, full of animal energy. At first she did not think she could endure it. But slowly she gave way as his senses, his body ravished hers.

Edain whimpered as he pulled the neck of her gown down so that he could suckle her breasts and nip at them with his teeth. A big hand clamped in her crotch. Her feminine bud of desire was helpless under his tantalizing, grinding touch. But she could not deny that it inflamed her. In return, she bared her teeth and sank them into his shoulder, and heard his exclamation of surprise and pain.

His hand in her hair dragged back her head as he punished her love bite with hard kisses on her throat and face, nibbling her cheek and the curve of her ear until they stung.

Ah, this was so different! This lovemaking was no languorous falling among the golden stars; it was hard and hot and reeked of crushed dry grass and sweat and horses. Edain felt, as she allowed herself to fall into the searing flames, that their passion would burn them alive. She was as bad as he; there would be nothing left of them but ashes!

This was lust, there in the silvery meadow, yet it was also some strange part of love. Her straining, heaving lover whose body raked hers so wildly conquered her—and was in turn conquered.

In the next moment he convulsed with a roar, matching her own muffled shriek of release. He lowered himself, shaking and dripping with sweat, making strangled noises.

Edain licked her swollen lips. She felt mauled and scratched, as slick with sweat as he. And as wearily triumphant.

"Holy Mary, I can never leave you." His mouth burrowed into the warm folds of her throat and shoulder. "Edain—Edain," he murmured, "how will I live without you? It's true, you must be a witch. There is no other woman who I could find in this earth to compare with you!"

She looked over his shoulder, still trying to catch her breath. The white cat sat not too far away in a patch of moonlight, licking its paws. She barely managed to whisper, "Nay, I am not a witch."

"No?" He lifted himself to one elbow so that he could look down into her face. "Why do you say and do things that no one understands?" His hand stroked her wet hair back from her eyes. "Why did you call the stray cat that came out of the forest by a name, and say that he was a relation?"

Edain's gaze slipped away. "I—I do not know, sometimes, what I am going to say. Only that there is a Feeling . . ." Her voice trailed away, helpless. He would not understand. "I cannot explain. Only that it seems to come into my head."

He waited a long moment, staring at her, then he rolled slightly away from her, hauling up his hose to cover himself. "And running the ship up onto a sandbar so that we would not arrive in time to be attacked. Did that come into your head, also?"

"Yes." Edain sat up. The whirlwind of passion that had seized them but minutes ago was gone, leaving her feeling dull, her body slightly aching. She pulled her gown up at the neck, and bent and straightened the skirt.

She heard him sigh. He ran his hand through his tousled red hair. "Christ's wounds, what a tale this makes! I will be hard put to find anyone in Chester who will believe it."

His face was in shadow, but the light picked out the breadth of his bare shoulders and the slightly waving hair that brushed against them. He was strong and beautiful. Edain could not help remembering with a sensuous shiver the feel of that powerful body in her arms minutes ago, while they were making love.

"When I bring you back to my liege lord, the Earl of Chester," he was saying, "you must explain all this to him as best you can. I've got the earl's two tax ships and two crews, all lost, to account for. Do you understand? You may be my only witness."

There was a silence for a long moment. The cat strolled over to them and rubbed its side and tail against Edain's shoulder, purring. She picked it up and put it in her lap, aware in that brief moment that her world had tilted. And not for the better.

She said in a very soft voice, "You wish to bring me back to your lord so that I may testify that losing his ships was not your fault?"

He got to his feet and went to retrieve his padded knight's jacket from under the trees. When he came back he had put it on, laced it up, and he carried his sword.

"Believe me," he said, "for that message I will guard you with my life. I—this voyage as a tax collector has been a curse from beginning to end. Verily, it is too long a story to tell." Magnus was thinking about the drunken evening with the Frenchmen, losing all his tourney prize money to them, and the wild boasting that had led to shipwreck and disaster. "God's truth," he grated, "it is my honor—my *family's* honor—I seek to save!"

Edain stood up, the cat in her arms. She said even more softly, "Is that why you did not return to Chester, but took service with the Templar? You knew that he was searching for me, and you needed to bring me back with you?"

Something in her voice made him pause and peer at her, trying to see her face. "Uh—yes, that was the main part."

What was the matter with her? he wondered. She was glaring at him with emerald eyes shiny with what could only be tears. But by the saints, he was damned if he could see the reason for any trouble!

He was mad for her, Magnus told himself; no other woman had enchanted him so. When he was not with her he thought incessantly of the next time he could have her. But surely even she, an orphan from some threadbare convent on the northern coasts, had not been expecting anything more from him than what he had already given. He had never mentioned the word "love;" he had been careful to see that what happened between them never went that far. Even though, he had to admit more than a little guiltily, he *had* taken her virginity.

Well, that had been by mistake, hadn't it? He supposed he had been stupid to assume that she was de Brise's whore.

"Fear not, I will take care of you," he said, hoping to soothe her. "I will be your guardian before all, you do not have to worry that I will abandon you. And after you have testified to the earl as to the true story of what happened, I will see you safely to a convent in that city, if that is what you wish."

"Return to the convent?" Her low cry was incredulous. "After what you have done to me? I have lain with a man, most sinfully in the eyes of the church. Do you think they would have me back?"

He scowled. "You do not have to be a virgin to return to the holy sisters. You know this. If you are repentant—"

"Repentant?" Her shriek alarmed the cat, who jumped out of her arms. "Do you think I will pay penance for what *you* have done to me?" She turned on her heel, marching away from him. "Ah, how unhappy I am that I ever laid eyes on you!" she flung over her shoulder. "Christ in heaven, I will not repent for what is not my fault! No—I shall bring charges to the bishop that you foully seduced me, an innocent novice of the convent of Saint Sulpice!"

For a moment Magnus could do nothing but stare after her. He was stunned.

He had seduced a novice? Jesus God, he could not afford any more trouble. This was not the very worst that could happen, but it came close. *She was going to bring charges to the bishop?* He was astounded that she would say such a thing!

"Stop, where are you going?" She was headed for the big destrier under the trees. "Edain—stay. Let me talk to you. Are you mad?" he cried as she untied the reins. "Listen to me. And let go of that bridle. You can't ride de la Guerche's warhorse!"

At that moment they heard the distant blast of a horn. The stallion tossed its head and took a few steps, dragging Edain with him.

Magnus cursed under his breath. The Templar's big mount was plainly trained to a horn signal, and would come if de la Guerche kept blowing.

"Give me the accursed reins," he shouted, lunging for them.

He needed to mount, get the girl up behind him, and get out of there. Fast as the big horse was, they had a chance even now to outrun the pony and pack-horse.

It was too late. Before Magnus could get to them the horse reared, dragging the reins from Edain's hand. As the horn rang again, the destrier promptly bolted into the night-dark woods and disappeared.

Magnus stood with his fists clenched, glaring at the girl. He allowed himself the pleasure of shouting a string of blistering curses. In the distance the horn winded again.

He quickly bent and took his cloak from the ground. "All right," he snarled, "now we will have to run. The dark and the thickness of the woods will help us until dawn. Perhaps by then we will have found a village."

She did not move.

When he turned to look at her she was standing in a stray pool of moonlight, her wool gown and loosened gold hair almost silvery.

Something in the way she stood there made his skin prickle.

"I am not going with you," Edain said. "You only want me as witness to your blunders, nothing more. I am going back to the Templar."

She turned and walked into the woods the way the horse had gone. A small white shadow, the cat, got up from the ground and quickly followed at her heels.

The trees and the darkness closed around her.

Eleven

"Disappeared?" William the Lion roared. "How long ago? And what of the money?"

FitzGamelin was braced for the outburst. Fortunately, the justiciar had his answers ready. He only wished they were better answers.

"The ransom money was paid, sire," fitzGamelin explained, "to Constantine of the Sanach Dhu, as planned, although it was a—ah, a bit more than was agreed upon when the Templar left here. When that was done, the girl was released to him."

King William slumped in his chair and stuck his booted feet to the fire. " 'A bit more?' What does that mean? How much more?"

When the justiciar told him, William the Lion gave vent to another leonine roar of rage.

The king jumped up from his chair, scattering the Benedictine clerks who had been hovering, ink pots in hand, at his elbow. The castle steward, fitzAlan, motioned for the servants to gather up the wine cups and trays, then herded them out onto the landing out of harm's way and closed the door.

FitzGamelin, though, had to stand his ground.

"God is my judge," the king bellowed, "if what you say is true about the money, we have given that bare-legged sheep thief in Loch Etive enough to set up his own kingdom! Jesu, one finer than mine own, if the damned huge sum the Templar gave him is it!"

"De la Guerche did not have all that much of Scottish gold to give, sire," the justiciar soothed him. "Part of what was paid to Sanach Dhu, we may assume, was Templar gold."

"Templar gold?" The king sat back down in his chair. "Holy Jesus in heaven, what do they want with her? They never part with their money except to lend it at a mountain of interest!"

FitzGamelin shrugged. "In general, sire, we know nothing about the Templars, even those in their commandery here in Edinburgh. Except what they wish us to know."

With a tentative look at the king, fitzGamelin dismissed the clerks, and sent them outside. It was best to clear the room as there was more bad news. The justiciar had a fairly good idea where, in spite of the money King William had paid for her ransom, the girl might be found.

"By the tripes of Saint David," the king was saying, "it is as hard to keep the Templars out of Scotland's business as it is to rid a bed of fleas. And damned if the pious knights are not just as persistent! I remember the day their emissaries first appeared to say that they had come to ask permission to found a chapter house to help travelers and pilgrims. Even though there be not many travelers and pilgrims in our cold and distant land. Then in the midst of their happy building of church and cloister they suddenly produce letters and writs from Nurenburg and Rome that say the Holy Father has given permission for the Knights of the Holy Temple to audit the finances of various Scottish churches, and a few bishops in particular. The first thing one knows there are two or three well-constructed commanderies in the land, and the psalm-singing, sword-swinging knights of the Temple are patrolling the streets of the city, ministering to the poor, collecting alms in the king's name—until they are embedded in the flesh of the kingdom like a thorn, half invisible, and damned near unmovable!"

FitzGamelin could not disagree. William the Lion of Scotland had thought in the beginning to settle a few Norman families in his desmesne, but he had not counted on the Templars who had followed them.

The justiciar had often wondered if the Templars had already offered their financial services to the Scottish exchequer. And whether William had accepted. They would, in time, he was certain; Scotland was a poor country.

"Perhaps," the justiciar allowed, "the Templars wish to keep the girl a few days to examine her so-called extraordinary gifts. Their interest in miraculous things is said to be avid. They may well wish to—ah, interrogate her."

William the Lion hardly looked pleased. "And who gives them leave? *I* am king here! Would the Templars be so bold as to take her out from under my nose? And after I had sent one of their own, de la Guerche, to fetch her? He left to ransom her before the feast of Saint Andrew and now Advent approaches. Where the devil is she?"

Somewhere in Edinburgh, fitzGamelin was fairly sure. The justiciar was not pleased himself at the girl's failure to appear at William's court within the expected time. They had paid de la Guerche to go to Clan Sanach Dhu and ransom her. Now the gossip in the city was that the Templar and the girl were back, but that de la Guerche was obeying the orders of his Edinburgh commander, and not those of the King of Scotland.

With a few murmured words, saying that he would go at once to look into the matter, fitzGamelin bowed out of the king's chamber. The stone stairs outside were crowded with clansmen waiting for an audience with their monarch. As he pushed past them the justiciar could not ignore that even though it was not yet Yuletide, William was calling in his chiefs for the war he so looked forward to in the spring. When he hoped to regain some of his borderland.

The war, fitzGamelin reminded himself, for which William wanted this girl, especially. So that, as he understood it, she could bring her great powers as seeress to the castle rock and unerringly guide William the Lion's battlefield strategy.

FitzGamelin hurried out into the courtyard filled with more armed clansmen. He did not know what to worry about first, that was the truth of it, he told himself as he hurried along. With the king so strongly set on having the girl, he did not dare delay a search for her whereabouts.

And what if she *were* being kept at the Templar's commandery there in the city? the justiciar fretted as his groom brought up his horse. With the Templars' zeal to explore all that was exotic and mysterious, a practice that had unfortunately given rise to so many rumors about them in the Holy Land, the knights could very well have subjected the girl to a little judicious torture. And God in heaven knew William the Lion of Scotland would not stand for that. Any probing of the girl's powers, with or without the use of torture, the king would insist on doing himself!

The justiciar swung himself into the saddle and spurred his horse through the gateway of the castle, on his way, in a great hurry, down into the town.

When the bell rang for prayers at nones the Templar servants and a few knights who elected to work in the winter fields would put down their rakes and hoes and file up to begin devotions.

Edain could see them from her window that was covered with a fine brass grille, pretty to look at, but as imprisoning as any iron bars. When the bell rang for midafternoon prayer it was the signal that the work in the fields was over. She pressed her face to the grille and watched the Templars walk up the hill.

After nones, the knights would gather in the chapter house to question her again. The interrogation had gone on for days. It looked as though it would go on forever.

No one knew she was there, Edain was reminded. Dear God, probably no one even knew she was in Edinburgh! She had not thought it would work out that way.

She could not stop thinking of Magnus and where he might be. And if he thought of her at all, except to concern himself with finding her and bringing her back to England with him. She was his witness—his very own words—to present to his liege lord to explain the loss of the tax ships and their crews!

It was plain he had felt nothing for her, Edain told herself. Nothing except the wicked lust of a young knight for a maid. It was an old story, one the nuns had warned all the orphans of repeatedly. And she, like a fool, was the last person on earth one would think to fall easy victim to his handsomeness, his easy, persuasive passion.

In the middle of the night she often lay awake tormenting herself with thoughts of her terrible mistake, and how stupidly she had trusted him. She worried about being there forever in the Templar's bare, austere barracks, held prisoner until she was an old woman. While they went on through the years questioning her endlessly.

And what questions!

She had found that the Templar knights standing in assembly with their close-cropped heads and identical white surcoats with red crosses, were fascinated with magic, with seers and seeresses, especially Scotland's plentiful Celtic variety. It was plain when they questioned her that they wanted Edain to perform for them as they had seen magicians do in the East, in the Holy Land. And were very disappointed when she would not. They seemed to feel, the commander especially, that if they kept on coaxing her, she would finally give in.

Can you levitate? they asked her one time.

The question had baffled her. She did not know what "levitate" was. When it was explained to her, she was surprised. Why would anyone, even a magician, want to do that?

The second in command, the Templars' prior, had wanted to know, *Can you understand the language of birds, and beasts?*

Edain thought long on that one. She had to admit that the answer could only be no, she probably did not. Not in the way they expected.

Now, standing by the window, she could not help but feel a deep sense of foreboding. *Show us your powers freely, and do not be frightened,* the commander had told her.

But the light in the depth of his eyes had hinted that their interest could give way, when their patience ran out, to something less pleasant.

She turned away from the window.

At first there seemed little reason to fear anything. The Templars would not seduce her and humiliate her the way Magnus had betrayed her. After the long journey with Asgard de la Guerche from Loch Etive it had been comforting to arrive at last in clean, safe surroundings. The monkish routine of so many armed knights had been somewhat strange at first, but the sound of the Templars chanting at their devotions ran like a peaceful, silvery thread through the hours of the day. Life at the commandery was simple, pious, and even comfortable, very like the one she had known in the convent. And after the hardship of the shipwreck, and being lost in the Scottish Highlands, it was nice to know that the fields and gardens around the place produced meat and vegetables, milk and grain for their particularly hearty fare. It was wonderful just to sit down to the meals the servants brought her.

Edain had been told that she was there to rest and recover from the journey from Constantine's broch. Although what would come after that had not exactly been specified.

That first night a bath in an iron tub had been prepared for her, and she was left alone in a great stone room to scrub her body and her hair thoroughly with yellow lye soap. Neat, white woolen garments, looking a little like a nun's habit, had been set out for her, as well as linen underclothes. And there were felt peasant's shoes, a little too large but comfortable, plus a brown linen cloth to cover her hair.

She had worn these clothes ever since. Only when she was in the chapter house was she allowed to uncover her hair. Someone, she thought it had been the commander, had said that seeresses were known for the beauty of their hair, and so this was requested of her, every time. They brought a long-legged brass stool called a tripod for her to sit on when they questioned her, saying this was the seeress's chair.

At first Edain had hoped to convince them that she had no powers. That what others declared they had seen was a trick played on their eyes, or ears. Or that they had simply misunderstood. It had worked in the past.

Edain could see Asgard de la Guerche's face among the rows of Templars, and she thought she caught a glimmer of sympathy in those blue eyes.

But a persistent unease began to grow in her about the Templars' assemblies and their continuing questioning. She was beginning to feel the need to defend herself. And as in the past she told herself her best chance was to pretend innocence, and deny everything.

But there were a few, she felt, who were waiting patiently until they could force the truth out of her.

She put her fist to her mouth, and paced the floor.

Holy Jesus in heaven, what *was* the truth? How could she explain the mysterious Feeling that had always been with her? She did not know what it was herself. Nor even when it would choose to make itself felt!

Talk about powers! The terrible thing was she had no power over *it!*

She turned when the door was unlocked from the other side and breathed a sigh of relief when Asgard de la Guerche came in, as he did every evening, to fetch her to the assembly.

She could see right away that something was bothering him. He looked as all his brother Templars did with soft leather boots and a long robe with the surcoat with the big red cross over it. Against the chill, damp weather that penetrated the stone walls of the commandery, he wore a close-fitting leather cap with a string to tie under the chin that he had not bothered to secure. His perfect blond handsomeness was unruffled, but she was beginning to know him well enough to notice now the lines about his eyes that betrayed that something was not as it should be.

She could not hold back a start as he suddenly dropped to one knee, took her hand, and lifted it to his mouth to kiss her fingers. Alarmed, Edain tugged at her hand, but he held it fast.

She felt her knees begin to shake. He had never kissed her hand before; he made it an intimate gesture, wholly unexpected. Was this an omen? That something dire was about to happen to her?

"Allow me, demoiselle," the Templar said huskily.

Before Edain could stop him he had pulled her close and quickly loosed the laces at the front of her gown. He leaned his big body forward and thrust his face and mouth against the warm skin of her breasts. She heard him take a ragged breath.

"I want you," he said in a muffled voice. "I want you. I cannot help myself."

For several long seconds he did nothing. He stayed on his knees, his hands clasping the folds of her woolen skirts while his mouth and lips rested lightly against her flesh, savoring her warmth and nearness.

Edain was frozen with fright. She did not know what she was supposed to do. Templars and their brother fighting order, the Hospitallers, were known for their chastity, and purity. In the Edinburgh commandery she took her meals alone, and went to chapel alone. Few Templars spoke to her. When any of them passed her in the cloistered hallways they lowered their eyes. The atmosphere was that of a monastery. She knew they would blame her if she raised a passion among any of them, no matter how innocently. And especially in that perfect knight, de la Guerche.

Edain's teeth and jaws clamped together in terror. She told herself she dared not move.

After a few minutes de la Guerche's grip on her skirts relaxed. He shook his head as if to clear it, then slowly got to his feet. She expected him to say something about what had happened, but he did not. He only said in a low voice, "Unbind your hair."

They were going to act as though nothing had occurred. But it was several moments before she could say, "Are we—am I—to go to the hall now?"

He nodded.

So except for the Templar's strange outburst everything was to be as usual, she thought as she removed her coif and let down her braids. But she was shaken, her thoughts confused and whirling. At some time the questioning had to come to an end, and then what? Would the Templars honor the ransom King William had paid, and finally turn her over to him?

Something had to happen, Edain thought as she laced up the front of her gown. The memory of Asgard de la Guerche's mouth on her skin made her fingers tremble so that she had difficulty untying the braids' end bindings and raking her loosened hair.

Why had he done it? *He wanted her.* The words were dismaying enough. She could not let anything like this happen; she was frantic now to be free of the Templars' prison. And it *was* a prison, for all its cloistered air.

The tall Templar stepped in front of her and opened the door. The white cat, bored with being shut up in the room, bounded down the arched stone hallway that led to the assembly chamber. By the time they reached the stairs it was out of sight.

The assembly chamber was situated under the Templars' circular church. The Templars' round churches, with the altar in the middle and the mass sung by a chaplain surrounded by the congregation, were their hallmark, and equally famous all over the world.

The stairs were lit by smoking torches in brackets on the walls. Beyond the assembly hall lay the dark shadows of the burial crypts.

The cat knew the way. Edain hurried after it, wanting to stay ahead of de la Guerche. When the Templar opened the door the cat raced past them and into the center of the crowded room.

It moved almost too quickly for the eye to follow, as though it knew who was waiting. It jumped into the arms of a monk in a ragged brown habit who caught it, examined the ring in its ear, and held it and stroked its head as though they were old acquaintances.

The hall was filled with half a hundred Templars. They followed Edain with their eyes as she came in with de la Guerche. The commander stood by the monk in the brown habit wearing a white, pointed hood and mask that had slits for eyes and mouth.

Edain had seen the commander in the white mask before. No one had explained to her why he, who was also the Master of the Order, was masked when he appeared in the subterranean assembly room; she gathered it was a part of a ritual that went on before they ever called her.

"She is very beautiful," the monk in the brown habit said. He had a deep, carrying voice. Without putting down the cat, he beckoned to her.

Edain pushed through the crowd. When she was close enough she saw the great gold cross with the wheel of the sun that lay on his chest. She felt a small whisper of hope rise in her heart, even though she could not help staring.

She remembered the nuns of St. Sulpice saying there were not many Culdee monks left. In all the long years only two had visited the convent, old men traveling from Ireland, and they had used the guest house only one night before resuming their journey.

The sisters had gossiped about the Culdees for days, and what had become of their once-powerful arm of the mother church. The Pope in Rome did not favor the few Culdee monasteries that still existed, or the Culdees' strange observances, among them the old Irish church's way of the reckoning of Easter and other holy days. Which did not match the Roman calendar at all.

That was only one of the differences. It was widely believed the Irish monks had wives and mistresses. It was said a bishop of Clonmacnoise celebrated mass with his five grown sons assisting!

Hundreds of years ago according to the sisters, when barbarians overran Rome and held the Holy Father the Pope captive, the Irish monks had flourished in their chapter houses and monasteries in their peaceful, faraway island. Eventually the Irish church became so strong and the Roman church so weakened by barbarian hordes that only the Irish fathers were able to send missionaries and scholars to the court of Frankish kings, even Charlemagne himself, and into Saxony to convert the Germans. Most marvelously, the flourishing Irish monasteries taught Greek and Latin and Virgil and Aristotle, and produced the finest painted and gilded illuminations of holy books in the world. The church in Ireland had become almost as important as Rome itself.

But as always happened, things changed. The Roman church finally asserted its power through those very kings the Irish Culdees had ministered to. The

Culdee fathers agreed at the synod of Whitby to give up their ancient observances and follow the Roman liturgy, and for many decades they had slowly faded from the main body of the holy church.

Edain looked up into the strange amber-colored eyes of the Irish father. He was not old like the Culdee monks she remembered; he was middle-aged, with a long nose somewhat flattened at the end, and a wide, ironic mouth. A big man, rather fleshy, but with a strong body and broad shoulders.

But it was his Culdee tonsure, his head shaven from ear to ear across the front of his head in the style, it was said, of the old Druids—and not in a round spot in the back like the Roman clergy—that made her stare.

Where had the Templars got him? she wondered. And dear Holy Mother, for *what?*

She watched as his big hand with the curious, knobbed fingertips continued to stroke the ring in the ear of the white cat. "Ah, Fomor," he murmured to it, "where have you managed to find the last of your old friends?"

The silence in the underground chamber was broken by a restless whisper that rippled through the throng of Templars. Behind her, Edain knew Asgard de la Guerche took a step toward her. The cat jumped out of the Culdee's arms and landed at the Culdee's feet, rubbing against the hem of his habit, eyes slitted.

The Irish monk looked around him with a penetrating stare and the room quieted.

"In the Book of Invasions it is written," he said, "that the children of the Fir Bolg came to Ireland from the land of the ancient Greeks and lived in Eire in peace and prosperity. They were farmers and gardeners, and each carried his leather bag to gather the soil to make great terraces, and grow marvelous crops. The earth was like an Eden, and Ireland was green and filled with the stone houses of the old gods. And the Fomorians raised great rings of standing stones as we see in the land today."

When he stopped speaking the silence seemed to echo in the stone vaults above them. The cat rubbed against his leg, purring.

"Then came the tribes of the goddess Danu," the Irishman went on, "called the Tuatha de Danaan, tall and fair and rich in beauty. There had never been a race like them. They came to Ireland in a cloud of mist so that the Fomorians could never see them until the fair Tuatha de Danaan filled the land and triumphed, and seized all the kingdoms for their own."

The commander stirred behind his mask and said something to the Culdee that Edain could not hear.

The Irish monk never took his eyes from her.

Slowly, he began to recite in an eloquent tongue that sounded to Edain, faintly familiar.

When he was through he paused, then declaimed in singsong Norman French, " 'Her hair was the color of the summery iris, of pure, beaten gold . . . Her hands were white as the snow of the night, and her lovely cheeks were soft and even, red as the mountain foxglove. Her eyebrows were as black as a beetle, her teeth were as of rows of pearls, her eyes were blue as hyacinths . . . Her hips were white as foam, long, slender, soft as wool, her thighs were warm and soft, her knees were small and firm . . . It was said of her that all who might before have been thought beautiful are as nothing beside Edain; all the fair women in the world cannot match her.' "

Edain stared at him, transfixed. It was about her, she knew at once: a whispering among the Templars there in the underground room broke out until it was almost a roar in her head. She put out her hand but there was nothing to steady her.

Edain, princess of Ulster of the old songs that the filid *sang.*

Edain was a goddess, kidnapped by the evil Midir. She did not know how she knew this, but she did.

The Templars' whispers rattled in the stone arches above them. The room turned around and around sickeningly. Edain heard the cat meowing.

It began to grow dark before her eyes. Something terrible was happening. Her stomach turned over, and there was a salty taste in her mouth.

As from a long way away she heard the commander say, "It is the Tuatha de Danaan, then, you are sure?"

And the voice of the Culdee monk, lifted over the cat's strident yowls: "Ah, yes, a great race, the people of the goddess Danu. You see, even the name fits her. When my own tribe the Milesians came and defeated them, the Tuatha de Danaan went into the hills and the stone tombs and the stone circles to live. For they were always great magicians."

Magicians.

It was the last word Edain heard. Asgard de la Guerche's arms came around her to hold her and kept her from falling.

But she had already fainted.

Twelve

The crofter's widow stood in the doorway of her hut watching as Magnus finished chopping the last of the wood.

It had begun to rain, or mist or whatever it seemed always to be doing in these hills. The widow did not come out into the yard but stood under the overhang of the thatch as he laid down a log on the stump and swung the ax. The wood, being still somewhat green, split in two, sluggishly, and the pieces fell off the stump into the mud.

He could tell without looking that the widow was not impressed.

"I'll not keep a fire going," she yelled from the doorway, "if you fling dry wood into the muck like that. Might as well drown it in yonder pond!"

Magnus only grunted.

He had stripped to the waist to do the woodchopping, something the widow seemed to appreciate from the gleam in her eye. Now the deepening rain was growing cold on his sweating bare back and shoulders. But he had another pile of logs to do when he was finished with this one, and what he lacked in skill he was accomplishing, he thought somewhat sourly, with sheer strength.

The widow had wanted him to do the milking, too, as part of the payment for a meal. But even she could see Magnus knew nothing whatsoever about milking cows, or even goats, so she had sent the sullen half-grown boy, her son, off to do it, and put him to hauling a pile of fence logs. It was work that anyone could see was more properly done by a mule, but Magnus had done that, too, and done it well. Now he was chopping a mountain of wood for her fire.

She was not a bad-looking woman, he thought, watching her out of the corner of his eye. Still young, with large breasts and a trim waist, and a roguish pair of black eyes that had sized him up as soon as he entered her yard. She'd known what he wanted almost before he'd asked for it.

Magnus had not eaten since helping a wild tribesman find his cow and newborn calf in a river thicket the night before. A task that had earned him half the cowherd's haggis as his reward.

Just the memory of it made Magnus wonder if starving to death, rather than being faced with yet another rancid oat pudding cooked in a sheep's stomach, was not the better part of valor. But then he'd come through the rain to find the widow's steading, and after she'd come out and looked him over thoroughly, she'd promised him bread and beer. And had even hinted at a bit of cheese.

He bent over and picked up another log and put it on the stump. He already had a sizable pile of firewood, but when he thought of the cheese, he wanted to do everything he could to make the widow doubly generous. He was beginning to think he could not get to Edinburgh at all unless he had food more regularly; it was a chancy business, travel, when one had no money, not even a copper farthing. And virtually nothing to trade now, except his sword.

He was beginning to have a new appreciation for villeins and beggars and gypsies and all the hungry, ragtag foot traffic he'd once passed so unconcernedly. The world was vastly different from the back of a knight's charger.

And now, he thought, as he put another piece of wood on the stump. And *now?*

Well, now Sir Magnus fitzJulien, that gallant poet, that handsome, peerless troubadour of fair English ladies' solars at the earl's court in Chester was hoping to chop enough wood to cozzen some dead crofter's widow into giving him what would be, thankfully enough, his only meal of the day.

Suddenly the thought of a little piece of roast mutton made Magnus swing, and hit the piece of firewood off center.

It separated with a crack and flipped off through the air. As the oak billets flew past the doorway the widow ducked just in time, and gave a muffled scream.

Magnus shrugged. He put another log in its place.

Yes, he told himself, bitterly, here we have Sir Magnus fitzJulien, undefeated tourney champion in virtually all the north of England, undisputed master horseman and swordsman, victor of over twenty melees at Chester's court alone. Men stayed away from him in battle unless they sought to make their reputations. And by God, he'd made his *father* proud, a difficult thing to do as the Earl of Morlaix was a champion knight himself.

Magnus remembered someone at court had written a song calling him the perfect young paladin knight, the "dauntless devil of the jousting lance." Which he had always thought a bit flowery and overblown. Even though most of it was true.

What he would really sell his soul for, he thought suddenly, was a bowl of hot beef and barley soup.

He saw the widow pick up the pieces of oak wood that had flown at her and tuck them under her arm. She started across the yard, holding up one corner of her shawl to shield herself from the drizzle. Magnus put another log on the stump and clove it, this time a little more neatly.

The widow sidled up to him and laid the split wood in the bin. She never took her eyes from Magnus's bare torso as he swung the ax again and muscles in his arms bunched and rippled.

Sighing, she ran the tip of her tongue lightly across her upper lip.

"You won't catch your death in this weather," she asked, "working out here half naked as you are, now will you? I'd hate to have it said I gave you a fever by making you work till you was sick."

Magnus slowly and deliberately split two more logs and tossed them into the pile. "I won't get sick. Not if I get enough to eat to keep my strength up."

The widow thought that over.

"Och, keeping it up," she agreed with enthusiasm, "that's important, it is, for a fine, bonnie braw lad like you." Her expression was somewhat dreamy as she touched his bare shoulder with her fingertip. "Ah, it's all wet and cold you are!" She looked around for the boy, making sure he had gone off to the barn. "You'd best leave the wood now and come inside," she said hurriedly. "I'll see what I can find to ah, um—put a little solidness in your flesh."

Magnus put down the ax and faced her squarely. Two could play at that game he'd decided the moment she'd put her finger on his bare skin.

"Soup," he said. "I think I have my heart set on some hot barley soup with a big piece of mutton or beef."

And if she didn't have any beef and barley soup, he told himself, he'd wait until she made some.

The boy came back with his pails of milk while Magnus was finishing the last of a mutton broth the widow had whisked together in a remarkably short time. He put down his buckets and flung himself into a seat by the fire to glare at them. The widow looked annoyed to see her son back so soon.

"Now," Magnus told her as he scrubbed out the bowl with the last of the bread, "you said beer, and a little cheese?"

With a sigh, she went back to her cupboard.

But she was not out of ideas, Magnus found later. She'd fixed him a pallet on the straw in the byre among the cows, telling him there were more chores in the morning, especially a drainage ditch that needed cleaning out down by the pond, that would earn him oat porridge, all he could eat, if he did them well.

The widow lingered in the barn, giving him melting looks, until the boy came in to fork down bedding for the animals. When he left, he made sure his mother went with him.

Magnus lay down in the straw, the soup and beer and bread and a large piece of boiled salt beef the widow had eventually parted with heavy and comforting in his belly.

He did not go to sleep at once. The rain dripped off the eaves and the cows below moved about and chewed their feed and then rather noisily lay down for the night. In a flurry of scratching and clucking, the chickens flew up to roost against the far wall.

Magnus listened to the sounds of animals, and rain coming down steadily, thinking that to go to Edinburgh to find Edain was madness. Anyone would tell him that.

He stretched out his big frame on the straw and put his hands behind his head and stared up at the thatch of the barn's roof.

But he was damned if he was going back south, across the border, without her. Of course at the moment he was in a cursed beggarly state. He lacked a horse, his hauberk, money—all the possessions that assured him knightly privilege. As of the day the earl's tax boat wrecked itself on Scotland's shore he'd become just another penniless, nameless fighting man. He could choose to look for a Norman household and pursue ways of borrowing a sum of money, but he would have to reveal himself as the famed Earl of Morlaix's son and heir. And under the circumstances, that, at the moment, might not be too wise. For in wild Scotland he might end up ransomed himself.

As for Edain, he did not care what she thought of

him. It was for her own good that he had to get her back from William the Lion and the all-powerful Templars, no matter how ill she'd taken his explanation there in the forest. He thought he had sensibly allowed that he wanted to bring her to England to testify concerning the loss of his liege lord's tax ships. Certainly logical enough.

He hadn't had time to tell her that was not all of it. That the truth was he wanted her for her own sweet self. She had been cruel and scornful to accuse him of blundering selfishness and base motives. If she were right there in the widow's yard at that moment, she would see for herself how much, God help him, he *unselfishly* wanted and needed her! Look what he was enduring!

The Holy Mother knew that he wanted no other mortal woman. In such a short time, the days they'd spent together since the shipwreck, she had stolen his heart.

He knew it would make her toss her head, disbelieving, to hear him say it, but as God was in heaven it was true! The saints knew he could stomach little more of these wild Scots females who persisted in throwing themselves on him and pinching him and mauling him. He had no doubt he had not seen the last of the hot-eyed widow.

Two days before, after Edain had so treacherously left him and returned to de la Guerche, he'd had to beg half a loaf of black bread from a farmer's wife. It pained him even now to think what flattery he'd had to go to, to even get that crust. And that the farmer's wife had mistaken his purpose and chased him halfway down the road before he finally managed to outdistance her.

Magnus gave vent to an audible groan. Edain—beautiful, warm, tender Edain—ah, how he missed her! From the time that she lay naked in his arms she'd enchanted him. That soft, lissome golden body, her delicate ways, her sweet hands that knew just how to best caress him, her low voice that so entrancingly spoke his name.

Making love with her was like nothing he had ever experienced. Those strange little lightning bolts. It was like sweet music. He remembered there was even a perfume like summer wildflowers there on the cold shore. And shining gold motes that danced in the air.

"Ah, there you are," a voice said. A head appeared at the top of the ladder to the loft. "Haven't gone to sleep yet, laddie, have you?"

Inwardly, Magnus cursed. Then the widow held up, shoulder high, what she carried in her hands.

"Ah, I thought they'd take your fancy!" she crowed. She came up the rest of the way into the loft and knelt down beside him, her eyes hungrily raking him as he lay stretched out full length. "If your feet is as big as my dear, late husband's was, then you're as grateful to me for the boots as a son to a mother."

"You're hardly my mother," Magnus said, keeping his eyes on the boots she held up before his face. "You're—ah, too young for one thing." She gave the boots a teasing waggle. "And much, much too pretty," he added hastily.

He made a grab for them to examine them at close

quarters. For what he was about to do, he wanted to make sure he got value for value.

The boots were worth their weight in gold, Magnus could see that at once. They were not horseman's boots, but iron-sturdy sheepskin, well tanned, with the fleece inside for warmth. They looked almost new. They were not home-crafted; some cobbler had made them. They were neatly finished, with tough cowhide soles on the bottoms.

Magnus knew even before he put the boots on and turned the fleece back to make a cuff that he was going to look, from the knees down, like some clod-footed Highland rustic.

God's wounds, he'd make a strange sight indeed with this footgear mixed with his fine knight's cape and his prized sword! If he came into Chester's court in such a getup—a knight to the knees and a Scottish sheepherder below—he'd be greeted with such a chorus of hoots and laughter and taunting *baa-baas* from his knightly companions as to drive him out of the place altogether.

Strangely, as he lifted one foot and then the other in the air to look at them, he found he didn't care. His own riding boots were just about gone, and torture to walk in what was left of them. These sturdy mudhoppers would get him to Edinburgh and halfway to Flanders if he wished.

He turned and looked at the widow, who was watching him closely. He supposed now he could be properly grateful.

She surprised him, though, when she seized the front of his shirt, her fingers working at the lacings, and said huskily, "Now my lamb, tell me what she's like, this girl of yours."

Magnus was dumbfounded. How did this Scottish crofter's wife know about mysterious, golden Edain?

His next thought was that he supposed news traveled far in most rural places. And the fact that Edain had been kidnapped by one of their chieftains thereabouts, and then ransomed by the Templar and taken off to far Edinburgh, would make a story for the tribes worth repeating for months.

The widow pulled the shirt over his head. When he looked down into her face with its thick nose and knowing grin he realized she'd probably heard nothing at all.

"How do you know about any girl?" he said.

"Y'mean yer sweetheart?" She gave him an arch look. "Och, such a handsome huge boyo as you wouldn't lack long in this life for a sweet, loving little dearling, now would he?" Her fingers worked on the cord to his hose. "She's a little thing, isn't she, with black, curling hair, tits rich and round as October pumpkins, and great snapping black eyes?"

"Uh, no," Magnus said, annoyed.

He supposed she was describing herself. And the picture of willowy, golden-haired Edain had just risen up in exquisite detail in his mind and he hated to lose it. He felt his intimate flesh rising with Edain's vision as the widow pulled off his boots and then rolled down his hose.

She put her hand around him quickly and stroked him, exclaiming over his size.

"Close your eyes, love, and think of her," she whispered in his ear. "I want you hot for me, laddie, so think hard of your precious lambkin."

Well, Magnus had to admit, that made it easier. He supposed he should be grateful that she'd suggest such a thing. But when she slid out of her gown and made as if to straddle him, he grabbed her around the waist and rolled her over on her back.

He could close his eyes and think of Edain this way, he thought, looking down at her. He drew her knees up to his hips and drove into her in one practiced thrust that made her cry out in throaty surprise and delight. But by God, he was tired of women sitting on him and pounding! If there was to be any pounding, he'd do it himself.

Edain, Magnus thought, *Edain.*

It took a great effort of will while he was doing what he was doing to hold her dear image up close in his mind.

And just to be on the safe side, Magnus reached out and kept one hand on the boots.

Edain struggled coming down the stone stairs to the underground room, and nearly fell.

In the ensuing scuffle the Templar prior and the Culdee priest lost their grip on her. She had one moment when she thought she would get away, even as confused and dizzy as she was. But she only managed to stagger a few steps before they had their hands on her again.

"Did they not put the opium in her food?" the prior wanted to know. He gave Edain a shake to make her stop fighting him.

"In her food, yes, milord," one of the Templars in the back said. "We gave it to her twice today. But as you can see, she resists it."

"Bring the cup again."

They paused in the stone chamber outside the Templars' assembly room. The tall prior had the Culdee and a young Templar hold Edain while he pulled her head far back, forcing her mouth open, and lifted the silver cup to her lips. While she gagged and choked, most of the bitter-tasting liquid ran out of the corners of her mouth and down her chin and throat.

"Easy, easy," the Culdee monk warned. He took the cup from the prior. "Pouring such a draft down her throat can drown her, man, did you not know that? Besides, you don't need this. I'm sure it is that a trance will come over her."

The prior was impatient. "It's all well and good for you to say. But all these days, the endless examining, it will come to naught I tell you! Look at her. How can she resist enough belladonna to make ten women placid and helpful?"

The Culdee monk leaned over Edain, who was being held by two knights, to peer down into her frantic eyes. "Now, girl," he said in a kindly voice, "the good knights do not understand why you will not oblige them. They mean you no harm—it is a simple task they ask of you. They want you to prophesy for them. They have pinned high hopes on you, that they will at last achieve their own Pythoness, their oracle."

Around them, the Templar guard that had brought her down were putting on their tall, peaked white hoods with slits for eyes and mouths, identical to the one Edain had seen their Master wear.

The Culdee monk saw her eyes twist to look. He said, "The Templars' own secret order has worked long and hard in Paris to try to achieve what they hope to achieve here. But the girl they held in the Paris commandery was a great disappointment. Certainly something far less than they had hoped for."

"She was a whore," the prior said flatly. He took her arm again. "The results were most disappointing. But come, it was a failure, so we will not speak of it here, where we hope to do so much."

With Edain between them they filed through the tall wooden doors into the underground room.

The Templars assembled there had already put on their masked hoods. When they turned to look at the prior and the Culdee with Edain and the handful of Templar knights following, a half-hundred hidden eyes gleamed.

Edain could not help it, she trembled.

The last draught of the drugged drink that the prior had forced down her throat was having its effect. Her feet hardly touched the floor. She gave almost no resistance as the prior and the strange Culdee monk propelled her to the center of the room.

Edain lifted her head long enough to see the Master standing there. And beside him, the brass tripod.

Oracle. Pythoness.

"I don't understand." She found she could hardly hold her head up long enough to mutter the words.

The Culdee was talking. "Now, now all this has been explained to you, don't you remember? The Templars because of their enlightened years in the

Holy Land, seek to understand God's most profound secrets, God's revelations of the universe, and the unrevealed nature of man. Here they persevere in their most noble efforts to create the great oracle of the Greeks again!"

The words made Edain even dizzier. Taking her by the arm, the Templars' prior turned her around to face the Master.

"She who sat in the sacred smoke in the cave at Delphi," the tall masked figure intoned, "attended by her holy priestesses—the great Pythoness, Apollo's seeress, uttering the secret visions that only from the god head can flow."

Edain jerked her arms, trying to get free. "That's blasphemy!" She heard the Templars around her suck in their breaths, disapproving. "No, I can't—"

"But you can." This was the stern commander's voice.

He reached out his hand and seized her wrist and drew her toward the tripod. Underneath the tall legs of the stand a brazier of charcoal glowed, covered with green leaves and herbs that cooked and sizzled and sent out a head-spinning smoke.

"But you *can*," the commander repeated. "You foresaw the attack on the tax boats that had come to meet the Earl of Chester's vassal, one Ivo de Brise and grounded the ships most prudently on a shoal so that they escaped. Constantine of the clan Sanach Dhu says that his children swear you made blue candle fire of their fingers and amused them in other magic ways while he held you imprisoned in his broch. And now Bricriu of Benbecula, the Culdee monk who has come to give us his thoughts on your presence here, says that he, too, will swear that after seeing you and questioning you he believes that you come to your gifts because you are a member of the great Irish people of holy legend, the Tuatha de Danaan, who were noted for their sorcery."

While he was speaking, two Knights of the Temple had come to Edain and loosened the belt of her woolen robe and pulled it away. She was naked underneath. Her long hair had been loosened from its braids, as always when she came to the subterranean room, and fell over her bare shoulders and breasts and partly covered her.

She felt the hands of the Templars cool against her skin as they bent and took hold of her and lifted her to sit on the long-legged brass tripod in the midst of the smoke.

When they could see her perched up there, there was a stirring throughout the underground room among the white robes marked with huge white crosses and the tall, pointed white hoods that masked the Templars' faces. Somewhere a bell was rung.

It became instantly quiet.

Edain clung to the handles of the tripod, breathing in short, trembling gasps, unable to see. The smoke drifted up her nostrils and blinded her and made her want to sneeze.

The Templars were truly mad to do this to her, was all she could think. Their duty was to take her to King William, who after all had paid her ransom. Besides, she didn't care how much they protested, they *were* dabbling in blasphemy—and worse. Now they had made her a part of it!

The smoke from the leaves and herbs in the brazier seemed to have as much of a drugging effect as the draught they'd forced down her throat. Edain's head was spinning. She wanted to get down from her perch. If she did not get down she was afraid that, dizzy as she was, she would tumble off.

But when she opened her mouth to tell them, her tongue was thick and unwieldy, and she did not even know if she could speak.

Magnus, she wanted to shriek. He was far away. She groped for him through the drugged smoke and could not find him.

Magnus! she needed him to come and help her!

Before she could pin her mind to the thought of Magnus and call him to her, the tripod seemed to shift, then it began rocking from side to side like a boat, dancing on its brass legs. She had to clutch it even tighter to keep from being thrown off.

Holy Jesus in Heaven, Edain suddenly saw legions of Templars coming through the great door and filling up the hall!

She felt her eyes straining to see through the smoke. The great crowd of Templars marching in were pale, bloodstained men, their empty eyes reflecting despair. Their tunics were ripped and dirtied. They carried torn banners. While she watched in a drugged horror they put up stakes and other tortured, mangled Templars were tied to them, and fires lit to burn them to death. When the dead were consumed their charred bodies were taken down and others put in their place, all in silence. And they, too, perished in the fire. And still Templars came marching in through the door. There seemed no end to them.

The smoke of the fire under the tripod was making

Edain hoarse. Her eyes smarted and she knew that her hair drifted around her in a wild cloud so that she could hardly see. Whatever she was doing—and she heard herself speaking in a harsh croak, saying strange things—she could not stop, even though her throat was dry and raw and hurting.

The leading edge of the army of the ghastly Templars surged up to where the prior, the commander, and the Culdee stood surrounded by the young guard knights. Before that onslaught she saw the prior fall to his knees, his hands held out before him in supplication. And the Culdee turn away, covering his face.

Over the heads of the sea of dead and dying Templars Edain was aware of a huge lion coming toward them. It was wounded, for it staggered and then lay down at their feet, only a small space between it and the tripod where Edain crouched, twisting and coughing, tearing her fingers through her hair to hold it back from her face.

Then it stopped. The terrible Templar army disappeared.

As though someone had opened a gate, or a door, to let the noise in, the uproar began. Rough, hurtful hands dragged Edain down from her seat so that it scraped her bare backside and legs. There were shouts of *treason,* and *kill her* in the air.

The Culdee held the others away. He flung off a cord the prior had thrown around her neck and threw it back at him. "Get away," he shouted. "Will you punish her for the very thing for which you seized her and brought her here?"

Edain coughed spasmodically. Her head was clearing, but she could not seem to get the deadly, burning smoke out of her lungs. Then in the crowd she saw Asgard de la Guerche fighting his way through the rioting Templars. Beside her the Culdee monk picked up the heavy brass tripod and swung it in front of him to ward off hands that were reaching for her. It did not seem to matter that she was naked, helpless—they wanted to tear her to pieces.

"What is it?" Edain screamed.

The Culdee monk shoved her behind him as de la Guerche made the center steps.

"You have given them what they wanted, Pythoness," the Irishman shouted. "If you do not remember anything of it while in your trance, then I will have to tell you that you prophesied the terrible fall of the Poor Knights of the Temple of Jerusalem into disgrace, and that they will be destroyed. And you have seen the Lion of Scotland—who, as you said in your vision in the holy smoke, fell at our feet and expired!"

De la Guerche reached for her. His face was as white as the dead Templars of Edain's vision, but his blue eyes were blazing.

"You see this madness?" he shouted at the Culdee. "Look at them!" He flung his arm toward the shouting mob. "They say they seek God's secrets, but I have seen all this before. You do not know what happened in Paris—and at Acre!"

"I do not want to," the Culdee monk growled as he swung the tripod in a circle in hopes of clearing a way. "I want only to get us out of this place!"

De la Guerche yanked off his cross-emblazoned surcoat and put it around Edain. "Do not be frightened," the blond knight shouted. "I will protect you!"

Edain lifted her head and stared up at him.

She was not worrying about Asgard de la Guerche's protection. Her hands were clasped, fingers knotted together painfully. It did no good to be this terrified; her very teeth were chattering.

She was beginning to know that when she was frightened, things happened. She had no control over it. She closed her eyes, her fingernails tearing into her clenched palms.

Magnus! Edain voiced it in a silent scream.

She had never used the Feeling to call anyone so hard in her life.

Above them, the first huge crack appeared in the vaulted chamber of the underground room. No one heard it. No one saw it.

But they heard and saw the second.

Magnus came awake at once. Still foggy with sleep, he saw that he was in the loft, the crofter's wife sprawled on her back beside him, snoring slightly through her passion-swollen lips. Her right hand rested in his groin. Magnus lifted her hand away.

Magnus.

There it was again.

He sat bolt upright. If he did not know where he was, in the loft of a byre in Scotland, he would swear Edain was right there beside him, behind his left shoulder, her sweet little hand resting light as a summer breeze on his arm.

But she was not. It was her soft voice instead, whispering right in his ear.

Magnus shuddered. He quickly looked around just

to make sure. The widow felt his stirring and awoke and sat up. When she saw his face she put her hand out, not bothering to cover her big breasts. "Sweetheart, what is it?" she wanted to know.

Magnus turned from her, already hauling on his hose. Then lying on his back, he lifted each leg and pulled on the boots she had given him. He sat up again, and looked around for his shirt.

She handed it to him silently. Magnus shrugged into it saying, "Is it dawn yet? I must leave. I'm going to steal a horse."

He was still shaking from the eerie sense of the call to him through the dark night. *Edinburgh,* Magnus thought. It had to be Edinburgh; he had the taste of smoke and fire and death and falling masonry in his mouth as though he had been there.

Christ in heaven, she would not have called him unless she needed him greatly! Edain was in peril.

"Och," the widow was saying, "you cannot steal a horse in Scotland. They will castrate you and ream out your bowels if they catch you, and only after that do they hang you."

"A good horse." Magnus picked up his cloak and his padded gambeson from the straw. "I need," he said urgently, "to steal one that will match that damned black devil of a destrier that belongs to Asgard de la Guerche."

Thirteen

"What girl?" the commander of the Edinburgh Templars said, with an attempt at innocence. "Justiciar, you know the prohibitions against keeping women in any commandery of the Poor Knights of the Temple of Jerusalem. We would be hard put to explain to Scotland's venerated sovereign, King William, how we came to have a girl here."

They crossed the courtyard and he took fitzGamelin's arm as they came to a pile of stones the masons were moving. "Watch your footing, milord, we are rebuilding part of the crypts, as we have been unfortunate enough to suffer a foundation collapse a few days ago."

The justiciar, curious, looked around the inner court of the Templars' barracks. He had heard about the mysterious cave-in of an underground meeting room; the masons, who were working to repair it, had brought the story back to town. As far as anyone knew no one had been hurt, although the secrecy of the Templars was such that it would have been unusual, indeed, for them to admit anything.

To fitzGamelin it all sounded too much like the stories that circulated about the fighting order everywhere and not just in Edinburgh. Secret ceremonies and initiations. Strange so-called religious practices. Even experiments with the occult.

The Templars' commander guided him out of the courtyard noise and into the peace and quiet of the refectory.

"Asgard de la Guerche," fitzGamelin said, "one of your esteemed order carried a warrant signed by King William to search the western highlands for a girl suspected of being abducted from the convent of the Sacred Limb of Saint Sulpice. It is a matter of fact that I issued him this warrant myself. Now we seek his whereabouts, for we have reason to believe the girl is with him."

The commander pulled up a bench and gestured for the justiciar to be seated. As he did so, a white cat bounded out from the kitchen, ran down the hallway into the dining room, and leaped into his arms.

The tall Templar held the cat against his chest, fingering the jeweled ring in its ear. "Milord justiciar, I know the knight, Asgard de la Guerche," he said blandly, "but he is not assigned to us here in Edinburgh. He comes from London and before that, Paris."

FitzGamelin's lips tightened. That was no answer, he told himself testily, no answer at all. He'd asked about the girl. What games did these arrogant warrior monks think they were playing with one of the king's ministers?

A Templar servant came in with cups, and an ewer of wine, and the commander served them himself.

It was particularly galling, fitzGamelin was thinking, that the king had given a good part of the gold to ransom this very girl from the Sanach. Now, William eagerly awaited her. Although it looked as though the Templars were reluctant to give her up.

Time was growing short. The Lion of Scotland had already marshalled his vassals and knights and some of the Highland tribes on his southern borders; he was preparing to march against King Henry of England and retrieve some of the lands lost after the death of his brother, King Malcolm.

These past weeks King William had prepared for war with several relics like the recently rediscovered leg bone of St. Andrew in a silver and crystal monstrance, which would be carried into battle. And he was enthusiastic about the reported powers of the young seeress from St. Sulpice—the girl the Templar de la Guerche was supposed to have brought back from Loch Etive.

Eventually, King William had grown restless waiting for her to arrive. He had heard rumors that the Templar, de la Guerche, had indeed returned, the girl with him, but that they were both incommunicado with the Templars on the outskirts of his own capital.

FitzGamelin had not dared to tell the king what else he had heard. That the talk was that the girl was no more nor less than the Templars' prisoner, and that the destruction of the commandery's crypts, or foundations, or secret meeting rooms—whatever one wanted to call them—was related to some ceremony with her that had occurred.

As he studied the commander's gaunt face over the rim of his wine cup, fitzGamelin made up his mind. He was not particularly fond of his fellow Normans; they were far too arrogant and secretive for his taste. But it was dangerous for them to flout the

Scottish king. The girl was being hidden here, he was sure of it.

FitzGamelin decided he would order King William's own royal guard to come and make an inspection of the Templar commandery. The royal troops could come on the excuse of looking over ancient cisterns and underground waterways to make sure they had not been damaged when the Templars' cellars caved in. Someone in the king's chancery could provide records that waterways and cisterns existed. Even if they did not.

The justiciar wanted to smile when he related his concern about the waterways and cisterns to the Templar commander. That dour-faced personage promptly turned a resentful, dusky color as he tried to suppress his temper.

"No one has ever inspected here," the commander snapped. The cat, its fur ruffled, jumped from his lap. "We are monks, milord justiciar! This is holy ground."

FitzGamelin nodded. "You are right, of course," he agreed smoothly. The smile broke through, anyway. "Dear sir, King William will do his best to accommodate you. And as for ecclesiastical concerns, I will see that along with the ditchers and builders, the royal guard also brings Edinburgh's bishop."

Edain had seen the commander and a richly dressed gentleman, a royal official by his looks, go across the yard and enter the refectory just below. She could glimpse them if she pressed one eye against the brass grille and squinted. A moment later, there was a soft knocking at her door.

It was locked, she could not open it. But on the other side Asgard de la Guerche said in a low tone, "The king's justiciar is here. I think that you saw him from your window, did you not? The Templars are worried that King William will send someone to look for you."

Edain flew to the oak door and pressed herself against it.

"Why are you here?" she whispered. The Templar had carried her from the assembly room when the vaulted ceiling began to fall. But she had been returned to her room and locked inside, nevertheless. "You are one of them," she said bitterly. "Tell the Templars to let me go! Why are they keeping me here?"

There was a silence on the other side. Then the muffled voice said, "I swear on my honor I will not let them hurt you, demoiselle. God's wounds, you cannot know what is taking place here, but it is a nightmare! They are afraid, but excited, too, that what you said will come true, even the prophesy of our—the Templars'—own destruction. First they want to see if you have prophesied rightly and that William the Lion will die. They know you made the vaults collapse. They've seen your power."

Edain dropped her forehead to the door's thick, wooden boards.

"I did not say he would die." Her voice was heavy with despair. "It was a wounded lion, as in a dream. That's what I saw, don't you understand? And in the dream the lion fell at our feet." She took a deep breath. "Dear God, why do you say I had anything to do with the ceiling coming down? Was anyone hurt?"

He sighed. "Sweet demoiselle, it does not matte now. The commandery sat in session last night an their decision is that although they are angered b your dire prophesies of the future, you are the oracl they are looking for. Therefore, they are determine to keep you—if not here, then somewhere else. Som even talk of sending you to the fortress of the Tem plars in Paris, to the Grand Master."

Edain groaned.

"Yes, it is a very great danger," he agreed. "Yo understand I had to bring you here. On my swor oaths to the Master I could not take you first to Kin William. I confess this is my great sin, and I will bea the guilt for it for all eternity. You do not know ho I suffer! Alas, I cannot tell you all of it, what ha happened to these girls, these oracles they have trie and imprisoned."

"Then you must help me get out of here." He wa right, he was guilty of taking her to the commander instead of the king: she would not forgive him easil "I am afraid of the Templars, I don't know what the want of me. It was all false, what I said and did i the crypts. They made me take opium! You hear them say it."

He was silent for a long moment. She heard hin breathing on the other side of the heavy woode door and could almost picture him standing there tall and handsome in his white Templar robes, hi gilded head bent.

Finally he whispered, "Demoiselle, I swear on Je sus Christ and the Holy Virgin, I will not let then take you away."

"Away?" Edain pressed her palms against the doo

attacked by sudden foreboding. Holy Mother in heaven, she knew from what he was saying that her very life was in danger. "God curse you, Asgard de la Guerche, tell me!" She almost shrieked it. "What do you mean, you will not let them take me away?"

But he was gone.

Later, when it was dusk, the door was unlocked. The commander of Edinburgh's Templars stood there with the prior and some others Edain did not recognize. They all wore coats of mail with the cross-emblazoned surcoat, and close-fitting hoods of ring mail. The Culdee monk came in first.

She shrank back, but the prior quickly stepped inside and threw a fur-lined cloak around her shoulders.

"No! Stop!" Her shrieks were useless; someone quickly stuffed a cloth in her mouth.

Edain tried to struggle, but two Templars wound the cloak around her and tied it with cords. Then, bundled like a rug, they lifted her and carried her outside to the stairs.

In the courtyard there were knights and servants carrying torches. De la Guerche came up, mounted on his black stallion.

"Demoiselle." The commander bent over her as she twisted frantically. "You must do as you are told, for your own safety and ours. This has become a most delicate matter. We hope Asgard de la Guerche may convince you that your condition is far better with the Knights of the Temple, under our protection, than with King William of Scotland."

She wanted to scream at them, to beg them to tell

her where they were taking her, but Templars had gone to open the big wooden gates.

Magnus!

She tried again, a desperate wail that only she could hear that echoed around inside her head and beat against her eyes. She twisted helplessly in the ropes that tied the cloak, knowing that he would try to answer her. That is, if some terrible thing hadn't happened to him.

At that thought, a wave of desolation swept over Edain. When last she left him, on foot there in the forest, he was in no condition to be her knight errant. Dear heaven, how could he help her now?

As the Templars carried her toward the gates there was no sign, no whisper, that she had heard. That he was coming. *Nothing.*

At that moment the outer gates opened to show night falling, the shadowy road that ran before the commandery, the dark outlines of trees. There were several small carts waiting at the edge of the wood with a cluster of people and horses around them.

De la Guerche, a gleaming figure in his white tunic and silver mail, touched his spurs to his destrier. I moved out into the roadway, the commander and the prior a few paces behind. The commander of the Templars said to the Culdee monk, "Brother Bricriu, can these people get the girl through the city?"

The Irishman nodded. "Aye, they boast they make their living dodging the king's royal watch."

A figure stepped out of the group around the carts. Before it could speak a spine-chilling howl pierced the dark. The Templars carrying Edain started, and almost dropped her. Behind them, a the Templars' gate, someone lit a torch followed immediately by shouts to put it out.

Something came roaring out of the darkness upon them: a lone rider at full course on the dirt road, whirling a huge, gleaming sword that shot sparks in the moonlight.

Man and horse bore down on the Templars before the gate, scattering them. In the scramble the prior lost his balance and fell and several knights toppled over him. Asgard de la Guerche, who was still mounted, wheeled his black destrier to meet the howling apparition that had turned, and was coming back again.

The horsemen met with a clang of swords. "Rule! Rule, Templar!" a voice shouted hoarsely.

"Jesu," the Edinburgh commander cried, fumbling for a sword he was not wearing. "Is it a challenge to fair combat? Or an ambush? Who is this?"

Behind them Templars, mostly unarmed, poured out of the gate and milled in the road. The two carrying Edain dropped her and rushed forward to help their comrades.

The horses wheeled into a patch of light, the riders slashing at one another furiously. One of the horses reared and screamed, wounded.

Edain lay on her face as the feet of Templars thundered around her, her heart pounding. The voice crying "Rule! Rule!" was Magnus's. She did not have to be able to see to know it.

"Stand back, stand back!" The prior and the Culdee tried to push the Templars away from the wheeling, pivoting horsemen. The young redheaded knight wore no mail, no helmet, and carried only the great, gleaming sword that made a whining sound in the air as he swung it. The horses backed and backed again. Then, raked by their riders' spurs, they lunged at each other. One of the combatants gave a sharp cry of pain.

"De la Guerche is hurt!" came a shout.

The attack out of the darkness had happened so quickly many of the Templars were still standing in the road, not able to do more than watch. At the cry that a Templar had been wounded they surged forward to pull down the attacker. Hands reached up, grabbed at the redhead's cloak.

"Rule, rule," someone at the back shouted.

"Nay, it's an outlaw!" another voice cried.

A figure ran out of the gates, pulling on his jacket. "By the cross, I know that berserker swing—it's Niall fitzJulien's pup!"

The wagons under the trees were turning, horses whipped up to leave. The commander started toward them.

"That's no pup," he shouted over his shoulder, "that's a full-grown man, and dangerous. Pull him down!" He waved his arms. "Get these wagons out of the road! God in heaven, should we blow trumpets to announce what we're doing?"

Blood was pouring from de la Guerche's side. It looked black in the moonlight. Parrying his thrust Magnus reared back in the saddle. As he did so his sheepskin boot slid through the stirrup. While he kicked vainly to free it, the wounded Templar spurred his horse closer and caught him on the side of the head with his sword and knocked Magnus out of his saddle.

The panicked horse reared as Magnus lay in the

road, his foot caught in the stirrup. It sidestepped, dragging Magnus with him. Asgard de la Guerche clutched the pouring wound in his side and slumped over the pommel of his saddle, his sword dangling from his mailed fist.

The crowd of Templars would have surged forward, but the night came alive with noise. Horns blew. They heard the thunder of horses being ridden at the gallop. In the darkness a line of horsemen was coming over the rise.

"Back! Back!" the prior shouted. Several knights turned and began to run toward the gates. In the darkness someone bent to Edain and rolled her over on her back.

"Sit up, girl." The Culdee monk hauled her into a sitting position, jerking at the knotted cords that held the cloak. "King William has sent his guard," he yelled. Hands under her elbows, he dragged her to her feet. "The Lion still seeks you."

Edain slumped against him. The jostling mob of Templars seemed to forget Asgard and Magnus in their hurry to get back inside their fort. But the king's attacking knights blocked them, keeping the Templars penned outside in the road.

The Culdee monk dragged Edain into the trees, toward the already-moving wagons. When he was close enough, he lifted and dumped her into the nearest one. Edain hit the wooden side, then fell against someone. A woman, sitting crouched with a child in her lap.

People on horseback milled around the wagons, shouting to one another in some foreign tongue. Behind them King William's knights stormed the Templars' gate and blew their horns, signaling to one another. The wagons plunged off the road and headed through the black woods.

Gradually the sound of fighting and shouting and horns blowing began to fade away. The wagons lurched to a slower pace. Edain sat up and felt her head and face with her hands.

She had hit the side of the wagon when the Culdee threw her in. Now her lip tasted of blood and her fingers found a sore lump in the middle of her forehead.

Where were they going? she wondered dizzily. Who were these shadowy people around her, speaking in what was surely not Norman French, nor even Scots Gaelic?

Someone spurred a horse down the line, leaning out to peer into the wagons. Someone without a helmet, with a drawn, bloodied sword, still breathing hard.

Finally he found her. "Edain," Magnus cried hoarsely. "How fare you back here with the gypsies?"

Gypsies? For a moment, clutching the sides of the wagon as it plunged into a shallow brook and out again, Edain could not understand the simple words.

Her head and mouth ached, and her wrist hurt where it had been stepped on. She was battered and sore. She could barely understand, all at once, that the figure on the horse was Magnus, alive and reasonably whole, with the moonlight shining on his red hair. When last she had seen him with Asgard de la Guerche they were trying to kill each other.

"Gypsies, yes." He leaned far from the saddle to talk softly. "Some of the men have run off because of the fighting, but there are a few wagons left."

At that moment Edain wanted to scream out her rage and pain and relief. All that came out was a croak. "The dark—I saw you and Asgard—Holy Mother, I thought you were dragged and trampled by your horse!"

He leaned to peer at the woman beside her. "Yes, well, my foot came out of the accursed boot, that's what saved me. Listen, the king's knights back there are searching for you. The gypsies tell me the Templars paid them to get you through the city." He looked around. "But you need to hide."

He reached out and poked with the tip of his bloody sword at a sheepskin by the side of the woman, who drew back, clutching the child, and hissed at him.

"What the devil is this?" They were passing under a canopy of thick oak trees. When they came out into the moonlight again Magnus's sword tip had uncovered a man's hand sticking out of the pile.

With a cry, Edain dug into the coverings and found the top of a helmet. Then the pale, marble face of Asgard de la Guerche.

Magnus reined in his horse and looked down, cursing.

"He's dead. I killed him and some damned Templar had his wits about him enough to throw the corpse in with us!"

Edain touched her finger slightly to Asgard's bloodstained brow. But she knew before she spoke.

"He is not dead," she whispered.

Fourteen

It began to snow as they made camp the second night in the southern highlands, but it was not all that cold. The lightly clad gypsies did not seem to mind the dusting of snowflakes. They had picked their campsite on the side of a hill overlooking a small valley in a grove of beech trees, and the branches with their dead winter leaves made good shelter. Tyros, the headman, set the children gathering the leaves for bedding before the snow turned them wet.

Edain sat with the fur cloak the Templars' commander had given her wrapped around her, while the gypsy girl Mila rubbed stain made from walnut leaves into her hands and arms. She had already learned the disguise washed off easily, so she had to remember to stay a little dirty. Like the gypsies did.

"That's a nice fur cape, what you got," the gypsy girl observed, rubbing brown liquid not too gently between Edain's fingers.

Edain pulled back her hand. It was not the first time Mila had admired the fur-lined cloak. The whole gypsy camp had fingered it, down to the smallest child, the message plain in their eyes. She never let it out of her sight.

"There," the girl said, "you are my color now. At

least up to your elbows." Mila slapped the cup of stain into her palm. "You do your face yourself."

Before Edain could speak Mila got to her feet and walked away toward the wagon where Asgard de la Guerche lay, burning with fever. Whenever Edain was not with the wounded Templar, Mila managed to slip away to sit by his side. When she had first seen them together Edain had had the strange feeling they'd met before. Although that could hardly be true.

She dipped her fingers in the juice and rubbed it into her cheeks and around her mouth. Across the clearing Magnus made a passable gypsy with his stain-darkened skin, a sheepskin for a cloak, and his long, curling russet hair. But Edain did not need a looking glass to tell her that the walnut stain made a strange mix with her fair hair and eyes. Even when she wore the red veil the gypsies had given her, her eyes were startling in their bright greenness. The gypsy women thought it a great joke. Behind the red silk, they said, her strange *gadje* eyes made it easier to pass her off to the villeins as a fortune-teller.

Edain put down the cup and looked across the clearing to where Magnus squatted by Mila's wagon.

She knew he was still angry with her.

She had silently called him when the Templars held her prisoner, and he had come. Even though she was the one who had walked away from him in the woods and chosen to go back with Asgard de la Guerche. Magnus had reminded her of her perfidy at the top of his lungs.

Well, she would admit that what she'd done had been a mistake. Asgard had brought her to the Templars, and they had only meant trouble and terror.

But Magnus had heard her calling him and did not refuse her. In fact he'd willingly pledged his very life: stealing a horse, traveling by night, dodging the king's troops, and finally making a daring attack on the Templars when they tried to give her to the gypsy band to take her God knows where—perhaps to France, as Asgard had said.

What Magnus had done had been brave, wildly perilous; she would give him full credit for his courage and daring, Edain thought, watching him bend over the patch of ground curtained by his once-fine cloak.

Even now she couldn't help caressing him with her eyes. He sat with his long legs stretched out before him, wearing a pair of battered gypsy boots Tyros had sold him. Snowflakes speckled his red hair.

The Templar was handsomer, Edain supposed. Asgard had a fair, masculine beauty that made all heads turn. But Magnus's crooked grin, his swaggering, redheaded assurance, his big, virile body, was something few women could resist. All the gypsy women had instantly loved him. The men gave him more than grudging respect: after Tyros it was Magnus they turned to, in spite of the short time he'd been with the band.

But he was cruel, she told herself with a sigh, and difficult.

From the moment he had discovered the wounded Templar in Mila's wagon, Magnus had wanted to abandon him. He would not stop long enough to leave Asgard at a crofter's hut, nor even wait until they found a monastery. By the side of the road, in the ditch, he'd snarled, was good enough. Worse,

Edain had seen him take the Templar's money. He was counting Asgard's coins, even now.

The purse that Magnus had cut from the wounded man's belt was part of her ransom. From what she remembered, listening to the bargaining in the broch, she gathered the chief of the Sanach had not gotten all of it. Now she had to admit the silver was largely what kept the gypsies with them. Most had left the first night outside the city, claiming there was more fortune to be made going east and at the Advent fairs than there was to follow Magnus and go south. There were only four wagons left, mostly women and children, with Tyros and one other man. And the men did little work, and demanded more money daily.

Since they had been on the road Magnus had driven them all tirelessly. The only thing that made their escape from the north a little easier was the news of the outbreak of open war between William the Lion and English King Henry. South of a hamlet called Penculick, Magnus had ordered the wagons from the road and through the fields because of a pitched battle they'd blundered into between English knights and a part of King William's Scottish army.

Edain watched his bent head. Behind the cover of his cloak he was counting the silver and copper coins from Asgard's purse. It was true they needed the money; the gypsies were not the only ones to be paid. Scotland, even in the south, had few inns, and they had to bargain for food with the crofters and sheepherders. Since it was almost Yuletide, getting enough to eat in this poor countryside, even paying with good silver and copper, was not easy.

After taking the Templar's purse, Magnus had ordered the gypsies to take Asgard out of the cart and leave him by the side of the road.

"He's dying!" Edain had cried. She sat in the wagon, refusing to let the gypsy men put their hands on him.

"Sweet baby Jesus, let him die, will you?" Magnus still wore a bloody cloth around his head for the blow he'd taken in their fight. "The Templars paid the gypsies to get you past the king's troops in Edinburgh, and de la Guerche was going to take you the rest of the way. As he had taken you to Edinburgh from the Sanachs' nest in Loch Etive. Remember he was on his horse, damn him, waiting to be your escort when they brought you out of the place!"

Even the gypsies had agreed with Magnus. The dying Templar was bad luck. What would they do with him, a wounded man, if they were stopped? They would be blamed for his condition, no matter what had really happened.

But Edain had thrown herself across Asgard's body and refused to let them move him. If he was to die, he would die with them. And somehow they would find him a Christian burial!

Magnus lost his temper at her stubbornness. While he shouted and stormed through the camp the gypsies had tried to lift Asgard out of the wagon. The Templar had screamed out at their rough handling. With Edain's shrieks added, they finally gave up.

From then on Edain sat with him, holding his fevered hand when he was restless, helping the gypsy girl attend his wound with reasonably clean dressings and a salve some of the women fetched.

It was not the best sort of nursing, but there was nothing more they could do. When the wagons moved one got out if one could, and walked rather than endure the jouncing. Mila and Edain braced Asgard among the sheepskins and blankets, but he still suffered. The sword wound Magnus had put in his side bled until Edain worried that the Templar would die from losing so much blood. And always, his fever raged. Mila and Tyros's wife examined his belly and chest and declared that he had a broken rib that, fortunately, did not seem to have punctured his lung. Or he would be spitting blood as well as having it ooze from his side.

Through the cold, misty days as they moved toward Scotland's southern coast, Edain and the gypsy girl gave Asgard water when they thought he was awake enough to take it and not choke. With half-closed eyes that did not really see her, he also let Edain spoon milk and soup into his mouth. At night, under Mila's jealous gaze, Edain lay down beside him in the bed of the wagon and covered them both with her fur-lined cloak. It kept them wonderfully warm. After all she had suffered at the Templars' hands, the commander's gift to her considerably evened the debt.

They were making for Dumfries, Magnus had informed the gypsies, the port in the south where he would take ship for Chester.

He had not taken Edain aside and told her about any of this. She dreaded, with Magnus's all-too-frequent shouting and bad temper, telling him she did not want to go to Dumfries. Nor did she want to go with him to Chester to testify before his lord. She had had plenty of time to think as the gypsies took the back roads over the hills, and was beginning to feel that if she had a choice she wanted to return to the quiet life she had known with the sisters at the convent of St. Sulpice.

She couldn't help it. From the time she was a very small child the nuns had made her their darling, their pet, then the trusted novice mistress of the orphan school. With them she was always secure and well-loved. Furthermore, the nuns had long ceased to speculate on her strange gifts and where she might have come from before she was put in the orphans' turnstile, and who her father and mother might have been. They accepted her for what she was.

By contrast, this strange outer world Ivo de Brise had dragged her into was full of hurt, and cruel disappointment. The harsh life not only bruised her senses with its danger and disorder but she was finding people fought to possess her and use her, sometimes violently. This was not the first time it had seemed her very life was in peril.

And as if this were not bad enough, Edain felt strange things were happening to *her.*

She could not speak to Magnus about it, not in his harried, ill-tempered state. But when she had been so badly frightened in the Templars' underground chamber the knights had just managed to scramble out of the room before the arched stone vaults came falling down.

From what Asgard had said the Templars had taken it as a sign of her power. If that was true, Edain thought with a shudder, then she now had a power she did not want.

Then there was Magnus.

Sometimes, lying in the dark in the wagon, listening to Asgard's fevered mutterings, she tried to tell herself that Magnus was wonderful and brave, and if it had not been for him she would not be alive. Nor could she ever forget those sublime hours when he had made love to her.

But she was growing to believe that his efforts to rescue her from the Templars, and this wild escape across Scotland between warring armies really served Magnus's own purpose.

Hadn't he said before that he only wanted to return to his liege lord's court with her so that she could testify for him? In her darkest moods, Edain told herself that reason alone would be more than enough to make him do all that he was doing.

She was beginning to fear her feelings for him had made her blind to the truth. That Magnus was alarmingly like all the rest. He was violent, he was harsh—his savage battle with Asgard before the Templar's commandery would never fade from her mind. Nor the way he had treated the dying Templar afterward, wanting to abandon him in the road.

The only thing Edain was sure of was that Magnus wanted her. When she climbed into the wagon at night, he stood watching. Glowering. Not liking her to be in the arms of another, even a wounded man. Once he had growled at her, "Christ crucified, don't sleep there! Come and lie in the other wagon with me."

The whole gypsy camp had heard him, as he

wanted them to. Edain pretended she had not, and went to lie down beside Asgard and pull the cloak over them.

For a long time that night she lay awake, unable to sleep, haunted by what had happened the past few days, remembering the Templars and their mad search for a seeress so as to better know the future and God's secrets.

Magnus was certain King William still searched for her; he and the gypsies were careful to stay out of the way of the armies marching on the roads south of Edinburgh and any columns of knights they might encounter.

When she finally fell asleep her fitful dreams pursued her over Scotland's wintry hills. Magnus followed her from wagon to wagon in the gypsy camp, demanding to sleep with her until they got to Dumfries. But in the dream she turned away from him, and slept more peacefully in Asgard de la Guerche's arms. The Feeling was gone, not there anymore. As it had been gone for a long while.

When she woke, that was what worried her most.

In the crofters' villages they heard there was an Advent fair at a little town by a river called Kirkcudlies. The gypsies insisted on turning aside for it, claiming they had to make some money for the time when Magnus and Edain, and Asgard's money, would leave them.

They camped on the river in a farmer's pasture, a luxury to have water so near, even though Magnus paid well for it. Magnus and the gypsies went into town to see the market where the fair would be held, and pay the fees to set up a booth for the mending of pots and pans and trading a horse or mule or two. And whether the gypsies would be allowed to do some juggling and other tricks.

The village priest warned them that fortune-telling was forbidden. But the innkeeper took Magnus aside and told him if he would put a silver penny in the priest's pocket he would allow the telling of fortunes after all. Even some of the famous dancing by the gypsy women if they were careful about it and kept it well hidden. And invited the priest, of course, free of charge.

Magnus and the gypsies lingered at the inn and were quite drunk when they came back. They woke Edain up coming into the camp, and all the gypsies' dogs, and Tyros's youngest baby.

No one could ignore the uproar. Even Asgard's eyes opened and looked up into the dark. Then he turned his head.

Edain knew what he wanted. She put her hand on his forehead and found that she was not mistaken. His skin was cool, his eyes clearer. The fever had broken.

She climbed out of the wagon and went for a pot so that he could make water. When she went into the woods to empty it Magnus was standing under the trees, in the shadows.

"Jesu, now you carry around his piss!" he growled.

Before she could stop him he took the pot from her hand and hurled it into the dark. Then he put his arms around her and held her so tight she could not even struggle.

"I lie in the dark and think what I have done for you these past days," he told her. "That I have rescued you from shipwreck and kept you from starving, and attacked a whole barracks of Templar knights to keep them from sacrificing you to their mad schemes, and now I must watch you sleep with one of them and carry away his dirt! All to dishonor me before a gaggle of well-soiled gypsies!"

"Is that what you think I am doing, dishonoring you?" She pushed at him with both hands, making a face. She smelled wine, and knew he had been drinking. "Where is it you are taking me? You have not told me anything. You have not asked me if I wished to be given to your lord Chester to tell how you lost his ships! I do *not* wish it! Sir knight, it is my desire to be returned to the good sisters at Saint Sulpice. They will love me, and protect me from this cruel life!"

"You wish to return to the convent?" He stared at her, dumbfounded. "How can you say that when you know I— How can you say it when we have—"

He lowered his voice, looking around.

"When we have lain with each other," he grated, "and exchanged the tenderest, most passionate moments. Does this mean nothing to you? It is like nothing I have ever known, I swear. Sweet Jesu, woman, you have only to know how I have had to endure other—" His voice trailed off.

Looking up into his face Edain suddenly knew that since they had been apart there had been other women. She knew what he was thinking right at that moment was true: he had not wanted any of them.

When he'd made love with them he'd thought only of *her.*

It was better than anything he could have told her.

"Ah, sweetheart," he groaned. He dragged her to him. Then as he kissed her deeply, passionately, he pulled her into the night-dark woods.

Once they were in a place covered with dry soft leaves the furry cloak was spread on the ground. He wanted their clothes off in spite of the cold; Edain felt herself lowered to the fine, silky marten fur. As he pulled off her gown, then her shift, Magnus said huskily, "Don't shiver, sweetheart, I will cover you with my own body, and keep you warm."

She was not shivering from the frosty air. The fur that caressed her bare skin was like delicate prickles of moonlight; exquisite, tiny shards of ice piercing her flesh. The frozen stars above sent their silver thorns deep into her body.

As she trembled, Magnus tore off his jacket and shirt, then his boots and braies, his eyes drinking her in as she lay against the fur. Even by winter starlight, her flesh was golden. Naked, he crouched over her to kiss her.

"Golden Edain," he murmured, "when I am with you I could not ask for heaven. It is not like—ah, God, how can I convince you this is not like the others?"

His mouth trailed hot kisses across her face and under her ear and into her loosened hair. His hands moved under her to lift her and hold her as her head fell back in luxurious surrender, her body arched, her legs opened to him. Her soft, whispered moan brushed his lips.

They both had come to know each joining was glorious, almost, in its ecstasy, yet not very real; each caress, each touch, was searingly bathed in passion. For Edain it was as though her very skin was penetrated by almost unbearable sensuousness. As his lips caressed her warm breasts the nipples tightened and budded and she arched even more tightly in his grip.

His hands shaking with desire, Magnus went slowly. In spite of the starry chill that nipped at their bare flesh he nibbled his way from her breasts to her shivering belly and below. As Edain bit her lip to keep from crying out, the tip of his tongue found the tiny nub of her sex and opened it, and nipped it between his teeth. A goaded cry burst from her as his mouth dropped lower and repeatedly caressed the hot tightness of her feminine channel.

She was writhing, wanting him more than she could say; she could not help herself. Eyes gleaming, Magnus showed her how to kiss him intimately in return.

Edain wanted to make love to him. What had begun there on the beach after the shipwreck now became the loving, golden connection that only they shared. Eagerly she took his great shaft in her mouth and laved it with her tongue, then kissed him, hard, then softly and tantalizingly once more while Magnus groaned and writhed, his fingers clutching her shoulders.

"Golden Edain," he whispered hoarsely. "Dearling, make love to me. Let me show you how."

He stretched his long body out from under her and took her by the arms and pulled her across to straddle him. Edain gasped as she felt the big knot of his male flesh between her legs, hard and seeking. And then his hand quickly between them, guiding himself into her.

He thrust upward and she cried out. His possession was huge, ruthlessly demanding. And it took her breath away.

For a moment she was poised over him, naked and beautiful, her hair flowing over her shoulders and breasts like a golden sheath. Then with a sob Edain began to move. To possess him. To possess her own love.

He cupped her breasts in his hands and kissed them as she rode him. A moan escaped her lips as his hand slid between them and found the shivery little bud that sent fire through her body. He kept his touch on it as she opened to him. They were filled with hot excitement. Exquisite pleasure. Colors. A peak was reached as Edain cried out in unparalleled discovery. Magnus bellowing as convulsions of pleasure ripped through him.

It was the same this time as it had been before. In the dark they drifted, gasping and complete, through a golden afterglow.

Edain collapsed on his broad chest, her fingers locked tightly in his. He had told her that when they made love it was not like anything he'd ever experienced. That it was so exquisite he was not sure they made love in this world.

She smiled.

For her it was always the same, to be held by him. To be catapulted out of time and life itself by their passion.

His hand stroked her hair, and she heard him sigh.

"Do you smell it, my love? Flowers? Am I dreaming it?"

Edain squirmed against him, shaking her head. Beyond them the woods were filled with gold dust, drifting in the dark. And yes, there *was* the perfume of flowers. She didn't think he could tell.

For a while then they were happy, she thought. They did not have to talk about what would become of them. She did not have to tell him that the Feeling was back. And that it had warned her that something was going to happen when they tried to go south.

Asgard had not gone back to sleep when the demoiselle Edain left the wagon.

His fever had broken. For the first time in many days he could think clearly, unhampered by the heat and throbbing pain that had wracked his body since the combat in front of the Templars' commandery. Dimly he remembered the terrible journey, the wagon bed, and the jolting that was an hourly agony, the two women who had attended him through it all.

The dark one and *the fair one* was how he had come to think of them.

In clearer moments Asgard had known the fair one was the beautiful Edain. He became filled with the feel of her cool, gentle hands against his flesh, the sense that somehow she defended him against those who would do him some hurt. That as long as she was with him, he was safe.

Sick, and without his wits about him, the journey had been a never-ending torture made bearable only by her presence. And he could not help but wonder at her, and what the Culdee monk had hinted at: Irish tales of long-departed people called the Tuatha de Danaan, who had gone to live in the old tombs and the circles of standing stones. At times, when the fever was at its height Asgard could see Edain there in a blue cloak with her gold hair streaming in the sea wind. The white cat with the jewel in his ear ran through all the dreams.

Now that his fever was gone he knew he was lying in the wagon bed in a camp in a meadow by a town. The night air was sharp and clear. For the first time he could look up and clearly see a vast carpet of stars. He could also hear voices in the woods, arguing. Then there was silence.

Sometime later he dozed, and woke again when the demoiselle Edain got back into the wagon. She unfastened her cloak and spread half of it over him before she lay down beside him. Asgard started to ask her to bring him some water, but something stopped him.

She settled down beside him.

He watched her under half-closed eyelids. The dim outlines of her face were not as he remembered them. They looked swollen, tumbled, her beautiful hair in rank disorder and full of bits of dead leaves. His nose detected the telltale, musky odor of sex.

For a moment Asgard felt a surge of emotion so strong that it left his stomach churning. It was as though the same sword blow that had pierced his ribs had also penetrated his heart.

The devil take them all, but this was no bright-eyed angel who had tended him while he was wounded and helpless, but an all-too-earthly woman of base appetites!

In his weakend state Asgard's shock and disillusionment was profound. He trembled and felt sick, cold sweat breaking out on his hands and face.

She had been with someone in the nearby woods, he thought. Those were the voices he heard.

During his burning delirium he had clung to a dream of her. For days after receiving his orders to take her to the Grand Master in France, he had tortured himself with thoughts of disobeying. Of taking her instead, this beautiful angel whom he knew the Templars would eventually destroy, to some safe place. Dear Holy Father in heaven, he'd even thought of renouncing his vows and marrying her!

Now he knew the idea had been a sickness, just like his fever. She had put an enchantment on him, ensnaring and deceiving him with her fatal wantonness. He had half believed the Culdee's stories of Irish magic. Now he knew none of it could possibly be good.

The Culdee monk should have warned him.

She was sleeping now. Under the warm furry cover her leg moved, and her foot touched his. Softly, so as not to waken her, Asgard moved his foot away.

He did not know what he would do. But somehow he doubted they would ever reach Paris.

Fifteen

The Advent fair in Kirkcudlies had attracted a large crowd from the countryside. Since this was a grain and sheep-raising section of the borderlands between Scotland and England, the roads were choked with shepherds driving in flocks with thick coats of winter wool.

Besides the Yuletide sheep sale, there were livestock dealers with horses and pigs and cows, a bagpiper, two horn players and a drummer, an auction of freemen villeins looking for work, and a troupe of acrobats.

Shortly after sunup fifty of King Henry's knights and a column of men-at-arms under the English Earl of Tewkesbury set up camp just outside the town. In a short time the soldiers had poured through Kirkcudlies's streets to find the Advent fair, fill up the ale booths and search for friendly girls.

The weather was crisp and bright, exceptionally fine for that time of year. The gypsies set up their wagons at the far end of the field, making a rope pen to display Tyros's horses, two aged war mounts fit for plowing and a fine lady's palfrey. The women put up bright blankets for awnings over the wagon beds, and rounded up the children to go through the crowds crying out to customers about the repair of pots and pans, and to hint at fortune-telling and gypsy dancing.

Mila and Edain settled Asgard in the back of the wagon under their blanket awning, hidden from view. The gypsy girl went off with Tyros's wife and another woman to look over the soldiers and see what sort of money was to be made from them. Magnus announced that he was going to survey the horse dealers. Edain sat on the tailgate of the wagon in her fur cloak and the red veil, keeping watch.

But not for long.

"Ho, here she is, a gypsy fortune-teller!" Two of Tewkesbury's foot soldiers sharing a wineskin between them came up to the back of the wagon.

"Sweeting, let me see your pretty face," one cried, and made a grab for Edain's veil.

She dodged his hand just in time. Edain stared at them through the silk, biting her lip.

The gypsies had not told her what to do if something like this should happen. She was not even supposed to tell fortunes, only keep veiled, and watch over the Templar. Mila's wagon was at the back of the field, under the trees, in a place where the children had been told to stay. But the children were gone and Magnus, hoping to find a horse to buy with Asgard de la Guerche's money, was nowhere around.

One of the soldiers tried to climb in the wagon with her. "Come now, bright eyes," he smiled, pressing a coin into her hand, "read my hand and tell me what fair maid I'll find here at the fair to pleasure me."

When she pushed him away, he tried to put his arm around her. Dear God, Edain thought, fending him off, they were drunk as pigs and the sun was barely up in the sky!

She looked at the other ruffian, reeling back on his heels with wineskin in hand, a grin on his face. What was she going to do with them?

The first man pawed at her veil again. "Here," he said, taking her arm and trying to pull her down from her perch, "lift up yer pretty red drape so's to have a drink, sweetheart. A little wine'll put some heat into you, won't it, Rodney, lad?"

The younger one seized her other arm, trying to force her to take his penny. Rather than have them pull off the veil and see that she was not a gypsy, Edain cried, "Peace, peace—I'll drink your wine! Give me a moment."

She carefully lifted the bottom edge of the silk.

That seemed to satisfy them, for the burly man-at-arms stuck the spout of the wineskin under it and poured a red stream down the front of her gown.

"Heaven's angels!" She held the wine-soaked skirt away with her hand. What else would they do? She was frightened enough to tremble. Where was Magnus? Why had he gone off to look at horses, instead of staying with her?

Then there was Asgard in the back of the wagon, Edain thought. She couldn't have the wounded Templar discovered by English soldiers, she was not sure what would happen. And Magnus, curse him, was not there to ask what to do.

The bigger man stuck the wineskin under her veil

again. To please them she put her hand on it and took a small drink.

The sour wine nearly strangled her. "Now you must go away," Edain choked. "I am not telling fortunes today."

"Not tell fortunes?" They stood close to her, flush-faced, their bellies pressing her knees. "Don't be like that," the younger one said, "when you're sitting right here, waiting to take our money. Come now, have another drink."

Before she could draw back the other man wrapped his arm around her neck, forcing her head back. He pushed up the veil with the spout of the wineskin and uncovered her mouth, and poured a long stream into it. As she swallowed and gagged, the wine went down the front of her. The smell was strong. She was becoming drenched with it.

Edain was getting dizzy with just the little she had drunk. When the big soldier let her go she had to put her hand against the side of the wagon to keep from falling over. She never took wine. It must have been fright that made the strong drink go right to her head, was all she could think.

She hiccuped unsteadily. They grinned back at her.

"That's it, dearling," the younger one said. "Now you're ready for a good time." He tried to squeeze her breast.

She pushed him away, and took another drink from the wineskin. "Give me your hand," Edain told him, sighing.

They were not bad, not evil, she told herself, just

stupid and savage. They were like children—going to hurt her if it took their fancy.

The younger man-at-arms stuck out a grimy hand covered with calluses. Edain peered into it, trying not to hiccup again, not having the faintest idea what to make of the lines.

She had never tried to tell fortunes in her life. But because she was afraid, the Feeling was there.

Mother of God, they were both going to die, anyway!

She saw it all, in a pitched battle between the Kirkcudlies River and the Edinburgh road. The two of them would by lying side by side, dead in a ditch after a change by the Scots army.

She couldn't tell them that. They had only a few days left to live; they might as well enjoy it. The bigger one handed her the wineskin again and without thinking she took a big swallow.

The wine made her light-headed, and daring. Tossing caution to the winds she said, "There's a woman, a dark girl, who is here at the fair to pleasure you." She told the younger man-at-arms enough about himself, the second son of a freeman farmer who drank and beat his children, to make him believe her. At least he loved his mother, she thought, swallowing a furtive hiccup, poor downtrodden wretch that she was.

"And bet on the horse races, you are going to win," Edain assured the loutish youngster. "Good fortune smiles on you, nothing can go wrong. You will have the best time of your life here at the fair today if you stay with your comrade and do not part from him."

It was all true enough.

"A dark girl, not a fair one?" He leered at her.

Edain shook her head. "Look for the gypsies."

The Feeling told her this one was going to give one of Tyros's women nearly all the money he had. But that the gypsy was going to be excited by his tireless rutting, and allow him much more than he'd paid for.

The other soldier was just as happy to be told that his wife was pregnant again, and would give him a boy that they would make money on by apprenticing the child to a butcher. All his other children had been sold off this way. Including two of the older girls to a brothel. She told him, too, to bet on the horse races.

The Earl of Tewkesbury's men went off, waving the wineskin and drunkenly singing. A wind had come up and blew the dust behind him.

Edain looked around and found quite a little crowd had gathered. They'd waited for her, standing back, eavesdropping on what she told the men-at-arms. Now, from the looks on their faces they would not take no for an answer.

"I heard what you said to the English soldiers," a sheepherder said. "If you can tell them you can tell *me* what horse to play!"

A stout woman dropped a young girl forward by her arm. "My girl here wants to know when she'll meet her true one to marry. None of the lads hereabouts pleases her."

The wine had made her flushed. Edain pressed her fingers to her cheeks, trying to think of what to say to make them go away. The villeins and their women jostled one another, holding out their coins.

She couldn't think. "Wait here," Edain told them.

She lifted the blanket and crawled into the back of the wagon where Asgard was sleeping. She sat down among the pots and clothing and clutter of the gypsy wagon, wondering why the Feeling, which had not been with her since that night in the Templars' meeting room in Edinburgh was now so strong. It puzzled her.

For one thing, she'd been able to see the young soldier and Tyros's woman together quite clearly. As well as what had happened to the other man-at-arm's children. She put her arms around her knees and shivered.

Something was happening. These visions were not the gentle gifts she'd always had: her way with animals, the way she could silently "call" someone without their knowing it. Which she'd hardly ever used except for poor Sister Jean-Auguste and a few others.

Now she didn't know what to do. Things were not turning out right. The Templars were convinced that she'd made the stone vaults collapse. She had to be careful; she didn't want to provoke any powers that would make something else happen. They didn't need anything to draw attention to them here, between the English and King William's army.

But there was no way she could think of to get rid of the villeins when they had already heard what she'd told the English soldiers, and wanted her to do the same for them. Besides, Tyros and the gypsy women strolling the crowds had already promised as much.

With a sigh, Edain got up and ducked under the blanket and came out to where they were waiting.

The turbulent wind gusted again, raising more dust and lifting the blanket awning behind her.

There were not all that many. Perhaps if she pretended to read their palms they would leave.

"Give me your hand," she said to the middle-aged man who had wanted to know what horse to bet on.

Edain took a deep breath. The bay mare that would run in the final race was the one to put money on as the mare was a long shot, and the bet makers were giving great odds. The mare would pull out ahead of a very strong field at the last turn.

When she told the burly villein exactly that, he was overjoyed and promised to come back when he'd won and give her more than the copper penny he'd put in her hand.

Edain looked down at the coin. There was more; the Feeling was very strong.

Before he could turn away she went on to tell him that his wife was stealing his money he had buried in an iron pot in the garden, and was using it to buy gifts for her lover. She'd almost seen the lover standing there, tall and blond, somewhat younger than the villein's wife. He was the middle son of Kirkcudlies's butcher.

For a moment the villein could not speak. He turned red in the face. "My money," he gasped.

He took off, running, across the grass in the direction of the fair's sheep pens.

Edain hiccuped. The crowd laughed.

Thank the saints in heaven, she told herself as she took the next half a dozen hands in turn, that no one else was about to die. Although one woman was going to fall carrying her Monday basket of wash and break her leg, and an old man was about to have a terrible toothache and lose most of his teeth.

Unfortunately, the crowd found this funny when they heard it, and teased the old man unmercifully.

When she came to the mother with the girl who was looking for a young man to wed, she told the woman that her daughter would find him only when she visited the mother's sister in the next town. Her aunt would put the girl in the young man's way, for he was quite a catch, being the son of a rich wool merchant.

While they were still smiling, Edain said, "But he will get your daughter pregnant and only wed her reluctantly, as his family will not be too happy over the connection."

The woman put her arm around her daughter's shoulders and pulled her away from the wagon. "Bah, what a thing to tell a sweet, innocent maid!" she cried. "A curse on you, gypsy trollop! Say what you will behind that red veil, I'll not pay you a good penny for a fortune such as that!"

Edain shrugged.

As the woman and her daughter started back across the field she thought of calling out to them that the girl's father did not know she was not his very own. But decided at the last moment not to.

The fortune-telling did not go as smoothly after that. Edain's words came too close to the truth for some, for a young couple went off disgruntled when she told them one was barren, and they would have no offspring. Finally one of the men went to get the priest, saying the gypsies should not be allowed to practice the devil's arts. The wind was picking up.

Edain could only speak while she held the veil pressed to her face with one hand. Low-flying clouds like those before a storm came scudding across the sky. Some of the villeins who still stood in line waiting for their fortunes grew tired of the wind's buffeting and the swirling dust, and went away.

Something was going to happen.

Magnus circled the horse dealers, thinking of Castle Morlaix's own fine stock that had been so carefully bred. These horses were not bad, but it was plain they had changed hands several times; the riding stock in particular rolled their eyes and looked as though they would take weeks to train back to the saddle. His practiced eye told him that came from taking them cross-country, herding them together at night, and not riding them enough.

There were other gypsies at the fair trading horses besides Tyros and his band. The country folk stared openly at the swarthy people. The north of England, and Scotland, were not so familiar with the "Egyptians" as folks called them. Although the gypsies had been coming into Britain since early in King Henry's reign, many of them following the Crusaders back from the East, Magnus knew them fairly well. For a while they had been as plentiful as fleas in Wales and the Welsh marcher country, including Morlaix. His father had been lenient with them until the gypsy women started trouble with the village men.

Magnus had found them good enough horse people, although prone to cheat. If the country folk mistrusted the gypsies the feeling was returned, with plentiful contempt. The *rom* as they called themselves, hated the villeins, whom they regarded as stupid, and so greedy they were easy to fleece.

A big, barrel-chested bay that looked as though it could run flat out for miles before being winded caught Magnus's eye. The dealer was an Irishman who traveled up and down the northern coasts. He came up to Magnus while Magnus had his head against the big bay's ribs, listening for any telltale noises that he was wind-broken.

They were a pair, the man told him; he wanted to sell a black mare to go with the stallion.

When the Irishman named a price, Magnus walked away. The man followed, as he knew he would. "The bay alone is worth the silver," the Irishman shouted. "I'm only throwing in the mare because she's that mad about him, the poor filly!"

Magnus had to laugh. "I don't need a pair of lovebirds, I need a horse."

Nevertheless, he waited while the Irishman mounted the mare and put her through her paces. The little horse was nicely gaited. She tossed her head and lifted her feet as though she knew she was being watched, and Magnus was charmed. He found himself thinking of golden Edain. The mare would be a handful, he would have to ride her himself for days before he could get her properly in hand for an inexperienced rider. And yet he couldn't help but think of how they would be together, the two lovely female things.

He found himself imagining the big bay stallion covering the little black mare. Horses nearly always connected for sex violently with the stallion biting and kicking the mare into submission, forcing her to her knees before mounting her. The size of that great shaft plunging into the filly's small opening as she squealed. Her body seemingly too small to contain all of it.

Flames were suddenly licking in Magnus's groin. The mare and the stallion had blended into memories of lovemaking in the woods with Edain in his arms. He wondered what they were doing back at the wagon. Who was about except for the infernal everlasting presence of the wounded Templar.

Magnus paid the Irishman as quickly as he could. While he was doing so, a fight broke out around the sheep pens.

"There's going to be trouble," the horse dealer said, nodding in that direction. "I wish they'd run them out of the country entirely, the filthy beggars."

He was talking about the gypsies. Magnus hoisted himself up on the bare back of the stallion, waited for him to dance and buck a few times and then settle down, before taking the lead for the black mare from the Irishman's hand.

But by that time he could see Tyros and some other gypsies running as fast as their legs would carry them.

"Does she have a name?" Magnus wanted to know.

"Anything you want, anything you want, sir," the Irishman shouted. "She'll be sweet and agreeable for the right rider, you can count on it."

Magnus kicked the bay into a trot and started off. He had the right rider in mind. Mares and stallions and rutting. His head was spinning with it. All he needed was a few minutes' peace and quiet.

* * *

Edain saw the gypsies coming back. They hurried across the field with Magnus behind them riding a bay stallion without a saddle, and leading a little black mare. He pulled up before the wagon, taking in the small knot of people around the tailgate with a flick of his tawny eyes.

Something was wrong. Edain could tell it at once.

"Get ready to move," he shouted to her over the wind.

Mira came running up to untie the mules and hitch them up to the wagon. In the distance a crowd seemed to be straggling across the field.

Like the gusting wind, discontent ran through the fortune-teller's crowd. There were muffled shouts of *witch*. "You have my money," someone cried. "Give it back!"

Magnus circled his horses, waiting for the wagons to get started. Tyros already had his heading back down the Kirkcudlies road. Another gypsy woman ran over to help Mila harness the mules. Edain threw the handful of copper pennies she was holding into the crowd of villeins. They forgot their complaints for the moment, and scrambled for them.

"Hurry up, hurry up!" Magnus shouted.

The wagon started up with an unexpected lurch, nearly throwing Edain from the tailgate. The crowd stepped back. A thrown rock hit the side of the wagon. Then another.

Edain held onto the wooden sides of the wagon with both hands. Magnus kicked his horse up beside her, his face tight.

"What have you been doing back there," he yelled, "starting a riot? Why are they calling you witch?"

Edain did not try to explain; the bursts of storm wind would take the words out of her mouth. She gave him a burning look.

The wagon hit a rut, sending her into the air from her seat. The gypsy wagons rushed away from Kirkcudlies's fair as though the hounds of hell were after them. A few villeins still ran behind the wagon, throwing rocks.

Magnus drove the bay stallion at them, making them scatter. He cantered back, his dark red hair blowing in the wind.

"They said at the fair the gypsies were stealing some sheep," he shouted. "We left at full speed."

Edain pulled off the veil. "Did you buy those horses?"

He turned the stallion in a wide half-circle, heels digging into its sides. He rode bareback, pulling the little mare with effortless grace.

"Yes, I paid." He gave her a wide, wicked grin. "I'm not the one they're throwing stones at."

Edain stared after him. Then she climbed into the back of the wagon to see how Asgard fared.

Asgard lay with his eyes closed, although he was not asleep. The wild bouncing and swaying of the wagon would have wakened him, anyway.

As it was, he had been listening to the demoiselle Edain tell the villeins' fortunes. It fascinated him, even as it made the hair on the back of his neck prickle uneasily.

Her power of divination was awesome, but so was her ignorance. She had no sense of caution. The clumsy way she'd dealt with the peasants, raising their amazement and fear with the bald truth of everything she told them, only invited trouble. He had heard their shouts, and guessed by the noise that a few had thrown stones as the wagons made their retreat from the field.

Now he watched her catch the edge of the blanket whipping in the wind and take it down. The cold air rushed in.

In spite of the bouncing she made her way back to him and put her hand on his forehead to see if the fever had returned. "You've been asleep," she shouted.

Asgard nodded. He was not strong enough yet to bellow over the racket. She knelt by his side and pulled the sheepskins up around his neck and shoulders.

He saw she had taken off the concealing red veil. Her long, gilded hair was plaited into tight braids wound around her head. The dark gypsy stain on her face made her jewel eyes glow.

He watched her thinking that it was possible she did not know her own power. Which made her even more dangerous. How could one forget the words of the Culdee monk who, when he had seen her, had talked of the ancient people of Ireland who lived forever? And who were famed magicians.

Under the blankets Asgard made the sign of the cross against his breast. This girl was surpassing lovely, but the church taught evil often had the look of innocence and beauty. Especially in women.

She sat down beside him and pulled her cloak around her. Up front they could hear Mila shouting to the mules to make them go faster. The storm was full of a cold wind that bent the trees and clouds of dust, but no rain.

Asgard closed his eyes. Lying still, he could feel it. No one seemed afraid, except perhaps the girl, who had a brooding look. But he knew all around them there was a demon-ridden force that was hurling them ahead of the storm.

Toward Dumfries, and the south.

Sixteen

"Henry Plantagenet is the best king England ever had," the first knight announced.

The rest of the table rather drunkenly agreed with him except for one of the Earl of Norfolk's men. "Nay, God rest the immortal soul of his grandfather," that knight said, raising his cup, "the Lion of Justice, Henry the First!"

Magnus sat in the shadows away from the main table, listening, his gypsy hat pulled down to his ears. There was a time when, properly wearing his mail and helm, he would have joined these fighting men and shared a cup. Although they were, even as knights, a rough sort working for hire to any lord who would pay them. They would no doubt have treated him, a knight of Chester's court and an earl's son in his own right, with more than a little favor.

He wouldn't get that now, Magnus thought wryly. His sword was hidden under his cloak, but it was all that marked him for what he really was. To the rest of the world, with his stained skin and ragged clothes, he was yet another shiftless gypsy; he'd even had trouble with the innkeeper letting him into the inn's common room until he showed him some silver.

The big knight at the table signaled for the innkeeper to bring another round. "Old King Henry the First had but one son to plague him," he said darkly, "and we can thank heaven Prince William died before he could bare his teeth at his sire. It seemed a great sorrow at the time to have the young prince go down with the White Ship and leave the old Lion to grieve, but look what faithless sons has done to his grandson, our good Henry."

"Everyone knows French Eleanor conspires with the princes," another knight put in. "It was a wise thing for the king to lock the bitch up and keep her there. At least it keeps the old drab from sending word to her boys to harry and provoke the king."

There was a round of loud agreement. Some of the knights went on to comment on the queen in the demeaning terms that had always plagued her. About her age when she had married the young king Henry, being eleven years older. And being divorced. And the mother of two girls by the King of France. Not to mention her loose reputation with that plague of any Christian state, the French troubadours she was so fond of.

More than fond, someone added. What with her carrying on with every singer that came out of Aquitaine it was no wonder the king had put her away.

A kitchen girl brought Magnus a piece of bread and a slice of cheese and laid it on the table before him. She was a fairly young girl in a dirty brown shift. She lingered, her eyes saying that he was only a gypsy and not worth her time but a strapping one, and wonderfully handsome.

Magnus broke the bread in two and stuck the

cheese between it, ignoring her. With a sigh, the kitchen girl went away.

He'd been hungry for some food a gypsy had not fixed and had taken himself off into the inn. Down the road Tyros and the other man were trying to sell the sheep they had lifted from the Kirkcudlies fair. Magnus knew he could take his leisure with his ale and bread and cheese. They were not about to sell anything soon, as the sheep's ears were notched with the Kirkcudlies signet, and buyers were leery that the animals looked stolen. Which they were.

Before anyone would buy them Tyros was going to have to take the time to crop the sheep's ears fresh and start all over again.

Virtue is its own reward, Magnus told himself, taking a big bite of the layers of cheese and bread. It was one of his father's favorite sayings, although he could never for the life of him see why: the earl never courted anything, with or without virtue, that did not also deliver a healthy profit.

A loud argument about the queen had broken out among the knights at the big table. Magnus, his mouth full of bread and cheese, slid down a little further in his seat and stretched out his long legs. Across the room, two black habit friars hunched closer to the fire. Knights in their cups were a rowdy lot. And whether Queen Eleanor was a whore or not was a dispute the holy brothers did not care to be dragged over to a tableful of knights to judge.

Magnus tilted the cup and drained the last of his ale. The queen, a good friend of his mother and father's, was an elder lady now, the mother of grown sons and daughters. And as far as Magnus was concerned, due some respect. He hadn't seen her since he was a downy-faced squire and the king and queen and their court had visited Morlaix. She had patted his cheek, surveying him with eyes that were still luminously beautiful and lively, and murmured something about his being a stealer of hearts even before he could properly shave.

The Queen of England had been to a half-grown boy the most beautiful woman on earth. And the most fascinating. When he had served the king and queen at Castle Morlaix's high table Magnus had not been able to keep his eyes from her. He remembered her looking glorious with her dark hair unbound, flowing over her arms and shoulders and down to her waist like a girl's, wearing jewels and veils and a dress made of some silvery, gleaming stuff. It was hardly fair now for some drunken knights in a tavern in godforsaken Scotland to call her a drab and a harlot. But then, he reminded himself, there were many who had never seen her. The queen had been imprisoned for many long years.

He lifted his hand for the kitchen girl and she came and got his cup and carried it off. When she came back with more ale her eyes gleamed. "Oh, sir," she whispered, leaning over him. "You're no gypsy, are you?"

Magnus realized that his cape had fallen away under the table and she'd seen his sword. He hurriedly stuck a copper coin in her hand and folded her fingers around it. "Seal your lips," he told her, getting up.

She followed him to the door, still eager, but he

slipped past her and went outside. Down the road the gypsy wagons were parked in a field.

The day was cold and overcast; in the gray light the gypsies' clutter of fires and tethered horses, underfed dogs, unsold sheep, and battered wagons, looked less than inviting.

Magnus leaned his elbows on the stone wall that enclosed the pasture, watching Mila and another woman cooking the noonday meal. The thought of the ale and the fresh-baked bread he'd just eaten back in the inn was comforting.

Nothing else was.

They were but a few leagues from Dumfries, and would leave for the port after the meal. Magnus intended to leave the wounded Templar at the nearest monastery and give him a part of what was left of his money. He would use the rest to buy passage to Chester for himself and Edain.

Edain, Magnus thought, wincing. There was the source of all his trouble.

He had not had a good night's sleep since they'd left Edinburgh, tossing and turning on the cold, hard ground. *Wanting her.* The memory of her in his arms, golden and thrilling and passionate, would not leave him alone. It was as though the fine webs of a spider's glittering enchantment bound him to her. The thought of possibly not being with her, of not being able to watch her during the day when she went about her tasks with the gypsies, or lie between the blankets at night and dream of her so near, and how much he wanted to make love to her, plunged him into the deepest despair.

For all his thinking and worrying about it these

past weeks he still had no good idea what he was going to do with her when they reached the Earl of Chester's court. Once there Magnus knew he would have to give a reckoning of this miserable trip. And receive discipline and fines, if any.

Sweet Jesu, he supposed he would have to explain why he, and not the Angevins he'd gambled with, had gone to collect taxes in the first place! That drunken episode and the folly of his dicing was not going to please Chester, his liege lord. Nor, he thought with a groan, his father.

Magnus watched the gypsy girl, Mila, carry a bowl from the fire into the wagon, obviously something she'd fixed for the Templar to eat. With de la Guerche recovering it was hard to keep the women away from him.

When he got back to Chester he would gladly take his punishment and even make restitution if it came to that. It would be a relief to get this sorry business over with. There was a possibility that since Edain could testify that the loss of the ships was not his fault, that he would not even be made to pay the full value of Chester's lost revenue.

On the other hand, the damned taxes were hardly what worried him. He was desperate to find some way to keep Edain. The Earl of Chester himself was lenient enough; Magnus supposed Rannulf could be prevailed to look the other way if he kept her as his leman. And providing there was no great scandal such as would occur if she wanted to return to St. Sulpice convent.

A cold chill ran through him. Surely she wouldn't choose to do that. She'd not slept with him for days, not since that night in the woods, and had given as an excuse that she was tending the wounded Templar. When he could see her eyes, the few times when she would let that emerald gaze meet his, there was a sweet coolness, even a faint, resigned distrust.

He supposed he knew the reason. She was his heart, his life, but she knew he could never marry her. As the heir to the earldom of Morlaix he could not wed without King Henry's permission. And even if the king were attacked by some untoward madness that would make him agree to such a thing, there was still his father.

Succession was everything to the Earl of Morlaix. As the son of the old earl's bastard, Niall fitzJulien had fought hard for all that he had. He would not let his fief be sacrificed in the next generation to an illegal marriage.

So there was nothing left to do after all these days of fruitless scheming but bring Edain to Chester. In his desperation he would try to peddle his soul among the power makers there to find a way to keep her. He could borrow money and pay enough bribes to keep Chester's bishops and churchmen from declaring her still St. Sulpice's novice, and therefore forbidden to him. And he had to somehow not let his father, who was a faithful husband and father and had never kept a leman as far as his sons knew, know anything about all this.

Magnus's hands gripped the stones of the wall until his fingers turned white.

Jesu, but he loved her! He would say it to anyone. Whatever the strange mystery that surrounded her, he'd vowed he would not leave her to the mercy of others, who would treat her as did the Templars Who would use her for what they needed, then brand her a witch and kill her.

The powers she had, whatever they were, did not bother him. Edain needed someone to look after her and protect her and cherish that sweet, loving smile those warm arms that crept so softly about his neck that beautiful body she'd given to no man but him

How could he let her go?

He couldn't, Magnus told himself. If he had to defy the king and the powerful earl of Morlaix, his own father, to keep her with him, then by all that was holy he would do it!

He would talk to her as soon as they got to Dumfries and he put the Templar into the nearest monastery and paid off the gypsies.

He jumped over the wall and started toward the camp. First they had to gather up what they had spread out all over the farmer's field, and hitch up the wagons. Knowing gypsies, it would be a marvel if they got it done before sundown.

Magnus worked hard the next few hours to get the wagons back on the road, even though Tyros's band complained loudly that they were not happy to see the journey end and Magnus and Edain and the Templar leave. Even though they would finally get the rest of their money. They had nowhere to go they wailed; Dumfries was unfriendly to gypsies, and since it was almost Yuletide people would be staying in their houses to celebrate and there would be no fairs.

Magnus at last got the wagons and drivers moving. The sheep were tied to the tailgates to follow behind Tyros's wains, but after a few feet they only milled about, baaing. Some fell down in the road and would not get up. The gypsy curs circled them, barking and snapping at their legs.

The wagons came to a halt.

Magnus rode back down the line, fuming. The damned sheep. Dumfries was so near and yet so far: they could be there by nightfall if the confusion that constantly plagued gypsies did not hold them up. He saw Edain, unveiled, come out to sit with Mila on the wagon seat. In the middle of the road Tyros struggled to tie an ewe by her feet and toss her onto a wagon bed. The wind was blowing fitfully. Magnus looked up into the gray sky. It looked as though it would snow.

At that moment a column of knights coming from Dumfries turned into the crossroads. The mailed figures in front proceeded at a brisk gallop beside a mounted standard bearer with green and white gonfalon snapping in the wind and a knight blowing a warning on his horn to clear the road.

Behind the knights were a troop of a hundred men in gleaming chain mail covered with green and white tunics. At the horizon were companies of men-at-arms carrying pikes, at their backs an array of seemingly endless supply wains.

"The wagons—move the wagons!" Magnus shouted.

His broad-brimmed hat flew off as he kicked his horse out into the road where the gypsies had run to help Tyros with the fat, wallowing ewe.

There was nothing to be done. They all saw that.

The mounted knights came thundering down on the gypsies' stalled wagons. The effort to come to a stop from a military gallop cost the leading riders. One, reining in his horse, was neatly bucked off.

A big horseman reined in his white stallion and it reared. With a fine display of horsemanship the man riding him bent over his neck as the horse pawed the air. As the destrier danced in the road, spume flying from its jaws, he reined it in steadily until it calmed. The other knights were less successful. Some had to gallop their excited mounts out into the fields before they could bring them to a stop.

The leading knight, a handsome man in his late forties with a face like granite, leaned forward in the saddle to survey the tangle of gypsy wagons, the sheep, the barking dogs, and screaming women that had broken up his column.

His expression changed into something even more inscrutable as he viewed Magnus, who was pulling the bleating ewe off to the side of the road with oak-stained hands, hatless, his russet hair blowing in the rising wind.

It was the dark face and red hair the lordly knight stared at.

"Magnus," he said in a gravelly voice. "Sweet Mary's tits, you're no gypsy! It's Magnus, my son!"

Seventeen

It was February before King Henry came to Chester.

Edain had been confined to the tower room, the one reserved for important prisoners, in Beeston Castle outside the city since Yuletide. From there she and her keeper, the Lady Drucilla, could see the king's troops marching across the countryside.

"Now, bless us, that's what you've waited for, isn't it?" the warden's wife said. "You ought to be happy. The king's come, now you'll find out why he's kept us waiting all these long months."

Edain leaned into the deepest window to see the Earl of Leicester's knights enter the castle courtyard, gonfalons billowing in the wind and horns blowing. She searched for the Plantagenet banner among men and horses.

"The king's not with them," she said, disappointed. "The flag is always carried for him, is it not? The leopards of the House of Anjou?"

"The king is coming, right enough," the older woman answered. "I know because my husband, Sir Maxim, was there when Sir Henry the castellan received King Henry's messenger only a sennight ago."

Lady Drucilla bundled up the sheets they had

been mending. All through the rain and cold of January they had repaired old court dresses for Edain to wear. When those were finished and she'd acquired a satisfactory wardrobe according to the king's exacting orders, they'd been given more commonplace tasks such as mending sheets and other household linens.

"Don't fret, dear," the warden's wife said, "now the king's come you'll have a bit more freedom. You won't stay shut up in here. I daresay you'll go about with the ladies of the court at the hunting and dancing, wearing the pretty clothes we sewed for you. Life will look a whole lot brighter."

Edain stepped down from the window and took the edge of a sheet and helped fold it.

The warden's wife and all the castle staff gossiped about why she was there, in the castle tower, awaiting King Henry. She couldn't help overhear them as they talked on the stairs while sweeping them and in the gardebrobe while cleaning it. They said that she was being held in Beeston Castle to await the king's pleasure. After all, the maids and the young soldiers gossiped, she was young and beautiful and Henry had a notorious reputation with women. One of the king's favorite mistresses, the Fair Rosamund, had just died after a short illness, and the king had already surrounded himself with attractive females. King Henry, the stories went, again kept women in his household service who roamed the London streets as his full-time procurers.

"Yes," Edain said, helping to stack the bed linens in the basket Lady Drucilla had brought, "it's good the king is coming. Not to have to wait and pass the time sewing clothes and bedsheets will be a great blessing."

The other woman gave her a sharp look. "It's fate, girl, that proper destiny that God wills us, and don't you forget it!" But she reached out to pat her shoulder. "Remember he's the king, a great man that the world looks up to, and not any common penniless sort who'd tumble you in a hayloft and walk away and forget even to leave you a bit of bread. They say—"

She took a cautionary look around the room, although there was no one to overhear.

"They do say King Henry is kindness itself to those sweet maids he fancies," she said in a loud whisper, "and looks after them surpassing well. Just as his grandfather did, the first Henry, may God rest his soul. Ah, that was a lusty man! King Henry Hotspur boasted he had more bastards than any man in England, and provided nicely for every one of them, as well as their mothers."

Edain managed a smile. She'd had the warden's wife as her companion—or jailor, she was never sure which—for most of the winter, and had grown fond of her. Lady Drucilla's comfortable ways reminded her of the nuns at St. Sulpice. The warden's wife had been kind, too, in the days following Edain's arrival at the city of Chester when she'd not known what would be done with her.

Almost at once Sir Henry, the castellan of Beeston, had presented the king's orders to the knight of the Earl of Morlaix's troops who had brought her there. King Henry's edict read that once one Edain, known as a novice of the Norman convent of the Sacred

Limb of St. Sulpice, was to be named ward of the king at Chester, to be treated well and housed most comfortably in the prisoners' apartments in the tower of Beeston Castle.

That was the last Edain had seen of the Earl of Morlaix's escort that had taken them from Dumfries to Chester's port. Mila the gypsy girl and the wounded Templar, Asgard de la Guerche on his bed of blankets, Tyros the headman of the band, the other gypsy man, the women, the dogs, and even the bleating sheep had all disappeared when they'd been taken from the ship to Chester's walled city. Earl Niall fitzJulien, who had discovered them on the Dumfries road had stayed behind in Scotland with his army. As had his son, Magnus.

The last time Edain had seen Magnus she'd had only a glimpse of him mounted on the big gray destrier he'd bought at the Kirkculdies fair, washed clean of his gypsy stain and clad in heavy mail, his long red hair cropped close under his helmet. He had looked, riding in a line of mailed horsemen of his father's army, the perfect grim-faced knight.

And not, she thought, the raffish, handsome scoundrel with the crooked grin who'd traded horses with gypsies at a Scottish fair, and whom women, seemingly by the hundreds, could not resist. He was the knight who had saved her life in a shipwreck, daringly snatched a wild tribesman's haggis to feed them, tramped the roads of Scotland in sheepherder's boots to look for her, stolen a horse and brashly attacked, all alone, the Templars' stronghold in Edinburgh to rescue her. And disguised as a gypsy, he'd commanded Tyros's unruly band and taken them safely all the way to Dumfries. Last but not least, he'd held her in his arms and made love to her so that the sun and moon and stars had stood still in the sky and the world had been bathed in gold dust and glory.

Choking on the memories, she could not bring herself to realize even now that it had all come to an end there at the crossroads when the Earl of Morlaix had ridden up at the head of his troops. Dear God, at that moment Magnus had been chasing a sheep to get it out of the way.

She would never forget as long as she lived what happened next. On his knees in the road trying to subdue a fat, struggling ewe, Magnus had stared up thunderstruck at the massive lord in helm and glittering mail.

Those two faces had been so alike in their outrage and horror that some of the mounted knights laughed.

A second later they'd been shouting at each other. Magnus bellowing at the great earl. The Earl of Morlaix roaring back.

"What is the matter?" the warden's wife exclaimed. "Ah, now, why are you doing that? Shame on you, weeping tears for a nice meeting with King Henry that any maid would give her all to have." She came around the basket of linens. "What is it, dearling? Are you beset now with silly worries? Are you fretting that you are a novice, and must get dispensation to wear the lovely clothes we made so that you can receive proper attention?" She sighed. "Ah, lay aside your fears, girl, there's none that will think the less of you for it. Besides, the matter is all taken care of by order of the archbishop himself."

Edain gave a shrug, wiping at her eyes.

She was a fool to cry, thinking of Magnus. But she could not explain to a pious soul like the lady Drucilla that King Henry was not keeping her at Beeston Castle to make her his leman. Nor what the Templars had wanted her for: to be their captive seeress and prophet, to foretell the future and give the fighting monks power over the world. Nor what it had cost Magnus to get her away from them.

Edain took a deep breath. She had come to believe Magnus could do anything. Horse thief, sheep-stealing Highland gypsy, vagabond—he could have been hanged for even a quarter of his crimes. Twice he had saved her life. But it was the underground room at the Templars' commandery that made her shiver, not the memory of being nearly drowned with him in the sea.

She looked at the other woman.

Poor Lady Drucilla. The warden's wife thought she wept at the thought of losing her virtue to King Henry. But she wept because she was so lonely for Magnus. He was her comfort, her strength—her love. All these months she'd been in despair, not knowing whether she could face the rest of her life without him.

Yet there had never been any mention that they might spend their lives together. He was a great nobleman's son and heir to an earldom. Already, someone had told her, betrothed to some girl of his class.

One had only to look at his father, the Earl of Morlaix, clad in armor worth a king's ransom, sitting the most magnificent of warhorses, surrounded by his knight captains and squires and body servants, to know how far removed Magnus's noble family was from a nameless orphan like herself, a meek novice from an obscure convent on the borderland coast. In all the hours they had lain together the word *love* had never passed his lips.

Nor was it going to, Edain told herself, closing her eyes against the familiar pain.

In quiet moments she had groped desperately for the Feeling. To woo it, to see what it would tell her about the one person to whom she owed her life, the one person she loved. Where was he now? Was he fighting with the English king's armies against William the Lion, like his father? Was he in peril?

She knew that he was. He had boasted that he was a tourney knight, undefeated in the battles staged at the courts of the nobles of England. But he had seen little of real war.

He was seeing it now, Edain knew. It was always in her mind, although it was hard for her to picture Magnus killing others in order to keep himself from being killed. Slaughtering others in the name of the English king's victory.

In the middle of the night she would wake from dreaming and sit up in bed and clasp her hands and pray for the Feeling to come to her. But no matter how earnestly she tried, it never did. There was not a whisper, not a picture, not a faint sense of anything. The Feeling simply was not there. Nothing.

"Here, girl." The warden's wife had gone to the chest and taken out one of the court gowns they'd mended, a dark green wool with a silken bodice and slashed sleeves to show orange fabric underneath. The dress was very fancy, made for the feasting and dancing.

"Now put this on," Lady Drucilla said. "You must wear your pretty robes from morning until bedtime, for we want to look smart for the king. Once he's here at Chester, he may visit you at any hour, that's what they tell me. He's a brisk, impetuous man, in spite of his age." She blushed slightly. "Well, that's the truth of it, might as well be honest. He's our blessed sovereign, he can come and go any hour he pleases, now can't he?"

Edain took off her everyday homespun gown and stood before Lady Drucilla while the other woman pulled a linen shift over her head, then the elegant wool and silk overgown. A woven silk belt in a flower pattern was put around her hips and fastened with a gold buckle. A gold brooch held a flowing green silk scarf to her shoulder and a coif of the same fabric with gold circlet was set on her hair.

The warden's wife fussed, obviously enjoying herself, to get the headdress to cover Edain's head but not hide all her gleaming hair. With spit and agile fingers, tongue clamped between her teeth, the older woman twisted shining gold strands to flow out from beneath the veil and over the gown's shoulders and sleeves. Then she stepped back.

"Ah, if you could see yourself!" Actual tears filled her eyes. "No wonder the king has sent to the wilds of the border to bring you out from some nithing convent! It's just like they say, beauty doesn't languish unseen for very long among the stones and weeds. Even the king heard of you!"

Edain lowered her head. The convent of St. Sulpice was not exactly an insignificant establishment; the abbess would be outraged to hear it described as "nithing." But she supposed she knew what the warden's wife meant.

They put the rest of the gowns, satins, wool, and velvets back into the chests and tidied the room. When the lady Drucilla let herself out Edain walked to the door with her so as to catch a breath of the fresh air, and to see what guards had been put at her door. A company of Gascons had come to garrison the castle; when the bailiff or Lady Drucilla were not around, they would sometimes leave the door open and talk to her.

Not this time. The Gascon guards were there, grinning suddenly at the sight of Edain, but Lady Drucilla's sharp eyes sized them up. She made the knights lock the door, reminding them of the harsh penalties for being too friendly with prisoners. Even if they were beautiful young girls.

Edain could still hear her scolding as she went back to the window. This was where she spent most of her time in spite of the cold air that flowed through the cracks in the casement. Now with the king's troops coming in, at least there was something to see other than rain and melting patches of snow on the cobblestones in the courtyard.

A familiar figure in a white cloak with a large red cross on the back came into view. She waved, but he didn't see her.

He was walking much better, she thought. She did not know where Asgard slept, but he was being cared for as he seemed to be recovering from the sword thrust in his side. If she leaned farther into the window she could get a glimpse of his face.

When he turned, she thought he looked pale, although he carried a staff to favor his bad side.

She wanted to see him. She had spent so much time with him nursing him in the gypsy wagon that she regarded him as a friend. Even though Magnus had warned her that the Templar had brought her not to King William but to the commandery in Edinburgh. Where nothing good had been intended for her.

She watched him as he crossed the courtyard and entered a barracks in the Old Tower.

She missed Asgard and the gypsies and Mila, she missed them all. But not as much as she missed Magnus.

Dejected, Edain stepped down from the window and crossed the room. She pulled up a chair by the fire and sat down and stuck out her feet to the warmth to await King Henry's pleasure.

Asgard had seen the flutter of a white hand at the window out of the corner of his eye, but he gave no sign.

He had made a habit of keeping his head bent as he passed when actually he always gave the prisoners' tower a thorough scrutiny.

Jesu, how could he *not* look at her every chance he got? This inhumanly beautiful woman who tormented his dreams?

He'd caught a glimpse of a fair, sculpted face as well as the hand before she stepped back. The barred window drew everyone's eyes as it was: stable knaves, kitchen cooks, knights riding their chargers out of the castle on patrol, all could not keep from looking up there where the enchantingly lovely demoiselle, it was rumored, awaited the king. She did not have much longer; the vanguard of King Henry's army was even now on the road from Wrexham.

England's sovereign was late getting to the war on the Scottish border. But then he had been much beleaguered the past year. Yet another rebellion by his sons Henry and Geoffrey had broken out in France, joined at the same time by the revolt of some of his own magnates in England. And in Scotland, William the Lion had made common cause with the princes and marched south to reclaim the borderlands. At this point, the King of England was being attacked on four fronts.

To add to Henry's woes, the murder of his onetime friend, Thomas à Becket, the Archbishop of Canterbury, had created a scandal throughout the Christian world, and brought the heavy censure of the church upon him. The Pope in Rome called for the extreme and humiliating measure of the king's public repentance, walking barefoot in the streets and in sackcloth and ashes, for being responsible for the archbishop's death. And then there remained Henry's queen, the famed Eleanor of Aquitaine, imprisoned for many long years in a castle in the midlands, who hated her husband, and longed to betray him.

As soon as the king had been able to subdue his sons' forces in France, Henry had brought an army to England and attacked his barons' strongholds, conquered them, and even now was marching northward to deal with William the Lion of Scotland.

The girl should have had little importance in Henry Plantagenet's plans, Asgard told himself. But he had spent enough time at the English court and knew the king's inquisitive mind well enough to know that Henry could not resist using her if he could.

God knows the Templars had not abused her, they only wished to explore her secrets and add the knowledge to their store of God's mysteries. The Grand Master in Paris was even now rumored to be exploring the sect of followers of the Rosy Cross, the Rosicrucians, to see what divine illumination could be gained from them.

It was too bad though that there had been difficulty in a similar vein when a seer, an old man, had been discovered in the far western islands of Scotland. There had been a kidnapping in which the king's men had carried him away. But after a few months of interrogation the old man had died without anyone learning much.

Asgard could not let that happen to the demoiselle Edain.

She was his.

She had been his from the moment he had ransomed her from barbarians in that stinking stone fort and brought her to the Templars' command in Edinburgh. Since then great forces had been set in place. They had all felt it in the assembly room that night.

He found that he had reached the far side of the bailey. He was trembling, although the winter sun was warm enough. He was thinking that through this girl the order of the Poor Knights of the Temple of Jerusalem could perform a miracle. One did not exaggerate when one said they were about to discover the meaning of the universe. Of the Godhead. Of life itself.

Asgard shuddered slightly.

On the other hand he well knew she was a wanton, imperfect vessel, a mere woman flawed by fleshly appetites. He had known she slept with the redeaded mercenary knight; perhaps she had also tumbled with Tyros and the other gypsy. These defilements might make her of no use to anyone.

But she could not just be let go. Most especially, she and her powers could not be left to be exploited by that debauched king, Henry of England.

That much, Asgard told himself, he must try to prevent.

Eighteen

"Hurry, hurry," Lady Drucilla said.

She pulled Edain down the tower stairs, followed by their escort, a burly little squire with almost-white hair, and two tall knights carrying torches.

At the bottom of the steps the warden's wife stopped to adjust Edain's headdress and pull her skirts into place.

"Don't duck your chin," she scolded, her hands working to pull the fabric into great flowerlike folds. "God save us, girl, but it's hard to rid you of convent training! Don't lower your eyes like that, look up! That's it! Lift up your chin, too, and your shoulders, and stand tall. I want your hair to show in spite of the veil."

She pounced on the sky blue silk and pulled it back, over Edain's shoulders. One of the knights laughed.

The warden's wife turned to give him an icy look. "Yes, well you may laugh, Sir Gervase, but if it wasn't the French fashion, and every woman at the king's court a craven slave to it I'd say pull the thing off. Coifs and veils and wimples wrapped around and under the chin—it's just a way to show off silly scraps of things common folk must save and penny-pinch their whole lives to own." She adjusted the veil slightly forward again, making a dissatisfied clicking sound between her teeth. "We need a bare face and a pretty one to let the blessed king have a look at her. Why else would he have summoned us to take a meal in the great hall, with him just arrived, travel stained and road weary, from the south?"

Lady Drucilla quickly stepped back, mouth pursed, to assess what she'd done. The knights stared at Edain admiringly.

The gown chosen for the summons to a meal in the castle feast hall in King Henry's presence was blue-gray velvet with bodice and sleeves embroidered in silver thread. The velvet was heavy and serviceable for all its dazzle, as it protected against Beeston Castle's bone-chilling drafts. Even better, it had a recent, stylish cut, unlike some of the others.

The warden's wife had decided the gown was French-made, that it may have belonged to one of King Henry's past mistresses. A shorter woman than Edain: they'd had to add a border of silver gray satin to make it long enough to wear.

Now she stood still before their scrutiny wearing a circlet studded with silverish beryls to hold the transparent veil in place; Lady Drucilla had decided against the wimple that drew a fold under her chin to frame her face. Instead Edain's own burnished gold hair spilled out from under the veil and covered her shoulders and arms. By contrast, the color of the veil seemed to make her eyes even more glowingly green.

The knights stared in silence.

"She's beautiful as the stars," the little squire said in a squeaky voice.

The other two turned on him, cuffing him for speaking out so boldly. They gave the boy a torch and thrust him out into the bailey to lead the way. Then they held open the tower doors.

The grassy sward was encompassed by the five towers of Beeston Castle, the keep, and the curtain walls. The sun was setting but the bailey was packed with nobles, government ministers and clerks, and the lord commanders and staffs of the various English armies that had come to meet King Henry for war on Scotland: the earls of Hereford, Leicester, Chester, and York, even High Bigod, Henry's sometime supporter, the Earl of Norfolk.

Not every person of importance could crowd into Beeston's vast banqueting hall. Tables had been set up with their own awning outside in the ward where local nobles, foreign ministers, and high-to-middling clergy celebrated the king's arrival. Roasting fires blazed in pits where whole oxen and sheep were cooked. Wagons trundled between the castle and out into the surrounding fields where most of the fighting men of the armies were camped, bringing bread and meat, and barrels of good Chester ale.

"Inside, we go inside," Lady Drucilla shouted into Edain's ear. The castle knights and the towheaded squire dropped back at the banquet hall door. A word from Lady Drucilla to the ushers allowed them to press on into the din of the hall.

Edain kept her head down, in spite of warning jabs from the other woman's elbow. The aisles were full of milling people and the trestle tables were full, and she could feel the stares. Even, it seemed to her, hear the whispers over the crowd's roar. Lady Drucilla propelled her off to the left of the hall, under the eaves to a corner reserved for wellborn widows and other pensioners.

The women all knew the warden's wife.

"Well, we've missed you, milady Drucilla," declared a woman in a black morning gown with a white wimple and coif like a nun. "Shut up in East Tower all winter mending clothes, I'd think you'd be sick of it by now." Her sharp eyes took in Edain as she took her seat on the bench beside her and accepted a bowl of porridge. "Is that blue dress one you were making?"

Lady Drucilla patted Edain's hand for all to see. "Have a care for a respectable work, my dame, sewing was what we were doing. The girl's our blessed King Henry's ward, a fine, convent-raised maid. I tell you, I've grown as fond of her as if she was my own daughter."

"Sewing's not what she'll be doing after this day," someone said under her breath.

The first woman lifted her voice. "I'd be fond of her as a daughter, too, if my pockets was full of the king's silver."

A few voices shushed her. "Ladies, peace." This was a stout woman at the end of the table. "Let us not fail to give thanks for our blessed king and his generous bounty."

"Where's the oatcakes?" a voice muttered. "Porridge and fish—we were promised oatcakes, too."

The widows, all eyes still on Edain, said a desultory prayer for the king's health. The conversation turned to other topics. When most of the diners around them had finished the second round of food they settled down to some heavy drinking. The king and his party arrived.

King Henry and his nobles had just come from war council by their looks. Many of the lord commanders with their phalanxes of knight bodyguards had shed their weapons and mail, but still wore their padded, sweat-stained gambesons.

King Henry was obviously hungry as he hurried down the middle aisle of the feast hall, outstripping his ministers and generals in his mud-caked boots, his crimson satin jacket open in front to show a stained undershirt.

Not a few of his subjects had heard the tales of Henry Plantagenet's indifference to fine clothes and grooming. His father, the Count of Anjou, had been a man of singular beauty. But his son, a stocky man of medium height with his ginger hair grown thin and a half stubble on his jaws, looked like the most disreputable soldier in his armies.

Yet he was still a king. There was no doubt of that.

Edain leaned forward to see the sovereign pass. His bulging gray blue eyes singled out familiar faces among the tables, and he shouted out greetings. In spite of his unkempt appearance the king was full of a fierce, demanding energy; some called him the greatest king in the western world. He made a fine, loyal friend and witty companion; intellectuals, scholars, and poets admired him. But there were those who well knew that he was also capable of the sort of vile treachery that had alienated his own sons, truly inhuman cruelty, and rages that dropped him to the floor to froth at the mouth and howl like an animal.

Edain saw him turn his head to look across the

crowd to the widow's table. A lightning glance; it was easy to miss.

In the next moment she told herself King Henry couldn't single out a woman he'd never seen in a crowd of so many people. But she felt a slight stinging of the skin, as though he had touched her. She pulled back at once to put Lady Drucilla in between.

When she could bring herself to lift her head again she looked to the front of the packed hall and saw the nobles gathered around the high table. The banners of Angevin leopards were there, the king's own. Hereford's boar. Then the green and white gonfalons of Morlaix.

A group of England's magnates, some with their ladies, had gone up to the high table to gather around Henry. Hereford was already there with Gilbert Foliot, the bishop of London and one of the king's main advisors, and King Henry's other good friend, Robert Beaumont, Earl of Leicester.

To one side, talking with the bishop of York, the tall Earl of Morlaix stood out in a green padded knight's short coat and telltale shock of dark red hair. What made Edain lean forward, clutching the edge of the table, was the sight of another tall figure standing behind the Earl of Morlaix.

His hair was newly cropped short and bowl-shaped in the Norman style. He, too, had just arrived from the north and had not had time to change. He had shed his mail, but his green short coat was not only sweat-soaked like his father's but slightly ravelled with wear. He looked weary, his face tight with fatigue. The wide, reckless mouth was now a somber slash.

She wanted to put her fingers lightly against that mouth, remembering its kisses, and caress it. Then she wanted to cover it with her own.

"Come," Lady Drucilla was saying loudly. "Pay attention, girl, don't you hear me? Here's the ushers and Sir Neville of the king's guard come to see that we move!"

She could not tear her eyes away from Magnus. Did he know she was there in Beeston Castle? Had they kept that a secret from him since they were parted? Or had he not cared enough to make inquiry as to what had become of her?

She tortured herself with that thought while people pulled at her, urging her to get up.

Magnus, Edain tried to tell him. Through the hot, smoky air of the feast hall she tried to call to him. *Magnus, I want you, I need you.*

Two of the widows and Lady Drucilla virtually dragged her up from the bench.

"Girl, what ails you?" the warden's wife hissed in her ear. "Have you taken a spell? Suddenly gone deaf? Do you not hear me saying we're to go up front now and be seated with Sir Henry Bellefleur and all his kin?"

Edain looked around, her mind turning slowly. The castellan would be far up front in the hall with the other nobles.

"I can't sit up there," she said. She would be right under the eyes of the king. Magnus and his father would see her.

No one paid attention to her protests. The king's knights pushed a way through the crowd. Cooks and servers and milling guests stood back for them to pass. The noise died a little. Stares followed them.

"Now, demoiselle." The king's knight made a courtly flourish with one hand. The castellan and his family, looking more than a little flustered, stood up at their table and made room for Edain and Lady Drucilla.

Edain hardly heard the warden's wife speaking. The castellan's half-grown boy, a new-made squire, stared openly at her. Sir Henry, with a quick look at his wife, said something about rare beauty always being welcome at his table. The lady Enid stared down at her plate, her face pale.

Edain saw that the castellan and his family had not expected they would be called on to share their board with what appeared to be the king's new leman. A Benedictine abbot from Wales sat next to the castellan's wife and began to talk animatedly, only pausing now and then to look down at her.

Edain could not tell from his expression what the abbot thought. As his eyes roamed over her she thought he merely looked curious.

A server brought Edain bread and a tin plate. In front of the high table a space was cleared for a harper, a Welsh boy who sang in that language as well as English and Norman French.

Sir Henry's end of the table was served roast hare and a haunch of venison by nervous kitchen knaves anxious to please their immediate overlord, the castellan.

Edain took out her knife and looked down at the piece of meat on her plate, thinking of the widows' table and their porridge. When she lifted her head she saw the harper in his space before the high table, his foot on a stool to brace his Welsh harp, and behind him all the nobles surrounded by their pages, squires, and servers.

Niall fitzJulien, the Earl of Morlaix, was far down to the right talking to the bishop of London. To his left a brightly painted woman hung onto the arm of the Earl of Leicester; it was hard to tell if she were the earl's wife or his leman.

Edain's gaze stopped at the middle of the table with a shock. King Henry's bulging blue gaze was on her, staring fixedly, not listening to Robert Beaumont.

The king knew she was there. He'd had her moved up closer where he could see her. She felt a little ripple of dread down her backbone.

Edain swallowed, and looked around. But the one she sought, Magnus fitzJulien, was nowhere to be seen.

Magnus had gone through the back of the hall and out into the ward to meet his next oldest brother, Robert, whom the king was expected to knight this visit, and Magnus's squire, Lorenz d'Arbanville. He had not expected to find his younger brother, Richard, waiting, too, and his sister, Alweyn. Robert kept his distance, but Alweyn and Richard threw their arms around him with cries of joy at seeing him whole and unscathed.

"There are too many of us," Magnus said gruffly. Robert had already told him where they were going to take him, and why. "All of us cannot fit into one dames' gathering like this. Where's Mother?"

"She's already there with the countess." Alweyn hung on his arm, looking up at him with shining eyes. "Don't worry, we'll fit, there are only five of us. Besides, the Herefords number more than we do if you count the smallest ones. The Beaumont girls may be there since they admire you so," she added with a sly look.

Richard burst into a ten-year-old's raucous laughter. Magnus saw his brother Robert did not smile.

As they pushed him toward the Beeston keep, exclaiming over the poor condition of his clothes and vowing that he would disgrace them, Magnus hoped the Herefords had not brought their whole family.

While England's magnates feasted in the great hall with the king, noble wives frequently retired to castle solars to dine and gossip and listen to minstrels. Having been subjected to these gatherings with his mother as a small child, Magnus well remembered they could be excessively nerve-racking.

"Have you seen her before?" Richard skipped a few steps as they straggled between the ward's tethered horses, soldiers, and sweating cooks.

"Um, yes, as a child." Truth to tell, he'd racked his brains and he could not remember which of the Hereford girls this Freudegund, his intended betrothed, was. Now he had Alweyn and Richard and a noticeably sulky-looking Robert dragging him to a meeting he would just as soon have avoided. He had just come from the borderland and was dirty and bathless, and needed clean clothes.

Moreover, he had promised himself time to inquire about Edain. He was not going to leave Chester until he found out what had become of her.

In a very crowded solar at the top of the main keep of Beeston Castle he found the countesses of Hereford and Winchester and their families, and his mother the Countess of Morlaix and several noble ladies he did not know.

And an army of children, Magnus noted, looking around, whose bedtime had obviously long passed.

His mother rose from her seat with a scream and flung herself on him. The smaller children, not knowing what it was all about, began to scream, too. In a trice, the whole place was wailing.

It was several minutes before Magnus could get his mother calmed enough to speak to her and show her that he had not been half killed by the Scots. Then he had to show his youngest brothers and the Winchester and Hereford boys the week-old scratch on his wrist a Scots clansman had dealt him in a skirmish. The children were so impressed Magnus was embarrassed.

Once that display was over, he did his courtly duty to the other noble ladies with a bow and flourishes, and inquiries as to their health and the welfare of their families. They just as politely asked about his battles. Magnus made suitable answers and said God favored their holy cause, while the little girls ogled him. He was glad when Alweyn dragged him by the hand to meet a tall young girl who'd been standing quietly in a corner.

Freudegund, his betrothed, Magnus realized.

He could have kicked himself for not remembering sooner that she was the fourth or fifth daughter of that very powerful magnate and great friend of King Henry, the Earl of Winchester.

For some reason his brother Robert came right in between; he had to push him out of the way to even speak to the girl.

Like most maids of fourteen she was shy, or pretended to be. Freudegund was pretty enough, if no great talker.

She did ask a few polite questions about the king's war with the Scots. Had he heard them speak their strange, barbaric tongue? Magnus told her that he had, but that the border knights generally spoke English, or Norman French. Magnus noted that her eyes were gray and her hair was straight, shining gold-brown, worn without a coif in the style of unmarried girls. She looked very young, although he had seen brides even younger. Somewhat surprisingly he found he did not even want to try to picture what she would look like with her clothes off.

He could only frown at her.

Jesu, he would have to start thinking like that when he married her! Bedding this brown-haired maid was a part of it, if they hoped to have children. That was the whole meaning of betrothal and marriage, wasn't it?

He noticed that she was studying him with a curious expression. "Sir Knight," Freudegund said, "how fare you? Do your wounds plague you? Are you weary or distressed in any way from your long travels?"

Robert was staring, too. Magnus drew himself up with an effort. "Nay, not distressed," he muttered, "but I confess I am weary, demoiselle."

She laid a small hand on his arm. "Come sit beside

me, and your brother Robert will fetch you some wine."

Brother Robert was looking at the moment as though there would be a large dose of poison in any wine he fetched. Freudegund shooed a brace of toddlers out of a window seat and they sat down. She held onto his hand. Robert hung about, looking murderous, until she reminded him of the wine.

A circle of little boys had gathered at Magnus's knees, wanting to know if he would unsheath his great sword and let them look at it. Freudegund sat quite close, her finger gently stroking the scab on his wrist.

Magnus watched his brother make his way across the room carrying the wine cups. Betrothal was intended to be as binding as marriage. He had an idea his mother preferred they be sworn while he was there, in Chester. Things happened quickly in wartime.

He could not shake off a sinking feeling. He did not know if he had the stomach to be promised to one maid while his heart belonged to another. Not only that, if he married Freudegund it was plain his brother Robert would hate him forever.

Magnus took the cup of wine from Robert's slightly trembling hand. Robert was seventeen and already almost as tall as he; King Henry would make him a knight within the week. Magnus took a deep drink of the wine. Unless he did something, he would be betrothed by then.

After the bell for matins at midnight, the feast hall gradually emptied. The nobles retired to apartments in Beeston's towers with their families, or to tents in their encampments in the surrounding fields. The process of cleaning up and cooking for the next day began. Empty provision wagons rolled out of the bailey and through the castle gates and down the hill to the city. Somewhere outside in the armies' encampments, horns blew.

Edain stood at the tower window listening and watching. The night was moonless and dark but the bailey was bright with torches for the horse grooms and sweepers and the night guard going on duty at the portal gate and on the walls. The feast hall would never sleep while the king was there: sounds of the kitchen boys' voices echoed across the still-crowded ward.

There were other sounds, too, that came and went in the tower, as now other guests were billeted there. But the footsteps never reached as far as the last landing, where Edain and Lady Drucilla were. That is, except for a very late, very heavy tread on the stairs.

Long before Lady Drucilla heard and got up from her pallet, Edain was at the door, waiting for the night guard to let the visitors in.

A heavyset man with broad shoulders, slightly drunk and carrying a chessboard under one arm, staggered in. Behind him, was the Templar, Asgard de la Guerche.

"Demoiselle, at last we meet," the King of England, Henry Plantagenet, said.

Nineteen

"Table," the king said, and gestured.

Asgard de la Guerche obediently jumped forward and swept a candlestick and a bowl from the one table in the room. He looked around for a place, then laid the things on the top of the cupboard.

Edain watched the Templar with an expression of joy and amazement. Asgard was there, in that very room! She'd not seen him for months except from afar, when she watched him cross the ward from her window. Now, so close, he looked strong, fully recovered from his wound. He was as she remembered him in mail and white surcoat with red cross, tall, angelically handsome.

She would have given anything at that moment to be able to speak to him, to find out what had happened to him here since they'd arrived. And indeed, why he was still there. But Edain knew she did not dare question him in the presence of King Henry.

Besides, she thought, biting her lip, she did not know what dangers might still surround them. Or even how freely they could speak if they had the chance.

"Hmm," the king said, clearing his throat.

She turned to see that King Henry had put the

chessboard and pieces on the table. Now he stood with his hands at his belt, his weight rocked back on his heels, surveying her.

"Gold," he murmured, his prominent eyes gleaming. "Hair and skin both, quite remarkable. And the emerald eyes. God's truth, de la Guerche, I admit I didn't believe it when they told me." His look traveled over her. "At least they were right when they said she was surpassing beautiful."

There was something in that look that chilled her. Before it, Edain dropped to her knees, the skirt of the court gown spreading out like a blue flower. Lady Drucilla had taken down her hair and brushed it a hundred strokes. She knew it was like a sheath of gold, catching the light of the candles.

The king couldn't seem to take his eyes from it. "De la Guerche tells me you are from Ireland," he said.

"No, my lord." She shot the Templar a startled look from under her lashes. Why would Asgard tell the king that? Unless he'd wanted to repeat the Culdee monk's fanciful stories. "I am an orphan, sire, left in the turnstile of the convent of the Blessed Limb of Saint Sulpice. The nuns will tell I only speak God's holy truth. I have no knowledge at all of parents or family."

While she was talking the king walked in a circle around her, looking her over. He paused to nod and say, "By the cross, girl, whatever the country you come from it must be some fairy abode as de la Guerche maintains. No earthly land could produce such perfection of face and form."

He came to stand in front of her. "Do you know,

demoiselle, that the Templars are full of profound theories concerning you? Theories that they greatly desire England's archbishops not even to suspect, much less discover? The Poor Knights of the Temple of Jerusalem are sore disappointed to have you slip from their loving custody." He smiled. "I see you remember."

Edain could feel the Templar's eyes on her. She kept her head bowed.

"Asgard tells me," the king went on, "that the Edinburgh commander wished to send you to their Grand Master in France, so that you might demonstrate your dazzling gifts for their learned scrutiny. But that at the last moment, observing his sworn vows to bring you to me, de la Guerche helped you escape."

Edain did not dare look at Asgard. *He had helped her escape?* When she still said nothing King Henry went to the table and sat down.

He pulled the chessboard to him and opened the box that held the pieces. "Know that I am much gratified," he went on in his high-pitched voice, "that de la Guerche honored the task that I gave him in London at Saint Martin's feast. Which was to find you, and bring you to me."

Edain remained kneeling, as the king had not given her permission to do otherwise, her face so stiff that the muscles in her cheeks hurt.

Confusion had rendered her dumb. But her thoughts were racing. Could Asgard have told King Henry that he had rescued her from the Templars in Edinburgh? If so, how had he managed to explain Magnus, who had really been responsible for it, and their escape with the band of gypsies?

She could not lift her head to look at him. She did not believe the Templar could tell such a twisted tale. After all, it was Magnus's father, the Earl of Morlaix, who had finally found them!

There was some reason for his pretense, she told herself. She could not expose him now. After all, he was the man whose intimate needs she had tended all those long weeks. Holy Mother in heaven, they could not help but be friends, when she had nursed him through a terrible fever when all thought he was dying!

Perhaps if King Henry knew that Asgard had had little to do with her rescue the king would be angry and punish him. She did not want to see that happen. King Henry's rages were famous.

On the other hand, she could not forget Magnus's words. That the Templar had come to Loch Etive with King William's money to ransom her, but when it had been paid he'd taken her not to William, but to the Templars.

She lifted her eyes. Asgard de la Guerche was standing at attention before his liege lord in sword and mail but without his helm, so that his uncovered head shone brightly. With that beautiful face, it would be hard to believe the Templar anything less than the very spirit of knightly honor.

The king looked around and saw her. "What are you doing, girl? Get up from the floor." He motioned for Asgard to bring a stool. Lady Drucilla appeared out of the shadows with cups and an ewer of wine. The king said something to her in a low voice. The warden's wife made a deep curtsy, then backed from the room. They heard her say something to the guard knight at the door, then the sound of her footsteps going down the stairs.

Edain sat down at the table facing the king, the chessboard between them. Henry lifted his gold and silver cup and drank. His hand was not steady. Wine spilled down the corners of his mouth and dripped from the base of the cup. He wiped his lips with the back of his hand, then picked up the chess pieces made of ivory and ebony wood and put them into place. Only the slow care with which he set the pieces down in each square showed how much the king had had to drink.

He pushed the ivory pieces to Edain's side of the board and kept the ebony for himself.

She stared down at them. All she could think was it was late, almost early morning; except for the lackeys and kitchen help moving about in the bailey the castle around them was dark and quiet, the nobles and soldiers and guests sleeping off the king's lavish welcoming feast.

Now that King Henry was finally there, in Chester, in this very tower room, Edain had expected to face the same questions the Templars had put to her, and demands to foretell the future, to do magic. Instead, the king had come to the tower room and seemed to want to make her think he desired to play chess.

Dear God, perhaps he *did!* Kings could do as they pleased. They satisfied every whim whether it made sense or not.

She watched as the broad, strong hand with freckles and red hairs picked up a rook and moved it forward one place.

King Henry said over his shoulder, "De la Guerche, there was an anchorite from Lindesfarne who could call the moves in a game of chess. It was very interesting. I had the old man brought to me, telling him that I was interested in the unknown constellations of God's natural law and wished to explore them, and so we played many a night together. Naturally, I told the ecclesiasticals nothing, fearing their wrath if they should hear of their sovereign and an unwashed hermit from the northern islands engaged in such a heretical pastime. That is, to see if one could foretell the moves of a simple amusement. The anchorite and I played chess for several months, but the old man's mind became dull after a while and he could do nothing. Regretfully, I had to send him away."

He picked up Edain's ivory queen, studied it, then handed it to her.

The Templar said, "And could he foretell, sire, what chess moves you could make before you made them?"

"Ah, yes." The king did not look up. "However, although his powers were entertaining, the old man could do little else. They were limited, it would seem, to chess. My squire, young de Clare, said he was a trickster. That he had watched the old man switch the pieces."

Asgard frowned. "Which did you believe, sire?"

"I've already told you." Henry held up his cup and the Templar hurried to fill it with wine. "Aristotle, the Greeks and Egyptians, especially the Zoroastrians, have all explored natural magic, but the Celts we have here with us in Britain's native climes seem to know nothing of any of it. As a people they appear extraordinarily backward, as they have no alchemy, no astrology, little of what is called witchcraft. What they do have, they ascribe to a marvelous fairy race from the mists of history, or something called the little people, or enchanted birds and the *sidhe*—those who live in the stone circles and ancient graves and are said to be the descendants of an Irish race of magicians. By and large, though, there is no body of learning. It's disappointing. I have been reading Hermes Trismegistos, and I had hoped for some proof of the Hermetic tradition, at least in a simple form of transformation. But with these wild tribes there is nothing."

King Henry put his elbows on the table and looked at Edain from under his brows. "From what de la Guerche says you are not a common roadside shell-switcher and gypsy fortune-teller, are you, my dear?"

Edain looked from the king to the Templar and back again. So Asgard had told him that, too.

It was very quiet in the tower room; in the bailey, someone drove a wagon across the cobblestones. Edain looked down at the board. "Sire," she said in a clear voice, "you must forgive me but I do not know how to play chess."

He did not seem to hear her. He looked down at the black-and-white chessboard, the pieces in place.

"I have moved a rook," the King of England said, pointing to the ebony piece. "Now the rules of the game are that *you* must move something."

Edain still held the ivory queen that he had given her. As he finished speaking there was a curious sensation, faint as a bee's buzzing, that responded somewhere in her head.

She looked down at the chess piece, not quite sure what had happened. The king leaned forward, eyes intent.

Uncertainly, she put the queen in its place on the back row near the king. It felt warm, as though it had been near the fire.

Suddenly she was tired. She felt dull with fatigue. Her mind did not want to apply itself to the chess game but wandered off, thinking of the feast hall and the widows at their table, and the court gowns she and Lady Drucilla had mended so that she would have elegant clothes when King Henry came.

She knew it would be useless at this late hour to protest that the dawn was fast approaching and that she did not have the strength to learn to play chess. With the king's eyes on her she picked up a white rook and moved it forward a space. He said nothing. She watched his hand hover over the board, select another rook, and move it. Unable to think of anything else, she did the same. The king moved a knight and captured her piece.

She stared down at the board in dismay, her ears ringing. She was sitting there because she did not know what else to do. But she could not imagine that the king saw any entertainment in this, watching an untutored girl like herself fumble with his chess pieces.

He was talking again to Asgard, who bent over his shoulder. Edain's eyelids drooped. It was an effort to see. She tried not to yawn.

"There are other openings," the king said as he

moved another chess piece, a bishop, into play. "Especially if one intends to use the Saracen defense."

Several of the candles had burned down and gone out. Asgard did not go to replace them. The king got up and picked up the poker and stirred the fire, then put a small log on it. The light flared, then grew dim again. When he sat back down he looked at the board, frowning.

"What have you been doing?" he asked.

Edain hardly heard him. When he moved his bishop, her hand moved her ivory knight and captured it, and a pawn.

The king sat back in his chair. After some thought he moved his knight to hers.

Edain put her head in her hand. Her skull felt heavy, as though she could not hold it up. She watched as the chess pieces moved, it seemed, almost by themselves.

It really was a battlefield, she saw, the armies arrayed against each other. There were the rooks, the common soldiers, always being captured and killed. And the dashing knights, the swooping bishops, the towers protecting the king with his queen.

She saw with a shock that the thing one had to remember was that in this game it was the queen, not the king, who was all-powerful.

Because the king, for all his temper and pride, would give in and carry a cross after all, just as the church wanted, as a true penitent for the murder of his once good friend, Thomas à Becket, whom he had made archbishop of Canterbury.

As though from a great distance she saw a tiny King Henry walking across the black-and-white squares barefoot and in sackcloth, just as the priests had commanded. When he got to the end of the board that troublesome presence, the Lion of Scotland, came up, tail twitching. But at the last moment it lay down tamely at Henry Plantagenet's feet.

"You see how she is playing?" a voice said softly. It, too, seemed to come from faraway.

"Demoiselle—" she heard the Templar begin.

The other voice interrupted him.

"God's wounds," the king said, "can't you see her face? If you must say anything to her, ask her to prophesy!"

Armies raged across the black-and-white board as Edain stared down at them. The queen came out of the tower with a proud, bitter face and waved her ivory arms. The four knights, two black and two white, rode up to stand in a ring around her.

The ringing in her ears grew louder.

Dear God in heaven, King Henry would never have peace! The young king, whom he had crowned himself, gave him no quarter in France. Neither did his second son and young Henry's ally, Geoffrey. As for the next son, Richard the Lion was his mother's son, and she was the only woman Richard would ever love. Sulky-faced Prince John, the youngest, was the one, alas, who would seize the throne after them all.

The king had been watching her. He said softly, "What do you see, demoiselle?"

She tried to clear her thoughts enough to speak. "The bear cubs will drag down the old bear and his golden crown, even though he loves them. A king's pride is put aside; forgiveness comes from the Pope. And forgiveness, too, from the one who is dead."

For a long moment Henry sat with indrawn breath, his face made ruddier by the light of the fire. Then he seemed to shudder.

"Ah, Thomas," he groaned, "will I never rid myself of the rebellious torments of my ungrateful brats, or your damnable ghost? Christ's wounds—I dare not say which I desire more!"

He abruptly reached across the board for her hand and turned it over.

Edain held the ivory knight tight in her fist: King Henry had to pry open her thumb to see it. Blood covered the little figure.

As they both watched, a red stream dripped down her palm and puddled on the black-and-white squares of the chessboard.

Henry Plantagenet lifted his eyes to her. His look was clear gray blue, suddenly sober.

"Come, demoiselle," the king rasped, "you have come all this way to tell me what no one else will utter. When will you say it?"

Still, she was very afraid. She could not meet his eyes. The armies still warred below them on the chessboard, unheeding. But they would soon come to a stop. The ivory knight lay alone in her palm, oozing mysterious red blood.

"The young king, Prince Henry," Edain said, "is dead."

Twenty

"Oh, what a shame not to take any of your beautiful gowns that we worked on," the warden's wife cried. "Some of the prettiest gowns in England, all to be left here with no one to wear them or do them justice, girl, the way that you would!"

She watched the two tower knights carry a small basket of Edain's belongings down the stairs to the soldiers waiting below, along with her own gifts of food and wine for the journey, and a warm blanket and a sheepskin saddle covering.

Lady Drucilla held her hands clasped before her in open distress. "Nothing—alas, nothing's to go, poor child," she wailed. " 'She'll need nothing fancy where she's going,' was all the castellan would tell me!"

Edain knew. The whole castle had heard the king's raging. There were reports he'd had one of his furious attacks where he'd been known to roll about on the floor and chew at the rushes.

King Henry had not believed what she said about his oldest son, Prince Henry. He'd thrown the bloody chess piece across the room, denouncing everything as the vilest of flummery. He'd been tricked by the

Templars, he'd roared. And it was a sorry mistake to have come to her tower room and listen to drivel.

That was a night and a day ago. And no longer important. For the courier had arrived from France with the news that the Young King, Prince Henry, who was to have ruled jointly with his father but instead fought him in open rebellion, had indeed died of dysentery.

Poison, some whispered. The rumor circulated without much conviction. In France the countryside rose up in convulsions of sorrow. The cities of Le Mans and Rouen that had supported Henry fitzHenry against his father had almost gone to war for custody of his beloved body. And in Queen Eleanor's hereditary lands of Aquitaine, he was already being immortalized in a song, "Lament for a Young King," by the troubadour Bertran de Born. Locked in her castle prison, no one had heard from Queen Eleanor.

For days the city of Chester and Beeston Castle were filled with weeping people. Those about the king reported that he was drunk and inconsolable, felled by grief. For all their quarreling and young Henry's treachery, the king had loved his son. Henry's advisors and close friends, Robert Beaumont the Earl of Leicester, and Gilbert Foliot the bishop of London, could not get him in sober enough condition to travel back to London. In the north, the war was uncertain; King William of Scotland had lost his ally in the young prince.

The castle boiled with rumor and speculation. The earls of Hereford and Norfolk moved their armies out of their encampments, hoping to attack Scotland while the news of young Henry's death was still fresh.

The roads were clogged. Regardless, the knights came from the king with orders to take the demoiselle Edain away at once.

The castellan had also come to her tower room to tell her that King Henry had decided not to burn her at the stake for witchcraft, nor even imprison her in the dungeon of Beeston Castle. Out of respect for her churchly connections Edain was to be exiled to her old convent, St. Sulpice. To go as a pauper, as she'd begun, with nothing but the clothes on her back.

The knights sent to take her had given her only minutes to prepare for the journey; no amount of pleading could buy any time. The few things Edain could claim, the fur cloak, a comb and a looking glass, some underclothes, were bundled together and thrown into baskets. The warden's wife stumbled about wringing her hands, the floor strewn with the beautiful gowns they had sewn.

Edain took Lady Drucilla by the arm and drew her to one side. "I need a message carried to Magnus fitzJulien. Will you do this for me? I know he is here, at Castle Beeston, I saw him at the king's welcoming feast. Ah, Lady Drucilla, will you not go to him," she pleaded, "and tell him that I am returning to the convent by order of King Henry? If I could only speak to him a moment it would ease my heart!"

The other woman gave her an astonished look. "Morlaix's young son? Is he not just betrothed to Earl Leicester's girl?"

Edain recoiled. She had not heard that; her plea had just come bursting out without thinking. Magnus was *betrothed?*

"Ah, girl." At the sight of Edain's face the warden's wife threw her arms around her neck. "Don't look like that! It's that fond of you I've become, I can't bear to see you so cast down." She drew back and dabbed at her eyes. "Now try to look on the bright side of things, dearling. At least you have your life, and they've not burned you at the stake."

A knight stood at the door, beckoning them.

Edain picked up her cloak. Magnus was betrothed! Not once had he come to her, tried to find out where she was being held. Still numb, she managed to whisper, "Yes, that is true. At least I have my life."

She came down the tower steps behind Lady Drucilla. A cold drizzle was falling. With the armies on the move it would take all day to make their way out of the city and to the roads going north.

At the bottom of the stairs was her escort, two mounted knights of King Henry's royal guard and the towheaded squire. Her heart leaped at the sight of another horseman in a dark cloak that, she knew, covered a familiar white surcoat emblazoned with a red cross.

"Sir Asgard!" As he dismounted, Edain ran the few steps toward him.

She seized him by the hand. His fingers were cold. "How fare you?" she cried. She wanted to hug him. "I have not seen you since the king—since that night—" She let her voice trail away.

What had happened was too terrible to put into words, even with Asgard, who had been there. She wondered if he knew she had no way of knowing what she would say. Or what the consequences would be. Edain had wished a hundred times since that night that the king had not come to her. Now people in the castle gossiped that King Henry was destroyed, that he would not move from his bed.

The Templar led her toward the palfrey. He said in a low voice, "I have good news. The king is now partly recovered, and will leave for London shortly. I am told by the lord Leicester, who attends him, that King Henry holds no ill will for you. He desires only that you be returned at once to the convent, where you will be safely protected."

And where he will never set eyes on you again. He didn't have to say it.

Looking up at his light-filled blue eyes, she knew his words meant she would remain at the convent forever. "Sir Asgard, are you to escort me there?"

For a brief moment she thought she saw something like a smile hover about his lips. "Yes, demoiselle," was all he said.

She sighed, thankful at least for that. As Lady Drucilla would remind her, she was not being stoned as she left Beeston Castle. Nor was she being condemned as a witch.

The Templar made a basket of his hands and boosted her onto the back of the little horse. She looked down at him, seeing him as handsome as ever.

Magnus, her rebellious heart suddenly cried.

How could she leave him with only that last sight of him to remember, at the high table in the feast hall? And thinking at the same time how much distance there was between them, a great noble's son and an orphan girl?

With a terrible effort, Edain fought down the yearning that tore at her. At least, she told herself as she turned the palfrey's head to follow Asgard's destrier, she had someone she trusted, a friend to take her back to St. Sulpice.

She turned in the saddle to wave at Lady Drucilla, who stood in front of the doorway to the tower, once more in tears.

By late afternoon the rain had turned the roads out of Chester into deep mud. The earls' armies moved slowly, and there was no escape; the few inns along the way were filled to overflowing. Asgard led the little party to the rear of the Earl of Norfolk's army, behind a troop of knights from the fen country of east England.

The talk among the knights of the Earl of Norfolk's column was somber. Prince Henry had been popular in England as well as France, and his death cast a pall. There was speculation about the borderland war, and whether William the Lion would continue fighting now that the Young King was dead and King Henry's enemies, the rebellious English barons, were subdued.

Edain guided her palfrey behind Asgard and the king's two knights to listen.

"Prince Geoffrey's the next for the throne," someone said. "Thanks to the old mare, the queen, there's still enough princelings to go around. And if aught should happen to Geoffrey there's the next, young Richard, and after him little John that they call Lackland."

"Nay, none can match Prince Henry," another voice put in. "Geoffrey stood in his brother's shadow, he did. It's like the troubadours say, we lost a good king in Henry, he had his mother's beauty and his father's crafty head."

Asgard pulled his horse back to ride with Edain. "How do you fare?" he wanted to know.

She lifted her hood to look at him. The misty rain beaded his face and made his mail glisten. He knew she'd been listening to the other knights.

In all truth she was hungry and wanted to ask when they would stop. And if he thought they could find an inn to stay the night. They had been traveling for hours and were all, down to the king's knights and the fat little squire bringing up the rear, cold and wet. But Edain did not want to seem to complain; their condition was no better nor worse than the plodding armies around them.

"I fare well enough, Sir Asgard," she said.

For a moment she saw a gleam of light strike his brilliant blue eyes. Then he nodded, and kicked his horse forward again to join the others.

A sigh escaped her.

She was fortunate to have Asgard escort her to St. Sulpice. She knew he would not let her come to harm. After all, he had come to her door in the Templar's commandery that night to tell her that he would protect her. She had not forgotten it.

That afternoon along the Mersey road she was thankful again that King Henry had sent Asgard in command. Half a dozen knights trying to catch up with Norfolk's vanguard drew even with them. It was plain that they were straggling because of a prolonged stop in a wine shop somewhere. The youngest one was so drunk he could barely stay in the saddle.

"Ho, there, Templar," one of them called to Asgard. His eyes were on Edain. "You are a long way from the Holy Land, are you not?"

The road was narrow at that point, and led to the ford of a small stream. Edain and the king's party were surrounded by Norfolk's foot soldiers, most of them villeins newly recruited from north England, armed only with pikes and spears. They milled around on the banks of the brook, wanting to take off their footgear before crossing as most of them, being countrymen, knew the hardship of marching in wet boots.

Asgard made no answer to Norfolk's drunken knights. His handsome face impassive under his helm and noseguard, he guided his escort far to one side of the soldiers wading the stream. The other knights forced their horses through, shouting and splashing, and galloped up the bank on the far side.

"Hoi!" one of them shouted, making a grab for Asgard's reins. "We're talking to you, Templar! Is this the girl they talk about?"

Another seized the palfrey's bridle while the third reached for the hood of Edain's cloak and pulled it back. At the sight of her white face, the golden gleam of her hair spilling out, they whooped.

"Aye, it's her," one of them shouted. "The Templar's not so holy he's above doing a bit of pimping for old Henry!"

The leader spurred up his horse. "Where are you taking her?" he yelled. "We have silver. Give us an hour with her and—"

He never had time to finish his offer. Almost casually, Asgard swung his mailed fist outward and caught the man in the belly. The blow knocked him from his horse and he fell sprawling on the stream's grassy bank. His companions, too fuddled with drink to act quickly, reined in their horses as the first Norfolk knight staggered to his feet, cursing. One of the king's knights drew his sword and leaned from the saddle and promptly knocked him down again with the flat of it.

Asgard had gone after the other two. One he grabbed by the arm, and with his great strength hauled him out of the saddle and dumped him into the brook. His mailed fist, reinforced with steel studs across the knuckles, came down on the side of the other's helmet hard enough to stun him. The youth slumped across his horse's neck.

It was all over with quickly, even bloodlessly. The king's knight sheathed his sword. Asgard had never even drawn his.

An escort knight picked up Edain's reins and led the palfrey away from the stream. She had not cried out, she'd kept her wits about her, but now she could not stop shaking. The knights had offered silver for her. The words echoed in her head. Only an hour alone with her, all three of them. That's what the first one had said.

And they knew she had been in Chester, with the king. Rumor flew fast in the armies.

When they reached the road Asgard spurred his horse up to the palfrey. After leaning down to see her face, her shaking shoulders, he reached down with one arm and drew her out of the saddle and up in front of him.

Being on the destrier was like riding a mountain. For a moment she could not get her breath. Then she leaned back against him with a sigh. Even through the layers of white woolen tunic and mail she could feel the movements of the Templar's hard body.

Gradually, she stopped shaking.

They found shelter for the night north of Helsby with a farmer who asked a staggering sum just to sleep in the loft of the barn. There was not so much traffic now on the road to the river Mersey. William the Lion's forces were reported to be deep in English territory and the armies from Chester swung east to intercept them.

Edain was weary, unaccustomed to such long riding on the back of a horse. She was so stiff she could barely walk when Asgard helped her down from the destrier. The farmer's wife, eyeing Edain's fine cloak, offered to give her a pallet by the fire in the kitchen for the night, but she refused; she did not mind sleeping with the knights as long as Asgard was there. The king's men were French, Angevins, as were all Henry Plantagenet's most trusted guards, and kept to themselves. Edain only knew their names: Giscard and Denys. After they had eaten the farmer's wife's hot meal of soup and bread and cheese they made their beds. The white-haired squire burrowed into the straw in the loft, rolled into a ball and went to sleep at once.

The rain died after dark, and the wind came up, damp and warm and smelling of spring. Edain lay with her cloak wound around her, listening to the gale moan in the eaves. Not far from her, between the squire and the other knights, Asgard knelt for his evening prayers. The light in the loft was dim, as the farmer's wife would not let them have a candle. Edain could only make out the glimmer of the white surcoat and shadowy cross and Asgard's pale hair.

He stayed long at his prayers. Lying on her side, watching him, Edain wondered what Asgard de la Guerche found to pray about at such length, and so fervently. Even why such a handsome man had found contentment in a monk's life.

She would say contentment seemed a proper word. Surely not happiness; there was nothing much of joy in that perfect, chiseled face. But then she did not suppose monks, even the fighting ones, were noted for gaiety.

At last he stopped praying and got to his feet, bending because of the low rafters, and took off his heavy hauberk of mail and his helmet. He spread them out carefully along with his sword and belt in the straw. Then he lay down on his back, and pulled his blue cloak around him.

"Sir Asgard?" Edain spoke before he could close his eyes. He immediately turned his head toward her. When that blue gaze met hers she fell silent.

What did she have to say to him after all? she wondered. That she wanted to be his friend? She remembered all the days she had spent with him when he was wounded, changing his clothes, bathing him, bringing him the pot for his needs. Could she say that in spite of his perfect image as knight and Templar she sensed that he was very alone?

As she was alone now, too, Edain thought. She wanted to talk to someone now that she was going back to the convent, now that she would be cut off from the world again. Her life had changed so much. The king was exiling her because she had used magic to tell him of his son's death. But he had been kind in his own way. Even in the midst of his grief he had not used the word "witch." He had allowed her to live.

She said softly, "I—ah, think there are mice in the hay."

Asgard lifted his head and propped it on his arm, frowning. "Demoiselle, I will go to the farmer and ask for his cat. All farmers have cats."

"No—no, my thanks." She might have known he would try to do something like that. "It will be all right."

She lay back down again, disappointed. Talking to Asgard would not do, she needed Magnus. Where was he now?

He was betrothed, she told herself bitterly. She could see him passing the time talking to the girl, dancing with her. He had told her that he was a tourney knight and a poet. Perhaps he was writing poems that he would read to her seated in a castle garden somewhere. Perhaps he was in a tournament melee with other knights, showing his battle skills to her.

Even that would not keep him long from the border war, she thought somewhat meanly. With the Scots armies moving southward he would have to leave Chester with his father's army. Going east.

Away from her.

She turned her face aside. Asgard was still watching her, waiting for her to speak. Edain rolled all the way over on her side, and put her back to him. And put both hands over her face so that he could not hear her weeping.

North of Wigan there was less traffic on the roads and they were able to stay at an inn, a structure of two stories with a common room for gentry and another for villeins and drovers. Asgard paid for superior accommodations: several benches and blankets on the stone hearth before the fire.

There was also a common room for women upstairs with two large beds. Edain shared them with a miller's wife and two lady relatives of a local baron going to London. The closer they came to St. Sulpice convent, the more people had heard of her. The nuns had been distraught when Ivo de Brise had abruptly taken her away, and the news had spread far over the countryside.

The miller's wife, who was on her way to Chester with her husband and a wagonload of flour to sell to the armies, told Edain that she'd heard of the girl from the nunnery who had been at royal court at Beeston Castle and attracted the notice of the king himself. Both she and the two elderly ladies wanted to know not about Edain, but young Prince Henry's death, and what his father, the King of England, had done when he heard of it.

"Things have been different," one old dame declared, "since the king shut up the lady queen in her prison. Eleanor of Aquitaine kept a rein on Henry, some do say. She's sore missed. If King Henry had allowed the boy to rule with him as he promised, young Henry would have been at home here in England all these years, peaceable and happy, instead of warring in Normandy against his father."

The other elderly lady waited impatiently for her sister to finish. "Is it true," she piped, "what they say? That the young King was poisoned?"

Edain shook her head. She still could not speak of it. Her own part in it, when she had foretold the prince's death, rose up in her throat to choke her.

Seeing her face, the baron's aunts gave each other meaningful looks.

"And where do you go now?" one wanted to know. "Do you follow our blessed King Henry? It's said bad feeling against him in France will keep him from going there to bury his son. So instead he will come and do battle with the Scottish king."

Edain closed her eyes for a moment. Like everyone else, the old ladies supposed she had been one of King Henry's women.

She said, with an effort, "I am returning to the convent of the Sacred Limb of Saint Sulpice. Where I was, before I left, mistress of the girls' classes."

All three women looked over the velvet gown she was wearing, and the fur-lined cloak, and said nothing. But as Edain left the common room she heard one of them say, "A beautiful girl, but it's plain she didn't please him. I'd give a penny to know why the king's sending her back."

Twenty-one

In the smaller, quieter common room a kitchen boy was serving plates of smoked herring, bread and cheese and ale, to the two royal knights. The white-headed little squire was not about, and neither was Asgard.

Edain thought of sitting down with Giscard and Denys to share the evening meal, but since they were talking and did not look up, she walked on.

She opened the heavy wooden door and went out into the night. Around the back was the midden pile full of kitchen garbage where the knights stood to piss. Beyond that the wooden structure that housed the jakes. Which in this countryside was a rude trench one had to straddle. In the darkness, Edain had picked a spot under the trees.

The wind was colder but still smelled damply of earth and grass and spring. Edain stood under the bare branches of the inn's oak trees, watching the last of the purple light fade low in the sky and the pin-pricks of stars coming out overhead. She sensed, almost before she saw or heard anything, that someone approached.

"Don't cry out," the voice said.

"Magnus!" she breathed.

"It *is* you." His voice was close, sibilant, in the dusk. He put his arm around her quickly, his other hand pushing back her hood. "I was looking for some spark of light to see your hair." His fingers twined in it. "Jesu, girl, I have searched like a madman since the armies turned east, hoping that the Templar would make for an inn. Two days! I cannot believe I found you!"

"You always find me."

She turned into his damp cloak, her hands going around his body under it, feeling the scrape of his mail, the odor of male sweat and horses.

This time, Edain reminded herself, she had not used the power to call him because there was no need to. There had been an ending, of sorts, with the news of his betrothal in Chester. And anyway, she had not made up her mind what to tell him about all the reasons she must return to St. Sulpice.

Now he was not thinking of any of that. He was Magnus, towering over her, strong and impetuous and full of passion, wanting only what she could give him. He held her face between his cold, slightly trembling hands and lavished sweet kisses on her nose, her eyelids, her mouth, until she was breathless.

"God is my judge but you are sweet," he whispered. "Ah, Edain, you are my heart and my soul, beloved, how could I let you go without any farewell between us? Without any lovemaking to remember? I would die a thousand deaths. And how could you leave Chester," he said, raising his voice, "with no more word for me than what the fat woman, the warden's wife, brought? That you wanted me to know you were being returned to the convent? And nothing more?"

Edain clung to him, listening to him. Everything was wrong. She did not know what she had expected; she was filled with wild, delirious happiness that he was even there, holding her, kissing her. Only Magnus would find her in a countryside full of marching armies.

But he was telling her that he had ridden from Chester for a lovemaking that he could remember. Those very words. That he wanted to tumble her one last time.

She tried to push him away but he held her tightly, his hand in her hair, lifting the strands, rubbing them softly against his cheek while he murmured that they needed to retire somewhere they could be alone.

She hated the breathlessness, the quick rush of hot, searing desire that met his. Plainly he was betrothed. He was lost to her.

She pushed at him as he tried to unlace her gown. "Holy Jesus in heaven, would you take me here?" she hissed. "Here in the inn yard, under the trees?"

"No." He could barely stop, his hands caressing her breasts. "Come with me."

Edain held the front of her gaping gown as he pulled her toward the back of the inn and a row of storage sheds.

"Here, this one," he said, pushing her ahead. He used his foot to open the door.

Inside, sacks of flour were stacked almost to the ceiling, and there were barrels filled with cider from the smell. Magnus fumbled along a shelf, found a candle and tinderbox.

"What have you done?" Edain peered into the darkness. "They will not let us in here!"

He gave her his dazzling smile as the tinder caught. He lit the stub of the candle, put it back in its holder, and returned it to the shelf. Shadows danced around them.

He sat down on a flour sack and pulled her to stand between his knees. By candlelight the planes of his face were harsh. War had put fine lines at his eyes and the corners of that wide, beautiful mouth. "When I saw de la Guerche in the inn yard I knew you were here," he said huskily. "Do you know I have not slept a whole day and a night, riding down one horse to near to break it, and having to buy another in Wigan, searching for you?" He opened the front of her gown again and lowered his dark red head to nuzzle her breasts. "I paid the innkeeper some silver for the use of his storeroom," he said, his voice muffled. "Then I waited under the trees for you to come out."

Edain stared down at the back of his head. This was Magnus, as always the earl's son, arrogant, cocksure. By his very manner she knew the inn people had been loath to refuse him anything he wanted.

"And have you told your betrothed," she said softly, "that you've gone to search for me? To have one last lovemaking, as you say, before I put myself behind cloister gates again?"

He looked up, eyes smoky. "Edain, by the cross—"

She pushed him away. She pulled her arms out of the gown's sleeves and pushed it down to her waist, then stepped out of it. She began to untie the drawstring of her shift.

"I love you, but you are not worthy of it, Magnus fitzJulien." She lifted her chin. "I owe my life to you, twice, but you still think you are above a poor orphan girl, especially one some now call a witch. But from the beginning it is *you* who have not been worthy, and not the other way around!"

"Edain, dearling," he said in a strangled voice.

She stood naked before him, having kicked off her shoes, her body gleaming golden in the candle's light. She began to take down her hair. It fell from the loosened braids like a gilded shower. She shook her head, making it fly over her shoulders in a light-filled glitter.

He reached for her but she stepped away from his grasp. He scowled.

"Jesu, Edain, have some faith in me. You are my own true love, I would do nothing to hurt you." When she only stared at him he burst out, "God rot it, will you listen? These marriages are not made in heaven, but between fathers of great families. They are blood contracts, approved by the king. To have you I must defy not only my father but my sovereign, King Henry!"

He reached up to run his fingers through his hair in a despairing gesture, and found it cropped short. The look on his face almost made her laugh.

She pushed him back against the dusty sacks, working at the straps of his hauberk. He had said she was his beloved, his heart and his soul, but he had never said that he loved her. On top of that he had ridden two days, looking for her, for this "last lovemaking." She didn't know what to believe.

With an oath he abruptly sat up and hauled the heavy hauberk over his head and tossed it away on the sacks. The padded gambeson and the rest of his clothing he yanked off and they followed it.

Magnus grabbed for her and drew her down on top of him, their bare bodies pressed together. His hands cupped her bottom.

"What do you want of me, Edain?" he said hoarsely. His legs moved between hers, pressing them apart, and the erect rod of his flesh probed at the entrance of her sex. "God's wounds, I have climbed mountains and swum seas for you, and fed you and saved your life, and fought your damned tame Templar and won. I cannot prove myself more. Jesu, there are times when I think I can't live without you. That I must see you, listen to you, speak to you, just have you near. I swear to you I would love you with my body through all eternity if that were allowed a mortal man!"

His look and his voice were so impassioned she could not answer. It did not matter, Edain told herself. She lowered her bare body to him, kneeling over him and kissing him softly in the hollows of his neck and his shoulders and the slightly hairy skin over his breastbone. His naked body was singularly graceful, so powerful and muscular. So male. Between her sprawled legs his big shaft strained to possess her; she could feel it pressing hotly, wanting to enter.

"I want you to love me," she whispered.

She covered his mouth with her lips. In a rush of tremulous feeling the kiss was somehow more new, more strangely thrilling than the first time they'd embraced. She knew he was feeling it, too. A tingling, like sunlight, invaded their lips and flowed through their flesh. It made him growl, grabbing her even closer.

He held her warm, naked skin against him tightly as he tore his mouth away from hers and kissed her throat, her bare shoulders, in a burst of hunger. His long fingers, then his lips, explored her breasts.

His hot mouth, his teeth tugging at her nipples sent streams of fire into her belly. She clutched his thick red hair, making wordless sounds of delight. She grew moist and swollen in her intimate places, and began to ache for the feel of him in her. She writhed as his fingers found the feminine folds of flesh and carefully, tantalizingly, invaded her.

"Edain, do you want me?" His eyes were hooded as he looked down at her, but he trembled with desire. Then his mouth covered hers in a passionate kiss, coaxing her surrender. His fingers spread to stroke over the silky flesh of her rounded bottom. He pulled back only to whisper against her lips, "Ride me, sweetheart, make love to me if you do."

As she knelt over him his hands cupped her breasts, his thumbs teasing her nipples, then skillfully stroked down her legs and inner thighs until they quivered, deliciously.

The candle flickered. The dancing shadows grew large on the storeroom walls. They were not Magnus's golden dust motes, or the scent of flowers. But there were perfumes like sandalwood and amber in the flour, and smoky veils of mist that drifted through the cider barrels like forest smoke. Edain straddled him and let her body surrender. Looking up, his eyes devoured her tangled blaze of hair, her kiss-swollen mouth, her little breasts with their glistening pink buds rising and falling rapidly. He entered her in one voracious thrust, making her cry out.

"Edain, love me, too!" he cried hoarsely as his body bucked under her.

He took her to a peak of writhing, mindless desire. The pressure of his flesh inside her created a driving heat that made her squirm and pound him. She pulled out, then convulsively thrust herself against him. The world began to spin wildly, filled with the essence of burning sandalwood, centered on a burning ache, hot with desire, frenzied with madness. Edain cried out, crushing her hips against him in a fierce burst of longing to have him forever.

The effect on Magnus was just as uncontrollable. He battered her with thrusts that drove her to the brink of madness, his breath harsh and ragged, his body rising to meet hers with a passionate ferocity. She was so intent on her own release she barely heard his rasping cry as he poured himself into her.

Edain collapsed against his chest, his throbbing shaft still in her. Quivering with the aftershocks of his release, Magnus gasped, "Holy Jesus in heaven! Edain?"

She was still struggling for breath and could not answer. It had been just as glorious as any other time they'd been together. She stared down into his tawny, thickly lashed eyes. Because he looked so wild, she panted, "How fare you?"

His handsome face looked up at her dimly. He cleared his throat. "I don't think I know."

For a long moment they regarded each other, gasping and dripping with wet. Then they both laughed together.

He lowered his face to her breasts and she saw only the crown of his neatly cropped head. Her own body was shivering, drenched with lovemaking, sweetly drained. She did not see how she could bear to leave him.

But she must.

They slept awhile, and made love again. The candle had burned down into a puddle of tallow. The shadows on the walls grew bigger, darker. The relentless pounding of Magnus's body swept Edain to the verge of a passionate madness. She took his strength, his raging need, as she arched and met him just as strongly. He held her clamped in his arms as though nothing would ever separate them. Until the world exploded into a shattering release that made her scream. Only his matching explosion touched her consciousness, his hoarse cry against her lips.

When it was through she put her hands around him and held him, awed by the ecstasy that was almost like pain as he poured himself into her. Edain stroked his shoulders and down into the quivering muscles of his back and onto the hard planes of his buttocks. She heard him grunt, his arms tightening around her.

They lay there for a long moment, savoring their closeness, the blissful happiness. Edain was the first to hear the sounds of people walking around outside in the inn's yard, and voices loudly calling her name.

She clutched at her cloak, not believing. It couldn't be, but then—

Dear Holy Mother, it was late, and Asgard and the others couldn't find her! She poked him. "Magnus!"

He lifted his head from her breast, listening. In the next moment he was on his feet. "Sweet Mary's tits! They know better than to seek me out here!"

He lunged for his hauberk, drawing the long mail coat down over his bare skin. Then his helmet. He was reaching for his sword when someone pushed the door open.

Edain crouched on the flour sacks and drew the fur cloak around her nakedness just in time. Asgard de la Guerche and King Henry's two knights crowded inside, filling the little storeroom with their big, mailed bodies. Edain saw the Templar's eyes widen as they sought and found her in the dim light. He went white to his lips.

Magnus, barefoot and with sword in hand advanced on them shouting, "Get out! This is none of your affair!"

Asgard still stared at Edain, his mouth working. She drew the cloak up across her breasts and turned her head, not wanting to meet those blazing blue eyes. One of the other knights snickered.

The Templar could hardly bring himself to speak. He tried several times before he blurted out, "Did you think this—this *libertine* would marry you?" When Edain shook her head, his face contorted. "Ah, Holy Mother, that is worse. You have committed a deliberate sin against God!"

Magnus stepped in front of him, lifted his sword, and brought the tip of it against the other's throat.

"Get out of here, de la Guerche," he ground out. He nodded to the others. "And take them with you."

For the first time, Asgard looked at him. "You have defiled her," was all he said.

He drew his sword.

There was not room in the storeroom to fight. The king's knights hastily scrambled back as Magnus swung first. The big Templar parried the blow, retreating through the door and into the night-dark yard. Magnus followed him, savagely attacking as Asgard backed across the grass.

Edain and the two knights stumbled after them. The fighters were like madmen, oblivious to the dark and wagons and fences. Their grunts and shouts, the clang of their swords, brought people carrying torches out of the inn. A crowd began to gather.

Putting her hands to her mouth, Edain moaned.

They were big men, young and strong, of almost equal height. Asgard was fully clothed, fully mailed, and wore his helm. Magnus was barefoot, naked under his hauberk, but he fought with a wolfish ferocity she had only guessed at that night in front of the Templars' commandery. He seemed an avenging demon. The crowd began to cheer for him.

She pulled at Denys and Giscard, begging the king's knights to try and stop them. They shook her off. The crowd was growing bigger as more people poured from the inn.

Edain realized she had no way of stopping them. No power at all, much as she would desperately want it. They intended to kill each other!

She was stiff with horror as she watched them. Asgard the Templar was cold and purposeful, the unequaled master swordsman. Magnus, with his heigh and strength and fury, fought like a man possessed

The rage that enveloped them went on and o without waning, a test of muscle and will. Then some one in the crowd groaned as Asgard seemed to favo his left side. The Templar went off balance, his elbo clamped to his ribs for a few steps.

"No!" Edain screamed. She didn't have to see to know that his wound had opened, the gash th she had spent so many hours tending after the flight from Edinburgh. She broke free of Giscard grasp. "Holy Mother, can't you see? He can't figh anymore!"

She ran to them. "Magnus!" she shrieked.

They didn't see her; as she rushed into the figh the whine of a sword in the air came perilously clos to her head. Suddenly Asgard faltered and wen down on one knee, holding onto his sword, the ti thrust into the dirt.

Edain threw herself down on her knees beside th Templar. Magnus saw her; there was just a split se ond for him to catch his sword in midswing and sta ger back, gasping, his sweaty face picking up the ligh from the torches.

"Get away from him," he shouted. "I'm going kill him!"

Asgard leaned on his weapon, his hand clutche to his side. Blood seeped through his fingers. Edai put her arm around him to hold him up.

Magnus's eyes widened. With a curse, he flung h sword on the ground. "Leave him!" he stormed. "G away from him! Can't you see the Templar wants yo

God rot it, Edain, tell me that he's never touched you!"

Edain gaped at him. "What are you saying?"

He bent over and picked up his great sword and rammed it in its scabbard. The crowd that had come out from the inn pressed closer, trying to hear.

Magnus rasped, "Come with me now, Edain. I will take care of you. King Henry does not have to know, he will never find out that you have not returned to the convent."

She stared at his grim face as though she had heard the words of the devil himself. Beside her, Asgard strained to rise to his feet. "Let me up," the Templar choked. "It's not over. I tell you, I am in condition to fight."

Edain's thoughts whirled. It felt as though the ground tilted. The torches made blobs of spinning red light in the darkness. There were suddenly voices, whispering in her head.

The voices said that she could never do what Magnus offered. He was right about this last lovemaking.

She could not speak. She only shook her head, her tangled bright hair hiding her face. She knew he wanted her to look up at him, but she could not.

At last she heard Magnus's indrawn breath, felt his anger and disappointment as he turned away. The crowd was close around them, pushing and shoving, holding up the torches to peer into Asgard's pale face.

"God and the angels, man," someone exclaimed, "look down at the ground! You're bleeding a freshet!"

Asgard held his red-stained hand to his side. There was blood all over the dry winter grass. The white-headed squire came trotting up and took Asgard arm and helped him to his feet.

"Take me inside the inn and get Giscard an Denys to take off my mail," the Templar said. H lips were stiff with pain. "Then we will see how muc I am opened up."

Edain nodded. She took Asgard's elbow, and sh and the little squire helped him limp away.

Twenty-two

"Before the great Flood in the Bible," Edain said, "fifty-three of the Old ones, led by a woman called Cessair, came to discover Ireland. Which was at that time occupied only by giants."

She was strapping Asgard's ribs with a piece of white cloth as he lay under some roadside trees. They had stopped so that she could attend the thin-stretched new scar in his side that had torn loose and caused so much bleeding. From the looks of it, with a little luck it would soon heal.

"In those days," she went on, "it was acceptable that a woman do these things—be the leader of a party of explorers. There were only three men with Cessair and the other women: Bith, Cessair's father, a son of Noah, which everyone recognizes is from the Bible, and Fintan and Ladra, the pilot of their vessel. The three men shared the women. It was Fintan who got Cessair."

Asgard winced, and not from the pain of his wound. "I don't remember any Bith, son of Noah, especially his going to Ireland with fifty women," he said. "I have been told these Irish stories are—uh, not very reliable."

She stopped and looked down at him. "Of course

they are reliable. They have been passed down fror bard to bard in Ireland for hundreds, thousands c years, it is a very accurate profession." She lifted u his arm and pulled the bandage tight around his ches and pinned it. "Unfortunately, there was troubl When Ladra the pilot died of too much, you kno lying in bed with the women," Edain said, avertin her eyes, "Bith and Fintan divided the women so tha they had twenty-five each. That was better. Then th Flood swept over Ireland. So you see if there was Flood in this story, Sir Asgard, then it certainly prove the story of Cessair and Fintan came straight from th Bible."

She lifted him slightly at the shoulders and slid hi cloak under him. "Now you will be more comfor able," she said, and smiled at him dazzlingly. "Onl Fintan survived, hiding in a cave which the Flood' waters never reached. And Fintan never died, bu lives on to this very day as a shape-changer, first on form and then another when he appears, keepin all the histories so that these stories shall not be lost.

Asgard looked past her to where Giscard and th squire were tending the fire. The escort had pause for him to take a rest, as his side was still painin him, and for all of them to take the noon meal. Jus a few feet beyond the ridge they could see a valle and a small village. By his reckoning they were onl a day or so, perhaps less, from St. Sulpice's conven

Edain sat down beside him, the cloak of her hoo thrown back, the wind tumbling her long gold hai Asgard watched her silently, thinking she looke more beautiful than ever, even though her dress wa stained and the rich fur cloak was beginning to show hard wear.

Inwardly, he sighed. Mysterious Edain was incomparably enchanting. Her glowing emerald eyes looked at his with such innocent directness that he had to look away. She was not innocent, not anymore, he told himself. Not after what he had seen last night.

It contributed to his everlasting damnation that he no longer tried to avoid looking at her or thinking about her. He had surrendered helplessly to a doomed passion. For, wicked or not, demoiselle Edain haunted him, filling his eyes by daylight, his dreams when he slept.

In so doing Asgard was fully aware that he was committing large errors of faith and Templar discipline. God knows his head was filled with impure thoughts; he writhed when he thought of them. He had even allowed himself to be provoked into combat over her in front of a crowd of tavern idlers, with her seducer, a carousing earl's son, a wastrel madman. And, God and St. Mary, he had even seen their naked bodies engaged in their illicit act with his own eyes!

Now Asgard could only bring himself to say, "Demoiselle, where have you heard these silly stories?"

"Everyone knows them." She leaned over him to gently brush his fair hair back from his forehead. "After Fintan came a descendant of Japheth—there, you see, there is another name from the Bible." She smiled again meltingly. "However, there was a king named Partholan who is the father of what is now the Irish race. He and his ships were stranded in the Orkneys, in the islands to the north, until a British chief told him that the land of Erin was fair, and there was room for them there. So Partholan came to Eire. After Partholan came Nemed, a descendant of a brother of Partholan who had stayed in Spain. These made two groups, of which the Fir Bolg were one. Then yet another nation arrived. These were the Tuatha de Danaan, the tribe of Danaan, the Great Goddess, the Mother of all the Gods. The Tuatha had been living in the North, and they landed in Connacht and built their kingdom there, and surpassed other peoples of Ireland in beauty, wisdom, and the arts, especially magic. After a big battle at Moytura, the Tuatha de Danaan and the Fir Bolg learned to live in peace. That is, until the Tuatha were driven into the fairy mounds by the Sons of Mil, the Milesians, the ones who are in Ireland now."

She looked at him and sighed. "It is a sad story. But it is all there in the Book of the Invasions, which all the bards and minstrels and even some of the Culdee monks know." She sighed again. "The Tuatha are my people."

The squire padded up with some bread toasted over the fire and some winter apples they had bought at the inn. Asgard took the bread and fruit and hiked himself up gingerly, careful of the wound in his side. He bit into the bread, watching the mountain wind as it played with Edain's bright hair.

It was a long and confused story that she'd told him, although he had heard part of it before from brother Templars who had explored Irish magic and mysticism. The account of how the Irish came to exist on their isolated isle did not particularly interest Asgard. He was content just to sit there with his back to the beech tree and look at her, thinking that if one were to create a golden idol to incomparable beauty, it would be this strange girl who cast a spell of allure for any and every man. He couldn't get the glimpse he'd had of her perfect nude body before she'd flung the cloak around it out of his mind.

He cleared his throat, frowning. "Tell me, demoiselle, how do you know all this? Did the nuns tell you?"

She lifted her head and those jewel eyes stared into the distance, thinking it over. "No, the nuns did not tell me." She was silent for a long moment. "I wish I could tell you, Sir Asgard," she said finally. "But the truth of it is, I do not know myself how I know."

She got up then, and picked up her cloak and wrapped it around her and went to join the others at the fire.

Asgard watched her as he chewed the last of his bread.

She left him no peace, that was the problem. He was so tormented that he'd thought perhaps he should believe what both she and the Culdee monk had said. That there were still peoples of the old races of Ireland living among them. The Old Ones, mysterious and unknown, with their gifts deliberately concealed. Or if they should happen to be shown, misunderstood.

Deep down inside him, Asgard's spirit shuddered.

He was a knight, a monk, a fighting man of God. To become a Templar one had to renounce the temptations of everything in this corrupt, disorderly world. When one had reached the higher realms of the spirit, when one had accomplished the rejections of the turbulent body, one at last had God's peace, bathed in the light and blood of the redemption.

But all that had changed when he had seen her, he thought with a groan. This girl, a notorious novice virtually abducted from her convent by some local brigand, who was now sought by the Templar brotherhood as a seeress, a beautiful magician—

Yes, and another man's naked wanton, he was quick to remind himself.

This girl had raised a searing, unholy hunger in him that had pierced his body and head with arrows of lustful desire. Instead of serenity she brought raging passion. In his dreams, it was to his everlasting shame that he felt liberated, delirious, wildly pagan. And awake, he could think and see naught but her.

No one knew, Asgard thought feverishly, how close he was to gibbering madness.

The squire was back with a cup of cold water from the spring. As Asgard drank the boy stood looking at him with bright, azure eyes. "There is a church in the town below," he said. He took back the empty cup. "And a priest what hears confessions."

Asgard looked up in astonishment. His first thought was to thunder a proper rebuke. To send the fat little squire scurrying for shelter for having the boldness to offer such a presumptuous suggestion.

Then Asgard considered it. A priest? His mind unexpectedly responded with considerable relief. Confession was, perhaps, just what he needed.

For what he was going to do.

The priest was in the fields with the other villagers, readying the ground for plowing. They had to send the tavern keeper's boy to fetch him. They waited a good part of an hour, sitting on the church steps in the warm sunshine, eating the rest of the apples. When the priest came up to the little church, he looked just like any other villein in his smock and braies. They waited another half an hour while he went into the church to change into his cassock.

King Henry's knight, Giscard, wanted to be confessed as well. Denys had fallen asleep on the steps; when waked he said his conscience was pure and needed rest more than absolution. Edain decided she would wait until she got to the convent at St. Sulpice. The squire took the horses off to graze and pretended no one had asked him.

Asgard went to be confessed after the king's knight had his turn. He stayed a very long time.

After some time had passed, Denys woke up, turned on his side and looked up at the sun, muttering, "Jesu, the Templar's telling the priest his life's story," and went back to sleep. In a little while even the squire dozed off in the deep dry grass by the grazing horses, his body rolled up into a ball.

When Asgard's confession was over he came out of the church and woke everyone, and they mounted, yawning, and started off to the north and the last of the mountains.

"We're almost finished," the king's knight, Denys, said to his partner. "Not much more to go now."

But Giscard, who had been shriven, was not in the mood to talk and only nodded his head.

It was Asgard, smiling for once, who said, "Yes, if we hurry perhaps we shall see St. Sulpice convent by nightfall."

* * *

By midafternoon, though, Asgard had tired again. Plainly fighting pain, he dropped back on the mountain track to ride in the rear. Giscard and Denys and the little squire were soon out of sight.

Asgard turned in the saddle to face Edain with a weary smile. "Come, don't let us stop here. If we are to rest, let us take this path. I can see glimpses of the sea through the trees."

Edain warmed to his pleasant mood. Since the village priest had heard his confession the Templar seemed almost happy. With Asgard leading, they turned aside and went down a path that edged the cliffs overlooking the vast indent of Ribble Bay. From there they viewed the old haunt of the dread Viking of centuries ago. It was still sparsely settled. The convent of the Sacred Limb of St. Sulpice was over the next ridge of mountains.

Asgard swung down from the saddle, favoring his side. He came to Edain and let her put her hand on his shoulder to slide down.

A westerly breeze from Ireland, damp and green-smelling, came to them from across the glistening water. They stood in silence, enjoying it. When Edain turned to say something about not letting the others get too far ahead, she found that he was standing very close, his brilliant eyes studying her.

She smiled, somewhat uneasily. "I know I have some speck of dirt on my nose, Sir Asgard, to see you look at me this way."

She lifted her hand to her face. As she did so he

caught it in his mailed mitt and held it. "Demoiselle, it is over," he said hoarsely.

Frowning, Edain gave a tentative twist to her hand, but he held it fast.

"Yes, it is almost over and it grows late," she agreed. She looked around, not knowing what strange humor had seized him. She gathered he was not pleased that their journey was ending. She hoped he was not going to try to kiss her. Or burst out with some declaration of desire.

Edain looked up, no longer trying to get her hand free. "Lead me to my palfrey, Sir Asgard," she said, "so that we may join the others."

Those clear, azure eyes seemed not to hear her. He whispered, still holding her by his iron grip, "Witch or seeress or from strange race of Irish demons, it does not matter—evil wears a beautiful face. I need no further proof. For I myself have seen how you ensorcelled and seduced Morlaix's son, and clasped him to your naked body."

For a long moment she could only stare at him. From what she had seen in his eyes, Edain had expected him to burst out with some declaration of desire. Not this.

"Is that what you have been thinking since we left the inn?" she wanted to know. "When you were being a pleasant companion? Of naked bodies?"

The Templar's beautiful face looked grim.

"Nay, not since the inn, demoiselle. Much longer than that. It is what I have been thinking since I first laid my eyes on you in the wild Sanachs' tower, and saw how you had spun your webs and spells about their chief so that he was tempted to keep you in spite of the great ransom I was bringing. And how you put your spells about Chester's mad tourney knight, and made him so besotted with you that he now defies his father the earl and even his sovereign king. And that you have affected even the Templars of the Edinburgh commandery, even the Culdee monk." He grimaced painfully. "And now me. It is my great sin that Asgard de la Guerche is no exception to your great magic. I have found that I, too, cannot live with your dagger of evil embedded deep in my heart."

The sudden pressure of his hand on her wrist forced Edain to her knees. She grabbed out at him, but her fingers connected only with the mail that covered his body, his arms, even his hands.

"Stop, stop!" She lunged about, trying to break free. "This is an evil spell but it is yours, not mine! I am innocent of all that you charge me!"

Asgard had pulled a cord from his belt. While he held her captive he worked with the other hand to circle it around her neck.

She could not believe what was happening. The man who was attacking her, her companion, her friend, still looked like an angel in his Templar's garb. As she felt the cord touch her throat Edain threw herself to one side violently, caught herself on her hands and knees, and scrambled to her feet.

Before she could turn to run, the cord twined around her throat and brought her up short. She was jerked backward against him, her hands clawing.

At that moment the Feeling swept over her. She almost sobbed with relief.

Let me go. The voice spoke to the Templar. *Whatever terrors you think to make me face, yours will be greater.*

She knew that he heard, for he shuddered.

Then he shook it off. With a burst of strength Asgard tightened the cord between his hands so that it bit into her neck. She felt the blood dripping from her broken skin and down into her collarbones. There was a smothering, suffocating sense of darting pain through her neck and head. In spite of her thrashing the world was growing black.

At that same instant a body came hurtling down the path, howling, and threw itself on Asgard's back. The Templar staggered, but did not let go of the cord.

"What?" he shouted. "Confound—"

He tried to reach around with one hand without letting go of Edain. But he could not get a grip on the clawing, scratching, spitting attacker chewing at his ears and reaching around to rake his face with its sharp nails.

Asgard staggered back, off balance, dragging Edain with him as he tried to rid himself of the squire who clung like a frenzied limpet to his back.

Edain was lifted off her feet, dragged about like a rag doll as the Templar yelped in anger and pain. The world was black, even sounds were fading, as the squire continued to maul the bigger man.

Dimly, Edain knew something was going to happen. She was certain she could not die like this. Then Asgard found that the cord in his hand was wriggling and trying to climb his wrist.

He screamed.

The Templar let go. Edain dropped to her knees

in the dirt and rolled over. The fat little squire did not budge. He continued to cling to Asgard's shoulders, still biting his head and neck, trying to kick him in the ribs.

It was not the squire nor Edain that Asgard was now trying to escape, but that which had once been the cord, the garrot with which he'd intended to strangle her.

It was no longer that. A thick-bodied, gray Highland adder was winding around his wrist and attempting to slide up into the sleeve of his hauberk.

Asgard screamed again, and wrenched his body about violently. The white-haired squire slid down from his back, landing on his feet in the middle of the path. Edain sat where she was, rubbing her torn throat.

She was thinking, somewhat breathlessly, that one could tell by the knight's ashen face, his wild, convulsive movements, that he was one of those who feared serpents above all the earth's terrors. Even as he grabbed at the snake with a sort of shuddering panic the black-patterned thing slithered across his arm, looking for an open place in his mail.

"Help me," Asgard choked. He kept backing away, as if to run from the reptile twining up his arm toward his chest. Behind him was the cliff, and beyond that, the sea. "Mother of God," he sobbed, appealing to Edain and the squire, "have pity! Do something to help me!"

The squire sat down beside Edain, licked at his fingers, then ran them through his white hair, smoothing it. He regarded Asgard's writhing figure at the edge of the cliff with interest. "Princess, would he have killed you?" he wanted to know.

Edain reached over and scratched him on the top of his head. "It's time you appeared." She put her hand to her throat, feeling the cut and the sticky blood that the cord had left. "It's a long walk from Edinburgh."

He only gave her a catlike smile. "Well, you are going home, so no matter." He pointed with his chin. "What of him?"

The snake had climbed around Asgard's neck. Both his hands clutched it frantically to keep it from disappearing into the hauberk collar. His blue eyes bulged, his handsome face was transformed; he looked quite mad with fear. Worse, he was at the edge of the little path. The cliff dropped off right beyond.

What of the Templar indeed? Edain believed now that he would have killed her. He was a man who did not know how to love, she thought, fingering her swollen throat. But the Feeling had let him live. It was up to her now to decide.

She told herself that if one looked so much like a tormented angel perhaps it was one's fate to search for that meaning in life that the rest of the Templars so eagerly sought.

She realized she knew just the place.

With a sigh, Edain got to her feet. She hurried to him in time to pull him back from the tall grass at the edge of the cliff. He went quite limp as she pulled the snake from around his throat and dropped it into the undergrowth.

When she looked into his face she wondered if he even knew where he was. Suddenly the Templar's eyes rolled back in his head and she thought he was going to faint. He was a huge man; she did not think she could hold him up enough to keep him from toppling into the sea.

She was just about to call out to Fomor to come and help when Asgard recovered from his swoon enough to stagger a few steps, holding onto her.

"The adder," he croaked. "I f-fear snakes more than the devil itself!"

"It is gone." She guided him away from the edge. "There is nothing to worry about."

Was this better than killing him? she wondered. Had she made the right choice? The Feeling had come to help her; before this was over she was going to have to use it again.

"I need to sit down." Asgard's legs would no longer hold him up. He sat down by some bushes abruptly. He lifted his thumb and held it up before his eyes. "I am going to die," he muttered. "I am bitten."

"Go get our horses," Edain told Fomor, "they have wandered off. And then go after Denys and Giscard. They have not even noticed they've left us."

With a flick of his hand that caught the sunlight on the ruby ring, the squire brushed his hair back and picked up his horse's reins and rode off.

Edain stood looking at Asgard, who sat bent over, his hands covering his face. She did not think he was going to die. The bite of Highland adders seldom killed.

She drew a deep breath, still holding her throat. She was glad Asgard de le Guerche was not truly in love with her, in spite of all his words. There was room for only one person in her heart. Magnus. And she could not have him.

Edain took a deep breath. This one last time, she would call.

She had a Feeling they were close by, and would answer.

Twenty-three

It looked as though the whole countryside north of the bay knew she was returning to the convent. The next morning as they made their way through a fishing village, people lined the streets, and young girls came out with bunches of holly and laurel to give to Edain. King Henry's knights were very impressed. They kept turning in their saddles to look as the villagers rushed forward to surround Edain, all wanting to tell the latest story.

"What is the matter?" Denys called.

"It is nothing," she called back.

It was silly enough. In the village of the night before, where Giscard and the Templar had been confessed, the chief's wife had given birth to triplets. The village priest had declared it a great sign of abundance, and God's blessing for the coming year. But the villagers themselves gave credit to the passing through of the Blessed Lady Edain, now returning to her home in the St. Sulpice convent.

The girls crowded around Edain's palfrey as they made their way out toward the convent road, wanting to touch her or have her bless the holly and laurel. Which later, she knew, they'd put under their pillows to dream of their lovers and the children they'd have by them when they married.

There was other news, the girls told her as they exclaimed over her unbound hair, the fur cloak and the much-worn velvet court gown she still wore.

The evil knight, Ivo de Brise, who had tried to force her to wed one of his villeins, had been called away to war by his liege lord, the Earl of Chester. He and five knights were now in Chester's vanguard of King Henry's, now fighting the Scots.

Best of all, de Brise's wife, the lady Horgitha, now had a new young steward from the western isles who was handsomer by far than de Brise—whom everyone hated, anyway—and the steward was said to be eagerly warming the lady Horgitha's bed in her lord's absence.

Edain could not bring herself to smile at the story the girls told her. Although it was rare justice after all the woe de Brise had caused her to have his wife cuckolding him while he was at war.

The girls ran back to the squire and made him stop his horse long enough to put a holly wreath on his bushy hair. And they gave a small bunch of laurel to Asgard, who rode nursing his snake-bitten hand.

The Templar had not said a word to Edain all morning, his perfect features as still and expressionless as marble. King Henry's knights knew nothing of what had happened, of course.

It would all come to an end soon enough, Edain was thinking; Asgard's and the royal knights' task was finished when they delivered her safely to St. Sulpice.

She rode ahead with Asgard bringing up the rear with Fomor. She did not have a chance to study the

Templar from there, but she knew him well enoug to know that he was suffering greatly from his di honorable attack on her there on the cliff, and h terror at discovering the adder in his hands. Sh found she was not afraid of him. Now that he seeme purged of his madness she no longer feared anothe assault.

The snake was different. Something in the Ten plar seemed to have been crushed when faced wit the one thing that struck absolute terror into h heart. The fear of snakes was something he had ca ried from boyhood; she was not sure, even now, h had made his peace with it. Asgard's shoulder slumped, brilliant eyes clouded. He rode with rein through his fingers, his bitten hand cradled in th other. There was little ahead for him now, Edai knew; what faith he'd had was gone. And there ha been little before she'd ever known him.

They stopped at the miller's ale yard to the nort of the outskirts of the town. While they ate the noo meal at the trestles, the village girls went off with th boys to sit under the trees and flirt. A cold sprin wind was blowing. The older men left, saying the had to go back to their plowing. The women staye on with the nursing babies and the younger childre who ran between the tables, screaming and shoutin and playing hide-and-seek games.

The little squire came up to her. "What are w waiting for, princess?" Fomor wanted to know.

Edain got up from the table and brushed th bread crumbs away with her fingers. "We are no waiting any longer," she told him.

Together they walked to where Denys and Giscard were holding the horses.

Either they had answered the call by now, Edain told herself, or they had not.

There were marshes beyond the village and long stretches of beaches of gray sand that followed the bay northward. Clouds scudded from the west across the wide expanse of sea and sky. The cobblestone road to the convent of St. Sulpice, so old it was said to have been built by the ancient Romans, could only be used at low tide. They had to wait again for the sea to recede, walking the horses up and down on sand sparkling with pockets of water and littered with brown seaweed and wrack.

Finally the tide began to ebb.

Edain was the first to start across. She was in a hurry to get to St. Sulpice, and besides, she'd known the old stone road as a child, and could follow it even when it was covered with a foot or so of water.

To the others lagging behind, who could not see the cobblestones, it looked as though she was riding her palfrey into the endless sea, the wind whipping out her cloak behind her. The little horse picked up its feet, shying nervously at shallow waves; it did not like the illusion of galloping on top of the water any better than the others.

Fomor brought his horse up beside her, grinning. They tried to urge the horses into a trot, but the splashing frightened their mounts and they would not go any faster.

"There they are!" Edain cried.

The horses could see the stone road rising out of the bay ahead of them and allowed themselves to be kicked into a canter. They burst onto the beach and the road that continued into the dunes. Behind them, Asgard and the two knights looked as though they were guiding their horses across the vast sheet of the bay.

The convent of the Sacred Limb of St. Sulpice was almost as old as the road. There was a story that it was built on what was left of a Roman villa with its high outer walls and courtyard, and the roof made of clay tiles. It stood on a hill in a grove of wind-stunted pines, with the road running in front of it. Before the gate stood Mila's wagon. And off to one side, Tyros and two of his women were holding a string of horses and mules.

Edain pushed the palfrey toward the wagon. The gypsy girl climbed down from the seat, her eyes glittering, and ran toward them.

"He will not come with me," Mila protested. "I know he will not!"

"Oh, yes he will." Edain smiled sadly. This was the end of everything, here at the gates of the convent where it had all begun the day that Ivo de Brise and his knights had come to take her away.

"It is you he loves," she said softly, "from the moment he gave you the bread on the road to Edinburgh castle. Do you not remember?"

The girl licked her lips, her black eyes darting to Asgard, who had reined in his horse and was staring down at her.

"How do you know that? How did you lead us here?" she cried shrilly. "Tyros said he heard voices

She went to Asgard, to look up at him. "It is true, then, what the Templars said when they gave us money to take her away?" Mila asked him. "That this woman is a witch?"

But his blue gaze was on her, transfixed. "The gypsy girl on the castle road." His handsome face showed that he could not believe it. "Yes, I remember you," he said slowly. "I remember another time when I was sore wounded, and you were Mila, who took care of me in her wagon."

Fomor laughed.

The squire kicked his horse into a trot and reached down and snatched off Tyros's wide-brimmed hat, turned his mount and cantered back to Asgard. He stuck the gypsy hat on the Templar's head.

"Now you are a Templar no longer," he announced, "but king of the gypsies!"

The hat that Magnus had once worn slipped down over Asgard's eyes, but he seemed not to notice. He leaned out of the saddle, showing Mila his hand.

"A snake has bitten me, a poisonous snake," he told her, worried. "Several times."

She seized his hand, looking up into his face. "I will care for you," she vowed. She kissed his palm and fingers passionately, and he did not resist. "You were always mine, never hers, my beloved!" Emboldened, she tried to pull him from the saddle. "Come, I will care for you where this evil snake has wounded you, and this time the witch will not be around to interfere!"

Giscard and the other king's knight, Denys, rode up, their eyes widening at the sight of the Templar leaning from the saddle, the gypsy girl pulling at his hand.

"Sir Asgard," Denys began. "These gypsies—"

He did not hear him. Asgard dismounted and walked toward the gypsy wagon leading his horse, the girl clinging to him. "You are very pretty," they heard him say. Behind him the other gypsies mounted, and turned their horses and mules toward the southbound road.

Giscard turned to Edain, astounded. "Demoiselle, we cannot—"

"Nay, it is all right. What else can he do? Nearly all his vows are broken" She freed her feet of the stirrups and slid down off the palfrey.

Mila's wagon was turning toward the sea road. Asgard had tied his horse to the tailgate and sat next to her, saying something quite earnestly.

He had never talked to her that way, she thought. He'd even forgotten to say his goodbyes.

Whooping, Fomor spurred his horse after the gypsies. *I will be back,* drifted back to her.

Edain sighed. She knew. He did not need to tell her.

She went to each of the king's knights to thank them, and wished them godspeed. She gave Giscard the palfrey, and told them to sell the little horse in Edinburgh and share the silver. To her surprise, both men began to weep.

"Oh, demoiselle," Giscard said, "you are too young and beautiful to choose the cloister! Pay no attention to those gypsies who call you a witch, they are an ungrateful lot. I am but a poor knight, but—"

"Nay," she said hastily before he could go further.

Poor Giscard, she didn't want to have to refuse anything he might offer. "Do not worry for me, I do this most willingly. Besides, the convent is my home, I was raised here."

Denys took off his helmet, openly blubbering. "Allow us to stay with you, and serve you then," he wept. "For we love you mightily."

Good heavens, she must get away from them! Edain had no idea such hardened men could cry like babes. "What would the good sisters do with such strong, fair young knights?" she chided. "You would cause such consternation they would never recover."

Edain tried to laugh to reassure them, but at the same time she backed away toward the convent postern gate. When she got to it she reached out for the bell rope and rang the bell. On the slope below them she could see the gypsies making for the sea, followed by Asgard in Mila's wagon, and Fomor not far behind.

The portress, Sister Constancia, answered, opening the small door in the larger one. "They told us you were coming," was all she said. But Edain could hear the joy in her voice.

She heard the bolt being drawn back. The big wooden door opened.

With a sigh, Edain stepped inside.

Twenty-four

The King of England was a changed man, there was no doubt about it.

In July, King Henry had made public penance by order of the Pope, walking barefoot and in sackcloth to Westminster Cathedral to repent and receive absolution for his part in the death of Thomas à Becket. Some weeks later, William the Lion of Scotland was seized by English forces at Aylnworth, and the border war was all but over.

The head of the commandery at Edinburgh watched the king cross the ward to the White Tower for their meeting, thinking one would assume that by now a visible burden would be lifted from King Henry's shoulders. That he would be able to put the most disastrous events of his reign behind him: the murder of the archbishop, Becket, and the death of his son Henry, the Young King. Not to mention the lesser embroilment of the war with Scotland.

But it was plain from the way Henry looked, with his burly figure now stooped, his face haggard, that this was not the case.

Of course, the commander thought, one almost felt a duty to feel sorry for Henry Plantagenet, since the man had suffered much. The king was genuinely fond of his unruly children, and the arrogant Becket had been his closest friend; when he had blurted out his unthinking words about Becket it was generally assumed the king had not meant them to be taken literally. But popular opinion throughout Britain held that both tragedies had been more or less caused by the king's own faults.

If King Henry had not cried out during a drinking bout, when he was not entirely sober, "Will no one avenge me of the injuries I have sustained from this turbulent priest?" then four of his court's knights would not have rushed out on that instant to murder Becket in his cathedral. The king's petulant words had produced results that would forever haunt him.

As for the loss through sickness and death of his oldest son, opinion was against the king there, too. It had never been wise to crown the boy England's co-ruler; no one had really expected the king to share his power. Henry Plantagenet was full of treachery, as all well knew. The old queen, Eleanor, who'd had her own kingdom in Aquitaine, had found that out. She now languished as a prisoner in a castle somewhere. And all of her former district of Aquitaine was Henry's.

Now, the commander thought as he watched the king's group enter the door below to the tower, one would hope that some measure of peace of mind and heart would come to this troubled ruler. But it was the death of his oldest son that marked England's king most deeply. Henry Plantagenet might survive the loss of Becket, his estrangement from Queen Eleanor, even endure the never-ending assaults of his quarrelsome princes. But the death of the Young King, Prince Henry, was the one thing that had aged and embittered him.

The commander heard footsteps on the stairs outside and readied himself. He was reminded that he needed luck in this interview with the king; he'd been warned Henry grew more bad-tempered, more unpredictable, by the day.

A knight threw open the wooden door. The king, in an elaborate robe of red velvet trimmed with ermine, came into the tower's suite of rooms. He was followed by several Cistecian scriveners and the elegant Gilbert Foliot, the bishop of London and one of the king's chief advisors.

The commander dropped down quickly to one knee, bowing his head. Red-eyed and unkempt, Henry walked past him, took a cup and ewer of wine from a cupboard, and helped himself. From the high color in his face the king had begun his drinking early.

"What is this?" he said to the bishop of London as he flung himself into a chair. "A Templar? Is this one petitioning us?"

The bishop of London bent to his ear to remind him, "This is Gervais de Bonriveau, sire, commander of the Poor Knights of the Temple of Jerusalem in Edinburgh, who humbly begs your attention to an urgent plea concerning one of their number."

The king turned and stared at the Templar for several long moments.

"Jesu, yes, the girl," he said finally. "She is not easily forgotten. I saw the petition. Gilbert, fetch it for me."

The bishop beckoned to the clerks, who were already digging for it in their cases of writs. Henry fixed his bloodshot eyes on Bonriveau as he gulped down the last of the wine. He motioned impatiently for the Templar commander to get to his feet.

"Tell me, Sir Gervais," he said, "why you wish this girl now, when she has been returned by my order to the convent of the Sacred Limb of Saint Sulpice?"

The bishop had produced the petition. He handed it to the king who let it dangle from one hand, unread.

The Templar commander licked his lips. The clerks of the Edinburgh commandery had prepared a speech outlining the salient points of the Templars' plea to have the girl returned to them. Bonriveau could see these long arguments would test King Henry's uncertain temper.

Get right to the point, he told himself.

"We most humbly petition you to return her to us," the commander said, "as she has ensorcelled a most worthy brother, one you know yourself, as he escorted her by your order to Saint Sulpice—Sir Asgard de la Guerche."

The king took another cup of wine from one of his knights. "Bewitched him? How can she do that? The girl has been cloistered since spring."

The commander looked around the chamber, arranging his thoughts. He hadn't been wrong; the king was in a capricious mood.

"We have reason to believe the dread event happened then, milord," he said. "It was Sir Asgard who returned Demoiselle Edain to her convent. But since completing his task our brother has sadly abandoned his duties—which we wish to say he performed to the great admiration of all who knew him—and has adopted Satan's accursed ways. Alas, Sir Asgard has renounced his vows, and roams the wild Scottish hills with a band of vagrants and thieves known as Egyptians, living a debauched existence. It is said the young witch called up these demons when he bade her farewell at the convent, and sent poor de la Guerche off with them."

The king had put down his wine cup to stare. "De la Guerche, that lofty, parfait knight, is living with a band of gypsies?" When the Templar nodded, he twisted in his chair to look up at the bishop of London. "Gilbert, is this true? Do you believe the girl has put de la Guerche under an enchantment that has made him go mad?"

The bishop cleared his throat. "Sire, there have been many rumors and tales, even though this girl we speak of is now behind cloistered walls again. Add to that, the proper concern in London in chancery, about the alleged acts of witchcraft."

"The chancery? You did not tell me of this." The king's countenance wrinkled. "And what of this witchcraft?"

The commander stepped forward, but the bishop of London spoke first. "She is said to be a seeress, your highness. That she is known to cast spells." Gilbert Foliot was discreet; he knew all about the king's session with the strange girl months ago. How she had told Henry the news of his son's death, and how much it had overset him.

The Templar said, "By your gracious will, sire, if the girl is returned to us she will be sent to Paris to be interrogated about these rumors and tales, and have them proved or disproved once and for all.

With this in mind, Templars have already been sent to find Asgard de la Guerche, with orders for him to return to his station. I am at liberty to say that our Grand Commander believes that once we are allowed to retrieve Demoiselle Edain from where she has taken illegal sanctuary at Saint Sulpice, and transport her to Paris, our brother de la Guerche will follow."

"Illegal sanctuary?" The king raised his eyebrows. His expression said that it was not up to the Templars to decide what was legal and what was not within the boundaries of Henry Plantagenet's kingdoms. "But you claim *your* sanctuary is legal, is that it? Especially in Paris, where you will have a trial and condemn her, and burn her at the stake?" When the commander stiffened the king added, "And no doubt burn noble de la Guerche, too. Come, this does not speak much of Christian charity and divine forgiveness, sir knight."

The Templar shot a look at the bishop, but there was no help there.

"Your majesty, I—I am told Satan-inspired bewitchments can be forgiven only by God," he spluttered. "The girl's interrogation and trial would of necessity be secret, as is Templar custom."

Henry's sharp, bulging blue eyes studied him. He misliked the powerful tentacles of the Templars, which at times seemed to reach across Europe without much, secular or churchly, to curb them.

On the other hand, if he did not turn the girl and Asgard de la Guerche over to them, he would wager that Gilbert Foliot and the other English clergy had no kinder fate in store for them. The Templars had secured their position in England with loans to the kingdom's treasury; it would be hard to refuse favor to one of England's largest lenders. On the othe hand he appreciated the Templars' dilemma now that they were faced with a defection of one of thei own. One seldom heard of this happening. Thei embarrassment was apparent.

And, Henry thought, watching the commande kneeling before him, they seemingly had no way o getting their errant lamb back into the fold withou first capturing the witch who had so enchanted him. Perhaps they thought that with the girl imprisoned in Paris her demonic powers would force de la Guer che to follow her.

He knew how much they hated to come to him he could see it in the commander's face. But the gir was Henry's subject; they had to get his permission

All this time Gilbert Foliot had been whispering in his ear that England's bishops voiced grave con cerns that tales of the girl's supposed witchcraft had spread far and wide. The churchmen were particu larly concerned with the popular belief that she was both a sorceress and a saint. Such an idea was both dangerous and impossible. It was not enough to leave her to live out her days in even so remote a spot as St. Sulpice; too many of her admirers would be eager to seek her out.

"Cease," Henry shouted, waving his advisor away.

Shrugging, Gilbert straightened up. A knight came to refill the king's cup.

Henry sat looking down into his wine, picturing the golden-haired girl. Jesu, what a demon-ridden night that had been. He'd been half drunk, which hadn't helped.

He remembered her absorbed, gravely distant air, her emerald eyes in the firelight like jewels. He hadn't expected her to be so beautiful, so luscious of face and body. The usual thoughts had crossed his mind, of how he could bed her after the fortune-telling was over. Then by some curious power she had managed to chase such ideas completely out of his head. Which was very clever.

He remembered, though, the feeling that a deft, forceful innocence poured out of her. He'd been convinced that this was how she used her gifts. And that she did not know much about them, nor what caused them.

She'd certainly made no attempt to "ensorcell" him, as the Templars complained. He doubted if the warrior monks, puttering about with their occult experiments in their cellars in Paris knew what the word truly was.

Then the king suddenly saw once again the terrifying moment of the blood dripping from her hand, the ivory knight clutched in her fingers.

Henry!

Dear God, the cry for his lost son still echoed in his soul with a scream of agony!

He abruptly put his trembling hand across his face, and groaned. Christ in heaven, how could he say that this beautiful golden child had caused any of his plentiful sorrows? He had been sitting right there at the table with her; it was his questions that had prodded her. He had seen everything, learned everything.

Just as he wanted.

She said the lion of Scotland would lie down at his feet and it had. King William now lay captive and defeated, in Henry's own prison. As for his quarrel with the Pope over the matter of the murder, he had made his agonizing, public penance, and it was to be hoped Becket, damn him, was satisfied, wherever he was.

And, just as she had said when he pried her hand open to see the bleeding chess knight, Henry, his beloved eldest son, was truly dead. Now the Young King's followers, who were many, hated him.

It had all come true, Henry told himself. Yet even at that terrible moment of revelation he was sure she was no more than the conduit through which the messenger of death sent the words.

The king held his head in his hands. Mother of God, who could blame him for sending her away? He'd hoped never to set eyes on her again. Now he was not a vengeful man. Only a melancholy one.

"Sire," Gilbert Foliot said, "speak to me." The bishop hurriedly beckoned the knight with the pitcher of wine. "Are you all right?"

Now, Henry told himself, the Templars wanted her, believing she had caused the downfall of de la Guerche. While England's bishops, not to be outdone in matters of rooting out evil, especially in beautiful young women, would also be happy to give her to the episcopal See at York or some other place to stand trial.

Abruptly, the king stood up.

"I will give her to you," he said.

While Foliot looked at him, astounded, Henry

handed the Templars' petition to one of the hovering clerks.

"She will be brought to your commandery in Edinburgh by one of my own knights," he told the Templar. "He is one of my own English knights whose honor and noble family is such that, on my oath, he will never surrender to mere witches' spells or enchantments. Gilbert," he said, turning to the bishop, "where have you put him? Send for the warden and turnkey. We will now seek out our own peerless candidate, and tell him the news."

Magnus had been half dozing. He stumbled to his feet when he heard the key turn in the lock, trying to straighten his rumpled clothes.

In the dim light of the lower part of the donjon he could not at first make out the figure that stood in the doorway, only that it was short and stocky and carried itself with unchallenged assurance. That, and the faded, ginger-colored hair.

The turnkey stood behind the man. Along with the warden, and two bailiffs. He peered at them.

Jesu, Magnus realized, it was the king himself!

"Sire!" It was all he could manage. He quickly dropped to one knee on the cell's straw-covered stones, and bent his head.

King Henry stood over him, both hands on his hips. "Ah, so this is where your father has put you," he observed. He looked around. "Only you in here? And unchained? Hah, I would not have seen you so comfortable, lad, if you had been mine."

"Yes, sire." Magnus was still trying to get the sleep out of his voice.

"I gather," Henry went on rather unnecessarily, "that you still refuse betrothal to Winchester's girl?" He walked up and down the narrow room, looking over the straw piled in one corner for bedding, the wood table, the one chair. "Poor maid, this has been a great humiliation for her."

Magnus knew it hadn't. "She—she loves my brother, Richard, milord," he croaked. "And the feeling is returned."

Henry looked at him from under reddish brows. "Your father did not tell me that."

Magnus lifted his eyes. "My father's will is iron, sire. He would not tell you because he wishes me to do what he wants."

"Hmm." The king turned back, his hands clasped behind him. "And so you sit in my jailhouse these past weeks, rather than surrender to his wishes and mine." Before Magnus could speak he said, "You knew my son, Prince Henry, who they called the Young King, did you not?"

Magnus hesitated, looking over the king's head to the bailiffs and the turnkey standing in the doorway. Their faces told nothing. But one never knew what would happen at the mention of the Young King's name. It was said the king was still prone to bouts of raging, inconsolable weeping.

"Since I was a child, milord," he said carefully. "When we were knighted we tourneyed together in Normandy, at Falaise and Coutence."

The king stood by the wooden table, looking

thoughtful. He scraped his finger back and forth along the surface. "So, you did not support my son?"

Magnus was even more cautious. "Nay, sire, and may God's peace be upon the holy dead. My father and I support you, as do all loyal Englishmen."

He saw the other man sigh.

"He would have made a good king of England," Henry said softly. "Fate, as you know, saw otherwise. To think that he, a beautiful young man at the peak of his strength, should be carried away by an illness of the bowels. It is not—"

Henry stopped, and turned away.

"Now, young fitzJulien," he said in a different voice, "I have better things for you to do. Since you wish to be released from this betrothal, I will give you the chance to earn it. The Templars have come to me with a petition that the demoiselle Edain has ensorcelled their most parfit knight, Asgard de la Guerche of Normandy, and caused him to go mad. So that the Templar now leads a band of wild Egyptians across Scotland, calling himself their king."

There was a second's pause. Then Magnus burst out with a laugh.

The king paused to stare at him. "I take it you find de la Guerche's condition droll?"

"Nay, sire." With an effort, he straightened his face. "It is most d-dire for proud de la Guerche, I should warrant."

The king waited a long moment, frowning. Then he went on, "The Templars' petition demands the return of the girl to Edinburgh, so that she may be sent on to their Grand Master in Paris for trial. The Templars believe that such is the power of de la Guerche's bewitchment that he will follow her there."

The king flung himself into the wooden chair at the table, and rubbed his face again, tiredly.

"Since you are proof against her spells, Sir Magnus," he said in his rasping voice, "I will send you with an escort to take her as far as Edinburgh, where you will turn her over to them."

For Magnus, the room seemed to reel. At the king's words he backed up against the cell's wall, feeling that his legs would give way under him.

"Sire," he said when he could speak, "forgive me for what I am about to say, but I am proof against no one's spells. I know this girl—"

"So I am told," the king said dryly.

"And she is no sorceress, no witch!" He had broken out in a sweat; he was beginning to glimpse the extent of the king's punishment. "Ah, sire, she is innocent of anything that ignorant people accuse her of," he burst out, "I swear it! As for de la Guerche, he is not enchanted, except with himself. I beg you—"

"Bah!" King Henry jumped to his feet. The men at the door stepped backward. "I have told the Templars that I would choose a knight whose valor and honor would render him proof against any witch's blandishments. One of my own, a knight of my court who can do what de la Guerche has failed to do. God's wounds, at last I will have my reply to these smirking, sword-carrying monks! Come," he told him, "take up what you have brought here and follow me. You are free."

Free? He was in a trap!

"I cannot!" It came out of Magnus as a croak.

"Forgive me, sire," he said as the other turned to stare at him, "but do not ask me to do this—to turn over this girl to the Templars for certain death!"

The king's face contorted with anger.

"Remember your honor," Henry shouted. "I speak not only of yours, fitzJulien, but your *father's* and your family's as well. *Sacred* honor. *Think* on it. Also, Winchester is not easily appeased; both he and your father have suffered weeks of listening to your brother's howls of insubordinate passion, and the girl's threats to do away with herself if she cannot have him, while you have comfortably rested your arse in my prison." Henry Plantagenet strode back to the door. "Yea, it is up to you now to redeem yourself!"

When the king reached the men waiting there he turned and lifted his arm and pointed to a spot on the floor.

"Down on your knees, Sir Magnus, and thank me." King Henry waited until Magnus slowly lowered himself, face flushed with anger, onto his knees in the rushes. "After you have delivered the girl to the Templars in Edinburgh, and only then, will I forgive you the dishonor of flouting my wishes and refusing your properly betrothed!"

Twenty-five

Someone was singing as they approached the beach north of the village. Magnus thought it was a fisherman on the bay, for the fog was reasonably thick. He could not catch the words, it might have been a man or a woman, but the melody was hauntingly plaintive. And as always in these parts, the song was in the language he never understood.

The knights of the escort listened to it for a moment, then shivered and crossed themselves. None of them had been in this part of the world before, but they had heard of kelpies and ghosts. Not to mention the real warlike bands that still roamed just south of the Scottish border in spite of the peace.

The fog made it eerie. Since they had come up to the old Roman road the knights peered around them with vigilance. One started violently when a fish jumped out of the water nearby.

"Come, it's a lone fisherman singing," Magnus assured them. "A mortal, not faeries. The bay is shallow, these people do not come in just because of bad weather."

They had brought a boy from the village along with them as guide, otherwise the knights would not have crossed the stone road over that seemed, with the tide at lowest ebb, to disappear in the water.

"Tell me, when does the tide turn?" Magnus called. The fog seemed to swallow his words.

"The tide turns in an hour," the boy answered. He seemed only a shadow in the whiteness, riding his mule just ahead of them. "You will have to wait for the next ebb in the morning to come back."

"Yes, sweet Jesus," one of the knights muttered loud enough for Magnus to hear, "by all means let us do that. I will sleep on stones, even in the mud tonight, rather than come this way again in aught but bright sunshine!"

"Don't worry," Magnus told him, "they will have a guest house at the convent, and a good meal. We'll not come back this way until the morning."

He pushed his horse up closer to the boy sounding more cheerful than he felt. As he looked down at the water swirling over the stones of the ancient roadbed, Magnus told himself he was as melancholy as the lone voice out there on the water.

In two nights and days of hard riding his head still churned incessantly with desperate plans. None of which, he knew, would work.

Christ in heaven, he wanted to shout—he loved her! She was his life, he knew that now. He had spent weeks in prison defying his father and the king to find that out.

Now he had made up his mind there was no power on earth that could make him turn Edain over to the Templars so that they could carry her off for trial in Paris.

On the other hand, he thought with another

plunge of despair, the king left him little choice. How could he condemn his family to eternal shame by breaking his knightly oaths? All who knew King Henry had heard of the depths of his diabolical vindictiveness. Had the king not displayed it time and again with his archbishop, Thomas à Becket?

Another plan. If he stole Edain from the St. Sulpice convent and took her away to Norway or the Orkneys, they might yet escape. But if he did so he was sentencing his father, mother, brothers, and sisters to utter ruin. The king would destroy all the fitzJuliens, imprison them, beggar them—those he did not put to death he would impoverish, turning them out on the public road.

At that moment his thoughts were interrupted as the horses left the half-submerged road and trotted up on shore. Glad to be free of the water, the destriers tossed their heads, cantering up the hill toward the convent through a grove of pine trees. The mounts were not alone; Magnus could hear the knights' audible sighs of relief.

He turned in the saddle. "Remain here," he told them, "for we will stay the night at the convent. Unsaddle the horses and I will arrange for the stable grooms to come and get them and take you to the guest house."

Magnus dismounted and handed his reins to one of the knights. Then he went to the gate to ring the bell to call the portress. A watery sun was trying to break through at the top of the hill. Flocks of birds in the oaks and beech trees greeted the light with eager twittering. It was still warm as autumn approached the Feast of All Souls; the orchard of apple trees on the crest of the hill still had branches bowed down with unpicked fruit.

The small door in the big wooden one opened. Blue eyes in a round face wrapped in a nun's wimple looked out at him.

"Magnus fitzJulien," he told her, his heart heavy in his chest, "on his majesty King Henry the Second's errand to the Abbess Clothilde. I am here to remove a servant of the convent."

The warrant was in his hand. Magnus lifted it so she could see.

The nun's head did not move, only her eyes, which shifted to view the folded parchment with its red seals and cords.

"We know of your mission," the portress said. "It is not necessary to admit you within, the sisters and the Abbess Clothilde are at mass, praying for God to give us some miracle to relieve us from the great misfortune you bring." She paused a moment, her lips quivering. "Stay outside. What you seek you will find in the rear, anyway, behind the guest house and the stables, in the kitchen garden near the orchard. Follow the wall."

The little door slammed shut.

Magnus looked around. The London knights had led their horses over to a stand of pine trees to unsaddle them. Two had taken off their helmets and were sitting on the ground, resting their heads in their arms after their journey over the hidden stone road. He started off, following the convent wall, as the nun had told him.

Even after days of torment, thinking about it, Magnus did not know what he was going to do.

He would never turn beautiful golden Edain over to the Templars to be tortured and killed, although that's what honor and loyalty to his king's orders demanded.

He could not run away with her, for Henry Plantagenet would take his revenge on his family for his disobedience in the most horrible way possible.

Finally, he had rejected all but the answer that was most terrible. That is, he could kill her, Magnus decided in an agony, and then kill himself.

Surely their deaths there in the convent would be a rebuke to the cruel fate with which the king had so entrapped a pair of innocent young lovers, whose only sin had been their desire to be with each other!

He could hardly bear to think of it. To live—to run away together and live in blissful happiness someplace where no one could find them—was the perfect dream. But it was a dream that would bring about the king's swift vengeance, the certain downfall of his father, the Earl of Morlaix, and all his family, including Robert, Richard, and all his sisters.

Inwardly, Magnus groaned. If they did it, if they ran away, he was forever a broken man. How could one live with the results of such a terrible deed?

Yet how could he, the one who loved her, do what the king had sentenced him to: escort her to Edinburgh to her death? To torture and burning at the hands of the Templars?

Jesu, what sort of monster would do that to his beloved in the name of incorruptible honor?

Magnus had come to the end of the convent wall. There was a gate for the kitchen garden and orchard. Almost blindly, he pushed it open.

He saw a girl sitting with a spinning wheel in a space between the rows of vegetables. At first he did not know who she was.

Then, Magnus saw, in the misty sunlight it was a vision, not changed at all. She was just as he had seen her that first time on the beach, with her hair all undone and the blue cloak wrapped around her. The sun struggled through the fog and lit her fair hair and skin and her glowing eyes in a golden haze.

For a moment he could not breathe, a painful, choking lump filling his throat because she was so lovely. He put his hand in the slit in the front of his hauberk and closed his fingers around the dagger.

He had thought to find her with her belongings packed, surrounded by boxes, ready for the road. But she was seated at a spinning wheel in the midst of rows of winter greens, quietly spinning. He plainly heard the hum of the thread as she pulled it through the spindle. There were baskets of carded wool around her, and just-picked apples from the orchard, one of them covered with a white cloth. Suddenly the big, fluffy white cat with the gold ring in its ear came out of the turnip row and rubbed sinuously against one of the baskets.

"Sweet Jesus, what is that thing doing here?"

It was not what Magnus meant to blurt out, but he was startled; he'd thought the cat had been left behind in Edinburgh at the Templars' commandery. He'd also been so dazzled by the sight of the girl he loved that his thoughts had fled.

Too late, he realized he had not even managed to give his beloved a proper greeting.

Edain had looked up at the sound of his voice.

"Magnus," she whispered.

He looked as he always looked, handsome and heart-stopping with the sun's light striking sparks from his helmet and his long mail coat. Yet nothing could disguise that wise, crooked mouth with a new, bitter turn to it. Or the tawny eyes full of torment and pain.

Yet he was her own love still, she thought, her heart pounding.

She watched as he removed his helmet and dropped it among the apple baskets. He ran his fingers through his thick, damp hair before he knelt before her. Then slowly he took her hand between his.

This was a different Magnus, Edain thought, looking into his amber eyes. Not the wild, reckless young tourney knight, nor the invincible berserker the other knights were in awe of, but someone trapped and tormented—and yes, very dangerous. A man pushed beyond endurance. She could look into his mind and see it and wonder who had done this to him.

"What is it, my love?" she murmured.

"They sent me," he said hoarsely, "to take you away from here." The word seemed to jam in the muscles of his brown throat. "The king. I have a warrant to return you to the Templars for trial for witchcraft, in Paris."

She put her hand to her cheek, her eyes widening. "King Henry has sent *you*? To take me to my death? Does he know we love each other?"

He was on his knees before her, holding both her small hands clasped in his. "I can take you away," he rasped. "We can run away to Italy, to Africa, to the far Indias and forget their damnable world. We can make our own happiness."

On the ruined lives of others, she knew at once. He did not have to say it.

Still, he was so dear to her she could not keep her fingers from caressing the dark red thatch of his hair. As her hand played with its softness he dropped his head to her knees, his hands clutching her gown.

"Or I can kill you," he said, his voice muffled. "I have been thinking on that. Kill you and save you from what they will do to you. And then somehow I will kill myself. There will be another war, the king will supply one, and it is easy to die that way."

When he lifted his head she saw his wet lashes, like spikes. Edain turned her face away. She could not bear to think of tears in those bold, tawny eyes. "You cannot do that," she whispered. "It is a mortal sin to take one's life."

His face contorted. "Curse it, don't you understand? We are trapped. I have done this to you!"

He reached into his mail coat for the dagger and she shut her eyes.

"Forgive me, Edain, my beloved," he cried, "but do you think me such a coward that I am not able to give us both a good death so that we can always be together?" His hands were shaking. "Jesu, my love, I cannot bear to think about it. I will not hurt you, I will be quick!"

But instead of the gold-handled knife he pulled out the folded parchment with its red cord and seals.

He held the packet in his hand, staring at it as though he had never seen it before. "Christ," he said finally, "the damned warrant! King Henry's warrant."

He started to toss it away into the rows of the kitchen garden, but she caught his hand. "You don't want it," he told her, "it is intended for the Abbess Clothilde. So she will release you to me."

"Yes, I know." Edain took the folded parchment from him and broke the red wax seals.

The cat twined itself about Magnus's legs, butting his shins with its beringed head and purring. Magnus reached down to grab it, hampered by his long mail hauberk, but the cat escaped him by leaping gracefully between the baskets. It crouched down behind the cloth-covered one, eyes gleaming.

"Get out of there," he told it. It vaguely reminded him of someone.

He reached for it. Instead of seizing the cat his fingers brushed the handle of the covered apple basket. Magnus pulled back the cloth.

Then something strange happened. He remained motionless, his fingers gripping the white napkin as though he could not let go, while Edain quickly read the king's warrant.

"Do you know what is in this?" she cried. "Magnus, the king has signed this himself! We do not have to run away! Nor do we have to die in a lover's pact."

Magnus's mouth worked. His hand could not let go of the cloth that had covered the basket's handle like a small tent. It was several minutes before he could say in a strained voice, "There's a baby in this one."

Edain was examining the king's seal, her face joyful. "Yes, her name is Maeve. The Red Queen, because she has your hair."

Magnus pulled off the napkin and dropped it on the ground. Inside the basket was a nest of embroidered linens, the type of work the nuns did so well, and in the middle of them was a baby's little face, folded and pouting with rosy sleep.

It was not his hair, he knew immediately, it was much brighter. A blazing, pagan treasure the color of red gold. Like his mother's.

"What a cross-grained man he is," his beloved was saying, "to torture you like this and make you suffer so, thinking that you must betray either me or your family. Yet I think he grieves greatly for Henry, the Young King. Listen to what he has written. 'The young and beautiful by God's grace should not suffer.' " She looked up in wonder. "He means us. What did you say to him?" She waved the parchment at him. "King Henry is sending you to Ireland, to be lord over your father's fiefs there! And he gives us permission to marry!"

"It is my daughter." Magnus held the basket in the crook of one arm while his finger tried to open the sleeping baby's fist. "I have had a daughter!"

Edain spread the king's writ out in her lap and smoothed it with her hands. "The next one will be a son. I have had a Feeling."

When he did not answer she looked up and saw that he had walked off through the turnip rows, the basket cradled in his arms, absorbed in the baby inside it.

"Bring her back," she called, "for I must shortly feed her."

The cat, Fomor, came and jumped in her lap. "No, not now," she told it and gave it a push. As it leaped down and stalked away, the ruby in its ear glittering, Edain laughed. "Don't be jealous," she told him. "Wait until she is older, you can teach her to ride."

Magnus came and stood beside her, the basket cradled in his big hands. "I could not have killed us," he said, "you know that. God knows the thought was stupid, but I had been thinking wildly for days. I was desperate."

Edain took the basket out of his grasp. "What would you have done, my love?"

"Whatever you would have made me do." He rubbed his hand through his dark red hair as he sat down beside her. "I could not live without you, Edain, you must know that. Everything else in this world is a sham, only you are real, for all that they say you a witch, and say that you can call people and bend them to your will. I have never found that was so. You are my angel, and my heart. What I have found is that whatever else you are, you need me to love and protect you."

Her eyes glistened. "Ah, you are so wise." She put her hand on his arm and bent forward and kissed him.

Magnus stroked her shining hair with his big hand. "I believe I would have taken you back to King Henry and challenged him. God's wounds, I would have refused before the king and all the nobles of England to turn you over to anyone! I would have claimed you as my beloved, my wife, and dared them to do their worst."

He suddenly leaned forward. "What a little mouth she has, like a rosebud! Are you going to feed her?"

Edain put the redheaded baby to her breast. Magnus's hand touched Maeve's tiny head, his big fingers cupping it.

"The Red Queen of Ireland?" The look he gave Edain over the top of the baby's head was full of happiness.

Edain smiled. "Red Maeve of Connacht was a great queen. According to what I have read in the king's warrant, because of his leniency in allowing us to go to Ireland we must show our thankfulness by naming our first born for him." She pursed her mouth mischievously. "Tell me, do you think our daughter will answer happily to the name of 'Henry Plantagenet'?"

She loved him when he threw back his handsome head, and gave a loud shout of laughter.

Author's Note

The Poor Knights of Christ and of the Temple of Solomon, known as the Templars, were founded in 1119 by a French knight, Hugues de Payens, to protect pilgrims traveling in the Holy Land from brigands and slavers. The Templars performed courageous service, and were soon the heroes of their day.

The Templars' efficient transportation and eventual network of treasure storehouses all over Europe made them the forerunners of modern-day banking, but they had their enemies; after the disastrous fall of the Templars' stronghold at Acre to the Muslims in 1291, the order was accused of sodomy, blasphemies, and other irreligious practices during their secret rites and initiations.

Edain's prophecy of the Templars' downfall by fire and ruin came true in 1307, when King Philip IV of France, who was deeply in debt to the Templars, had all its members in his kingdom arrested. Many were tortured to exact "confessions," then burned at the stake. Eventually, under pressure, Pope Clement V had the entire order suppressed. The last Grand Master, Jacques de Molay, was burned at the stake; the youth group of American Freemasonry, the Order of the De Molay, perpetuates his name. A secret pocket of Templars is rumored to have existed to the present day in southeastern France, its last Grand Master the poet and filmmaker Jean Cocteau.